When The Blind See

To the Alpers,
-Janelle Thornton

When The Blind See

Book One: The Prophecy Trilogy

Janelle Thornton

Original art on cover by Donna Holter of Sioux Falls, SD

Library of Congress Number:		2004195383
ISBN:	Softcover	1-4134-7996-0

This book was printed in the United States of America.

To order additional copies of this book, contact:
Xlibris Corporation
1-888-795-4274
www.Xlibris.com
Orders@Xlibris.com

26298

Contents

Preface

The tiny child slept nestled in warm blankets in a sturdy wooden bed made small to fit his size. A ribbon of moonlight rippled through the thick clouds like a shining river descending from the skies, threading its way into the boy's chamber. It fell through the glossy bay window, illuminating the smiling face of the young boy. He was small, with unruly brown hair, sturdy young bones, and a sweet face yet unmarred by the harshness of the world. One small fist was clasped around a medallion that he wore around his neck and never took off, it's largeness a symbol of his noble birth.

The queen, thin and gentle-natured, walked into the quiet, empty room to check on her sleeping son. She stood beside his low bed, watching how the moonlight turned his face pale like milk. Her eyes wandered to sweeping hills, broad fields of blue-green grass, and the thick forests that formed the Kingdom of Casan. The kingdom's land was surrounded on three sides by stately mountains that kept out danger from the Beyond, and a thick, nearly untamable forest bordered them to the east. The palace she stood in rested on the highest hill, near a stretch of wood, their boughs silver and their leaves pale in the darkness of night.

The clouds again covered the pearly moon, almost full, and cast the room into darkness, except for the one, low-burning candle. It flickered and smoked slightly but stayed alight. No one seemed awake at this time of night, a time when the entire world seemed to sleep. The queen watched her sleeping, smiling child and stayed beside his small bed. She loved him dearly, but he seemed destined to make her worry. Only today, he had wandered on his toddler legs into the stable and reached out to stroke the fieriest stallion in the herd. And it had allowed it, to the astonishment of all the grooms. A smile lay on the sleeping face, and the gentle queen knew he remembered too.

She stroked his soft hair away from his cheek, and then she smiled, stepping back. "Sleep well, dear child," she whispered, a familiar phrase she often said to him. "I'm sure you will have plenty more adventures."

Little did she know how his life would change that very night.

She slipped out of the room again, satisfied, but only moments after she left, the bay window opened enough to admit a rather large man with a dark beard and hate-filled eyes. His gaze fluttered around the room for a moment, taking in the emptiness and the stillness. Then his eyes fell on the young, sleeping prince. He was the one; they all knew it. He was the one of whom the prophecy had spoken. He was going to be the end of the free reign of the "evildoers". But they wouldn't have it; their time of freedom had been too good and too long for it to be torn from their grasp by some "new king". No, the line of the Par family would end here.

The man at the window swept up the prince with one hand, blankets and all. The boy awoke, prepared to cry out, but a large hand that tasted of blood was thrust over his mouth, nearly strangling him with the smell and force. He struggled, kicking with strong young legs, hoping to get away from the grasping hand. But it was not to be. In one silent motion the man swung out the window again, disregarding the child's kicks and growls, and onto a waiting rope. He landed on the ground with only a slight thump, tugged the rope from its perch, and grabbed a waiting horse. It fidgeted at the boy's struggles, unnerved by the noise and motion.

It happened amazingly quickly. The man holding the boy leapt onto the horse and spurred it into a run, clasping the struggling boy in one arm while he guided the horse by the reins in his other. Grass muffled the horse's footsteps, and a cloth wrapped around its hooves stilled the steady beating as it charged away from the only home the young prince had ever known. How long the prince was forced to ride, he didn't know. All he could think of was the fear in him, the darkness that pressed around him like leering phantoms, and the bloody hand that held him still.

Somewhere far away from anything he had ever known, he was tossed roughly to the ground. His captor stood over him and kept him from daring to run. The boy gazed around him in the darkness, looking up at the moon and wishing it would give him some light. All around him seemed still and black, the only sounds the horse's stomps and grinding teeth and his own heavy breathing. Suddenly, a circle of men surrounded him, whispering and moving only slightly, and he whimpered in pain and fright. One man stepped forward and appraised him like one who looks on with only faint pity at a witless animal. He raised his hands and said a strange word the little prince couldn't understand, and a light like the spark of a candle winked into existence. It grew brighter than torches, lanterns, or even the sun and continued to shine before his eyes. He tried to turn away from the blinding sight, but two hands held his face so that he couldn't move. The light was too strong for his young eyes and stung them to the core. He screamed and thrashed but it did no good; the light only burned all the brighter. The baby prince shrieked in agony, fighting with all his young strength to save his eyes.

Finally it became too much. Whiteness filled his vision, and he fell to the ground in a heap, tears pouring down his cheeks as he lay like a dead body.

"There is no prophesied one," the first man said calmly.

1

A Friendship and a Death

The half-elven boy stood stiffly at the edge of the clearing, facing into the woods, and waited. Birds cried from the treetops, their wings whispering in the breeze, but everything else was quiet. He was a half-blood, a product of a father from the race of elves and a mother from the race of men. But that didn't matter to him. To him he was an elf, an elf that had lived, and would forever live, in the Eastland.

"Yaja! Where are you?" The boy yelled into the thickness of the trees. He waited for an answer a moment before shouting, "You aren't funny! Come back!" There was silence for a moment, and then a soft giggle was the only answer from the shadows of the forest.

Half-blood though he was, the boy had hearing even better than an elf's. In truth, all of his senses were as good as any of the inhabitants of the Eastland. Except for one – he was blind. The only blind elf, even a part elf, in centuries, but he had learned to make do.

But no matter what he did, to his father, a large warrior pure and to the bone, the boy was a disgrace. "He will forever be depending on other people! He will never be a soldier or a hero as I am," the boy had overheard his father say once. "He is a disgrace to this family. A blind elf. A misfit. He's as good as worthless."

The boy, to prove his father wrong, had worked harder at enhancing his hearing and his sense of touch. Trees began to identify themselves beneath his fingers, voices taking shape, the sound of metal on metal in a blacksmith's shop becoming a landmark he could use to find his way.

He found gifts that didn't involve seeing, things he could do to prove he wasn't "worthless". Somehow he wanted to make his father proud.

Even though he was completely blind, he tried not to make it stand out. He had the uncanny ability to 'look' at people with his blind eyes, becoming used to looking into where he guessed peoples' faces were rather than looking away in shame. But despite all of this, deep inside he knew that his father would never be proud of him or even accept him. The boy's lack of vision stood as a barrier between father and son that was impassable. It always would. His name even showed his disgrace, the thing that set him apart. "Piaphin" meant "sightless" in the ancient, elven language.

Suddenly, with a flash, Yaja came racing out of the woods, shaking the boy from his thoughts. She was the Princess of the Elven People – sweet intelligent and beautiful – though right now she was only nine. But everyone knew she would grow up to fit that image. Her features showed the pureness of her blood – sharply pointed ears, smooth fair skin, and brightly colored eyes on a frame of light bones. Long, black hair hung down to almost her waist in wavy locks.

"Phin!" she yelled (which was the boy's name to friends and relatives) and jumped at him.

Phin, though unable to see, dodged aside. He didn't need to see to know she was coming at him; it was her way. His brown hair billowed around his head in unruly strands that came to rest over his ears, his neck, and his eyes. The eyes themselves were palest blue and people could tell by that, and the way they moved that Phin was blind. The half-blood's elven side showed through in the slightly pointed ears he had and his thin frame. His man-like side appeared in his thickly-muscled legs (though he wasn't exceptionally fast) and strong arms. There was an air about him, an air of dignity and understanding that people saw. But the people that knew him personally, like Yaja, saw his love for life and optimism in everything, despite his disability.

A half-smile played on Phin's lips as he stumbled back and forth away from the princess, feet catching on hidden clods of dirt and unseen clumps of grass. The sun shone warmly down upon them out of a blue sky, soft clouds floating by like boats in a wide, blue ocean. "Their" creek flowed along, always in a noisy hurry, beside the little clearing they called their own. The forest surrounded three sides of the grassy opening, and a smoothly sloping hill rose up on the fourth side. It was one of the last days in a purely beautiful summer.

Finally, the boy tripped and rather than scrambling away like he could have, let his friend get him. Yaja giggled, throwing his ten-year-old weight to the ground with a rather unladylike shove. Phin was an average ten-year-old boy: reckless, adventurous, and mostly fearless. That explained why he was away from the town in the deep forest with only his best friend, though there were tales of dangerous creatures being in the wood. He came and enjoyed it anyway, like he had been every day before this.

The two children finally stopped their romping and flopped down beside the bank of the stream, letting the sun soak into their warming skin. Phin listened contentedly to the bubbling of the water as it rushed along and the gentle hum of insects, feeling grass under his back and hands.

"Phin?" Yaja asked idly, watching the puffy white clouds float by.

"Yes?" the boy responded, knowing what was coming and smiling to himself.

"Is it hard to be blind? Do you like it?" the girl asked, rolling to her side to watch the boy answer. "I know I've asked before."

Phin chuckled gently, the familiar half-smile playing on his face.

"Yes, you have!" he said. "But is it hard? Nah, I guess it isn't. I mean, it's different, but I'm used to it by now. I can still hear and sense things around me. But do I like it? Sure, I guess. I mean it's all I know, right?" he answered with a disconcerted shrug.

Yaja snorted, displeased with this answer. Though she had asked many times, she always expected some new, better answer.

Phin laughed outright and turned to her, though it made no difference anyway.

"Did you expect something better?" he asked jokingly.

"I don't know," Yaja said. "You're just so relaxed about *everything*."

Phin chuckled to himself again. "Where are the horses?" he asked suddenly, sitting up. They'd left the two equines to graze on a more plentiful side of the hill but had neglected to tie them to something. They had been gone a long time.

Yaja shrugged. Then she corrected herself with an "I don't know." Phin laughed, knowing what she had done first, because people did it often in his presence without thinking.

"You don't think something could have happened to them, do you? Something might have gotten them." He called out his horse's name over the grassy knoll, knowing that if his young horse heard he would come.

Yaja looked around her. "They'll be all right. You'd think your horse was a champion war stallion by how much you worry about him." Phin shook his head.

Suddenly he heard the pounding of eight hooves, their steps smooth over the green grass. "That'll be Mage and Bayla," he said, getting up. "We'll be late if we don't head back now, and you know it," he added meaningfully.

Just as he said it, two horses came trotting over the small hill and splashing across the stream. The larger was a mare with glowing chestnut fur and a long black mane and tail that matched Yaja's flowing black hair. The other was – or so they guessed – barely a year old and was pure, almost gleaming white. Pinkish color filled the colt's eyes. He was albino – they thought – and that simply explained why the three scars on his right flank were pinkish as well. Many supposed these marks were from the claws of a forest cat, something that had happened to him before Phin had found him and brought him out of the woods. The city dwellers had no idea where he came from or what breeding he had, but he had too much spirit to ever be a carthorse or a calm riding stallion. He was completely wild, roaming like a deer in the forest, and kicking at people that tried to go near him with ropes or bridles. Only Phin had ever been able to get on his back, and people decided the strange, wild albino and the strange half-blood boy made a good enough match, even if the fiery stallion would have made a good war horse, had he been even slightly tame.

"You should get a different horse," Yaja said, mounting Bayla, who wore a soft saddle and a bright royal bridle.

"You're bluntly rude," Phin teased as he scrambled up onto the albino colt's sleek back. "But you can have your own opinion. I know every part of him and what each of his sounds mean. You couldn't find a better horse for me."

Yaja snorted and tapped Bayla's flank. Mage shook his snowy mane and walked up beside the mare, smaller hooves crackling on the dry leaves and brush. Slowly the two started down the well-traveled dirt trail.

The horses walked steadily and with a loose rein, or no rein for Mage. Their riders talked casually, discussing the way things were going in town, what other children their age were doing, and their plans for tomorrow's ride. Then they reached the city. There the sound of carts rumbling, horses stomping, mules braying, and the town's citizens talking and shouting drowned out the other noises. The streets were gravel or cobblestones and made a different kind of sound beneath the hooves of the horses – Phin's way of telling they had entered Niathorn once more.

Elves everywhere waved and called out to the young princess, and she waved politely back in the manner of her nobility. Phin and Yaja were used to this by now, having ridden out to the woods and back every day for the past months and they continued down the bustling streets, past the shops and booths and the many houses while elven children shrieked with laughter and ran around the horses' legs. Mage snorted with apprehension, and Phin stroked his neck. Then the king's royal palace appeared over the slope of a hill.

The two children dismounted at the great doors. Yaja took her mare to the stables while Phin stood with Mage, running his hands through the horse's soft fur while the colt nuzzled his neck. Phin enjoyed the noises of the town, though he was grateful that he didn't have to find his way to the castle alone. The boy couldn't find things if the sounds he was accustomed to moved like the city sounds did. Trees didn't change places and familiar paths had specific landmarks. Things didn't remain so stationary in a thriving city.

"Well, goodbye, Phin," Yaja said, her usual parting response when she returned from the stable.

He knew what would come next: he would mount Mage, ride to his own house and get greeted by his father's usual 'hello': "you're late," though he never was. That was why the boy was so surprised when he nearly stumbled into his mother as he turned to mount Mage again.

"H-Hello, Phin," she said, touching his arm to get his attention and trying to sound normal. Phin would not be tricked. He could hear the jerks in his mother's voice and knew she had been crying.

"Mother, what's wrong?" he asked frightfully, clinging to a fistful of his colt's mane.

She muttered something that sounded like, "Nothing, nothing, sweetie" as she pulled him into a hug. Phin pulled away roughly.

"Something *is* wrong. Tell me, mother; tell me what's going on," the boy persisted.

"It's . . . it's your father. He-he's . . ." his mother whimpered.

"Yes?" Phin persisted.

"Dead," his mother finished, "As he was riding through the woods at night. Wolves . . . wolves attacked the camp."

Phin was stricken. His father, dead? It couldn't be possible. It had to be some sick joke, or something.

"You can't be serious," he gasped.

His mother nodded solemnly.

"Mother, answer!" Phin snapped, and Mage jumped at the sudden rebuke.

"Sorry, dear. I *am* serious and I have decided that you and I shall move to the Northland, the region of my people," she finished. "It's for your own good, child," she added calmly.

Now Yaja gasped, and Phin stood speechless, his eyes staring off at something only he seemed to be able to see.

"But this is my home. These are my people," Phin said in shock. This was too much. The Eastland was all he had ever known, the elves all he had ever been around. How could she just uproot them when they would need the support of people they knew?

"Maybe," Yaja said suddenly, "maybe Phin could stay with us?"

"Oh, I don't think so, dear," Phin's mother answered.

"But we could take care of him," Yaja persisted, "and he wouldn't burden you at all."

Phin turned to face her a little, wondering if he should be insulted. His face had grown a bit red.

"Would you consider that, Phin?" his mother said, shock at the very thought written in her voice.

"Well . . . yes, I guess I would," Phin said shakily. There was too much to consider, too much in his mind already. How could he choose between his best friend and his mother, especially when his father had just died? Did he want to live in the castle, away from the mother who raised him, or in a strange part of the country away from his best friend?

His mother was having the same doubts. She loved her son, but, truth be told, he wouldn't be much help with getting money. It would be difficult now to have enough to keep them well fed since she would have to make all the money. Even when he was older he would be little help. Maybe knowing he was safe but without her was better than having him with her and worrying about how she would keep them fed.

Finally after much talk with the king and his mother and several days of preparation, Phin was allowed to stay in the Elven King's castle with Yaja, "until things are settled," his mother added. Phin wondered how long that would be as he hugged his mother for the last time and tears rolled down his face. Months? Years? None of them knew. His mother's last tear-jerked remarks were: "There will always be a place for you in the Northland, and if I don't come back until you're an adult, come on your own at any time. I love you."

"I love you too, Mother," Phin said, smelling her soft scent of flowers and forest and treasuring it.

2

Journey to the North

After five and one half years, Phin finally took his mother's offer. He decided he was man enough to go to the Northland and find her, because Yaja had changed and the two old friends had fought and split apart. The boy no longer felt any wish to stay in the Eastland, especially in the house of the person who now hated him and he now hated. The few belongings he owned were quickly packed into a bag and the rest were left along with his borrowed room. Phin took up his staff, a smooth pole he had used to be sure the ground was good for walking without seeing it, and pushed open the door. The rich tapestries and simple feather bed stared back at him from the huge room, but he heard only the silence of it.

Phin stepped down the long curving staircase, his staff lightly rapping each step to be sure it was where he thought it was, the pack thrown loosely over one shoulder by the strap. No longer did a half smile rest on his face, but a pure look of determination and spite.

"Piaphin?" came the voice of the king from behind him.

Phin turned back towards it, his face angled towards the top of the staircase.

"Thank you greatly, sir, for giving me a room for these six years, but I feel it is time I went to the Northland . . . with my mother," the boy said, his pale eyes seeming to stare into the man's face.

There was an awkward silence.

"You are . . . decided?" the king asked, trailing off.

"Yes," the boy answered immediately.

"Then farewell. I shall give Yajandalay your goodbye," said the king solemnly.

Phin cleared his throat with discomfort.

"With all due respect, I don't think she will care if I leave," he said and dipped his head in parting. Then he turned and went down the steps, leaving the king stunned.

Phin exited the castle and went into the streets. If people hadn't known him, none would have been able to tell he was blind. He didn't walk as they expected a blind person to: hands out in front of him, feet stumbling, and movements unsure. Phin walked with a strange dignity and authority, his staff tapping softly on the road as his blind eyes gazed forward.

By now Phin had memorized how many turns, left and right, it took to get out of the city. Soon he found himself in the natural stillness of the woods. Insects and birds sang and flew overhead, humming and chirping softly from the grass and the trees. A breath of early summer wind rustled the trees and the hair on the half-blood's head. Phin smiled and placed his hand to the smooth bark of a tall birch, noting the slope of the wood under his fingers. Slowly, almost lazily, he started forward again.

The dirt path beneath his feet wound in and out of the dense trees, passing around fallen logs and pools of rainwater. Phin knew the trail almost perfectly, as it was Mage's pasture and he visited his now full-grown horse often. The stallion could not be staked down, tied up, or fenced in – though many had tried. Soon the stake would be ripped up, the rope chewed through, and a part of the fence destroyed. So the half-blood had taken to letting the stallion wander, calling him to return when there was need. Mage always came to Phin and ran from everyone else.

The trail rose up slightly, and a ridge suddenly appeared before Phin's feet. He stumbled and fell hard to the earth, losing his staff and growling under his breath. Phin groped about for his fallen pack and stick and got back to his feet. He knew his approach with the walking stick wasn't foolproof, but it served him well most of the time.

A great white stallion trotted towards him suddenly out of the thick depths of the forest. His mane flowed around his neck, tangled and shiny while his large hooves stamped gracefully on the mossy earth. He had long, elegant legs, a sloping neck and a pearly quality to his coat that rippled as he moved. Had he been tamable, he would have been a rich man's prized stallion, even being an albino. Instead, he was Phin's. The horse's pinkish eyes stared intently at the fifteen-year-old boy before him.

Phin stopped and listened a moment more before saying softly, "Mage?" The stallion whinnied and ended the distance between them. His velvety nose pressed into the half-elf's neck.

"Mage," Phin said, smiling. He intertwined his hands in the mane and felt the softness and warmth of the stallion's coat. "Good to see you . . . 'touch you,' I suppose would be more appropriate." Phin chuckled, and Mage nickered kindly.

Phin circled around, keeping his hands on the body and running them down the neck and came to the horse's side. With a firm grip in the mane, the boy pulled himself onto the stallion's back, clinging to his walking stick. He tapped the horse's side gently with the staff's tip, and Mage started forward.

"We just have to get to Marigo. I'll ask a man I know if he would be a guide for us to the Northland," Phin said, half to the horse he was riding and half to himself. "And I have a general idea how to get there, to the other city I mean."

Mage walked quickly, avoiding the low branches he knew his rider wouldn't be able to duck. Phin held tight with his legs and his hands, tugging gently on the mane to signal a turn right or left. He could tell by the sound of the brush around the horse's legs or the sound of his hooves on the packed earth, if the stallion walked on a trail or not.

The day slipped on, long strips of sunlight falling on the path before them to signal the ending of the day. Phin, unable to see this, kept Mage going. The albino tramped on tirelessly, occasionally flipping his tail or turning his long head to sniff at the air or snatch a bite of grass.

Night insects and creatures began shifting from their holes and coming to life, starting out into the cooling air. The insects chirped, and the murmuring of cicadas filled the trees. An owl swooped down on silent wings, landing, talons extended, on a hapless mouse that squeaked in its terror. The sniffing of a boar digging in the dirt for grubs was one of the few other sounds.

Phin took much more notice of these signs and pulled Mage to a stop. He dismounted, standing upon his legs, which were shaky for a moment due to the constant riding, and leaning on his helpful staff. With the horse behind him, he journeyed off the path and found a safer place at the base of a large oak where the thick roots broke through the dirt in humps and tangled sticks. Phin cut an arrow pointing toward the trail in the earth with the hunting knife he always wore stuck in his belt, the only weapon he carried. Mage stood a few feet away, grazing contentedly on a patch of grass and clover.

Phin threw down his pack and unfastened it. After groping about with his hands for a moment, the boy found a loaf of bread and a few other small provisions he had hastily packed. He ate hungrily, not having eaten since that morning, though the meat was tough and salty and the bread coarse but filling. Mage wandered over, smelling the sweet scent of apples and wishing for some himself. With one bite he tore the fruit from Phin's hand and trotted back to his grassy knoll, pleased by the taste and proud of his accomplishment.

"Just remember that that food has to last me four days at the least," the boy warned. Mage made a noise that might have passed as a chuckle, had he been human, as he sloppily devoured the apple.

The night was warm and hinted at the coming summer days, the stars winking through the canopy of leaves above like candles being lit. Phin settled himself against the trunk of the great tree, his pack drawn close, and he closed his eyes, feeling once more for the arrow so he'd be sure to find the path they had been on again. He breathed the smells of the woods for a moment more and listened to Mage as he returned to grazing, before drifting off to sleep. The air smelled like coming rain.

A crack of thunder shook the forest, echoing over the mossy floor and through the many trees and trails. Great drops of silver-blue rain cascaded down, falling on leaves and the hard earth. Stormy clouds rolled through the sky like rounded waves on the heavenly sea. Creatures leapt for cover from the coming storm.

Phin sprang awake, his hair and clothes plastered to his skin from the rain. Another clap of thunder shook the ground. The boy grabbed his fallen pack and slung it onto his back, one hand grabbing the tree beside him.

"Mage!" Phin called. The wind howled over his words and forced them back into his mouth. The storm had blown in without any warning. How was he to find Mage in all this?

Lightening slashed across the sky like white scars while thunder rolled behind it like the torrent of a stampede. The rain clattered on, turning the ground into mud and soaked brambles. Phin stumbled along, searching for his horse, his staff lost, straining his hearing for any sign of an animal. He longed to find his horse and then get somewhere undercover.

Amazingly his ears picked up something. A sound, faint but clear to his trained ears, like the sound of dogs baying and howling, yipping and barking. The sound seemed to come from above, like a pack of dogs, puppies even, running along the clouds. It reminded him of an old myth he had heard as a child.

Suddenly the dogs were joined by other sounds, faint and strong at the same time. They were calling to him to follow them, to go home. Horses whinnied, eagles shrieked, cats snarled, birds trilled, wolves howled, but above all the dogs bayed.

Phin shook his head. The sound was probably just an echo, a trick of the storm. He was sure. There were no baying dogs, or other animals. There was no such thing as animals in the sky.

The boy held firm to his pack and yelled again into the wind. There was no answer from the horse or anyone else – just the thunder and the echo of the animals above him. He ignored them and, tearing his boots free from the mud they were lodged in, pressed on.

Another crack of thunder rolled over the shaking forest and muddied earth. Phin was pelted with rain as he stumbled through the brush and pools, falling almost as often as he stood. His clothes were splattered with mud, and his hair was pressed against his skin. Branches raked at his face and hands as he tore through the forest, lost and confused in the eruption of sound, but he was determined to find his horse. Sitting would do him no good, and who knew how far Mage could get if he decided to run! Phin would never find him.

How long he stumbled on, he never knew. It seemed like years. All he knew was that he had to find Mage. But in the wild shouts of the storm it felt as if he wasn't moving at all, but that the world was turning beneath him while he stood still.

Suddenly a bolt of lightning struck a tree ahead of him. The noise was deafening, and the ground rumbled and shook like an earthquake. Chunks of wood from the tree cascaded off in a shower of limbs and chunks of bark, like a nightmarish fountain. Phin's feet went out from under him and he fell, his arms and head hitting hard against a fallen log. The rest of him landed in a bog of mud created by the storm's waves of rain. Consciousness slipped away from him like water through a cracked bowl.

Faintly he heard a figure approaching, his steps slow and carefully picked. Phin slowly felt two hands grip him firmly and turn him over. But it all felt like a dream, or as if he was hearing it from far away. The hands gently put him over the figure's shoulder, his head lolling, but strangely there was no pain. Then all consciousness slipped away.

Sunlight streamed through the open window, the breeze fluttering the thin white drapes that were used as a covering. It was late morning. Phin lay asleep on a soft straw bed, his breathing deep and steady. The room was small, sparsely furnished, consisting of only the bed and two chairs with blank, wooden walls and a featureless door.

The boy's eyelids fluttered. He groaned, his head throbbing as if his heart had moved suddenly into his head and decided to beat out an angry rhythm there. His brain swam dumbly. The storm and everything afterwards were only a muddled blur, like someone had taken his thoughts, thrown them in a bowl, and blended them with a mixing spoon.

Phin forced himself to his left elbow. For a moment it seemed as if he was back in his own room in the castle, and the fight with Yaja and the journey to the Northland had only been a dream. But the pounding in his head, and the foreign sounds around him proved him wrong. He brushed a few dirty strands of hair out of his face.

The wooden door across from him swung open gently on well-oiled hinges that made almost no sound. Phin turned his face to it. A man with heavy footsteps and a large frame entered the room.

"Hello, stranger. How are you feeling?" the man's deep voice asked with kindness.

Phin groaned slightly. "Not so good," he answered, forcing himself into a sitting position.

The man chuckled. "I would have guessed that after you fell and hit that tree," he answered, chuckling heavily. "Who are you and where are you from? By the look of you, you're an elf or at least a part."

Phin nodded, which caused his head to hurt worse. He pressed one hand to his temple and leaned back a little.

"My name is Piaphin, but Phin is easier. I am from the elven city of Niathorn. And I am a half-blood," the boy added.

"Yes, I see that now. But why, pray-tell, were you headed north?" the man questioned. "I found you quite a way from Niathorn."

"My father is now dead. I was going to find my human mother." He would rather not get into details about the fight with Yaja. "Where am I now?" he asked and then added quickly, "Thank you for saving me."

"In the city of Stormwing, on the Rabba Plains. And you're welcome."

"How on earth did I get to the Rabba Plains?" Phin asked, surprised. Did Mage really walk that quickly or had he gone that far in his reckless walk last night? The Rabba Plains were north of the Eastland forest, practically a part of the Northland! The large man shrugged, but Phin waited for an answer.

"I guess you don't know," Phin said finally. "Please don't shrug or nod around me."

The man was surprised at the sudden strangeness of the boy and his disrespect in so bluntly telling a man what to do.

"Oh!" Phin said suddenly, unconscious of the other man's thoughts. "Have you seen a horse lately?"

"Of course, but is there a special horse you're looking for?" the man replied casually.

"Yes," the boy answered, "he's a big stallion."

"Well, we had one wander in from the woods this morning. But I can't just give him to you. You'll have to describe him before I can give him to you or even let you see him," the man answered.

Phin sighed. This could be difficult.

"He's got very silky fur, except for three long scratches on his back right flank. He walks lightly for as large a horse as he is. No pen, rope, or stake can hold him if he is determined to get out. He can give the most frightful war scream when he's angry, but the kindest nicker if he likes you. Does this fit the description?" the boy asked, wondering if he sounded like a real stranger because of his outlandish way of describing things. He rubbed his head.

It took the large man a moment before saying, "You could have just given me color, gender, and specific details."

"Oh, all right. He's an albino stallion with three scars on his left flank and pink eyes." Phin said. Then he added as an afterthought, "Or so everyone says."

The man said nothing but stared at him as if the boy was something that had crawled out from under a log, and he couldn't figure out what kind of creature he was seeing.

Phin sighed and blatantly stated, "I'm blind."

There was an awkward silence. The man cleared his throat. "I see. Well, come see, er . . . the horse," he said uncertainly.

Phin stepped out of the bed and walked up beside the broad man. By the feeling on his skin, someone had dressed him in fresh clothes from his pack. His head swam again as he took a step toward the large man. Though he was rather tall for his age, he felt dwarfed and insignificant next to the large man.

"Um, do you have my pack?" Phin asked.

"Oh, yes. It's over by the bed . . . never-mind, I'll get it," the man answered. He took one step, reached down, and handed Phin's light pack back to the young man. "Now to the horse."

The man cleared his throat again and then led the half-blood outside.

They walked down a large broad road for a while, and Phin's elven features instantly made him stick out. People shot curious glances at the boy as he walked, his face pointed forward, seemingly oblivious to the world around him.

In reality, he was drawing it all in. All the sounds and feelings around the strange city circled around him, but one noise rose above the rest: the sound of a stallion screaming in pure hate and rage.

"That's my horse," Phin said bluntly.

"You can tell just by hearing it?" the big man asked.

Phin tapped his slightly pointed ear. "I've been blind since birth, or so I've been told. My ears have grown rather attuned to the sounds I know," he answered.

By then they were near the screaming horse. Mage was tethered in a tight wood pen with ropes that bound his nose and throat and secured tightly to the beams of the fence. There was so little room that the stallion couldn't even move his legs, not to mention that they were hobbled tightly.

Mage screamed wildly, trying to rear. The close confinement of the cage was driving him crazy. Eyes rolling, nostrils flared, he looked possessed and maddened, even with his smooth white coat and gentle features. The blind half-blood drew slowly up beside the tight pen and the crazed horse while the people around stayed back from the insane animal and the men who had secured him held to the ropes to make sure they didn't break.

"Mage," Phin breathed, "steady, boy. I'm here."

The horse instantly quieted and thrust his silky nose into the boy's outstretched hands. He nickered gently, his pink eyes staring intently at Phin as if to beg for help.

"That's the boy's horse all right," said the man who had led Phin out, remembering the first strange description about the stallion's sounds.

The boy drew his dagger and sliced through the ropes that bound Mage's face and neck and the ropes that bound his legs.

"Let him out," Phin commanded stiffly.

"Who says we take orders from an elfling?" one man sneered as he stood idly besides the pen.

"Do as the boy says," the first big man said coarsely. Without a question of challenge, the men pulled the gate of the pen open. Mage whinnied and cantered into the nearby woods, his tail a waterfall of white.

"How will you get him back?" the first man asked, placing a hand on the boy's shoulder. "He seems the kind that will run from people."

"He'll come back to me on his own," Phin said securely. "He always has."

The sun hadn't even risen yet; it was just now shooting its first rays of light above the eastern horizon. Birds awoke from their night perches to begin to sing. Everything else around was still.

Phin got up off his bed in the inn quietly and pulled on a fresh set of clothes. His tunic was clean and loose, fastened at the bottom by a comfortable leather belt over his leggings. Then silent hunting boots were slipped onto his feet, and his knife was pushed into the belt. He was amazed by how much his few elven coins were worth in this town; he had gotten a room in an inn and plenty of food for his journey to the North whenever he wanted to leave. Clothes secured and new staff in hand, he then reached over to the low table beside his bed where the night before he had perched an apple for his stallion. He tucked the fruit into one of the pockets of his leggings, grabbed the new staff he had made from where it rested against the wall, and left the room, careful of the squeak in the door.

The boy had been in Stormwing for two days now. It was a safe, comfortable trading city with forest close by on the south side while fields dominated the western outskirts of the city so the citizens were provided with food. Men and elves came together to exchange goods there, crowding the many inns and making it so the taverns were almost never empty and the streets had some people in them at all times of day or night. Phin had spent much of the past few days wandering the shops, listening to people in the market places, and weighing out if he had enough coin to buy a certain thing. The things in the stores were as exciting for a blind man as for anyone else. His pouch of money was a bit lighter after two days in the exciting place because shopkeepers and market men were just as eager to get a blind man to buy things as they were a man that could see.

But at this time of morning there were more people sleeping than out exchanging goods or drinking themselves stupid in one of the taverns.

The streets were quiet except for a few drunks staggering home, an elf tending to his mount and preparing to leave, and a small group of men talking in low voices in a corner. No one noticed a lanky boy walking toward the forest with a staff except a skinny cat and a docile donkey tied to a fence. Phin walked steadily because the forest was what really drew him out at so early a time in the morning.

Huge ancient trees loomed before him, cloaked in shadows and clothed by the gradually growing sunlight. Though Phin couldn't see this, he could hear the cool morning breeze winding through the many dew-soaked leaves and branches, flitting along with the insects and song birds. Mage would be in there also, and in the stillness the boy could hear him move.

He entered the sanctity of the forest with slow, judged steps, his staff securely patting the ground to check for places where he could fall. Ruts and bogs were everywhere from the storm's fury two nights back, and the boy had to pick his way through carefully. Mage was close ahead, but Phin didn't want to break the stillness by shouting. He would find him when he would.

With one hand on the trunk of a tree he took a few more steps. That was when his feet hit something hard and smooth that he hadn't expected. He reached down and picked up out of the mud a perfectly formed bow. He rubbed the mud off with his fingers and felt beneath it silky smooth wood that was covered with engravings of strange letters and long looping vines that felt as if they had grown there rather than being carved into the wood. It was unclipped and felt as if it had just been polished. Phin stroked it once, and it felt like an elven weapon, or some hero's greatest treasure. It was as if a legend had opened up and dropped the bow on the forest floor just for him to find.

Phin felt it would be wrong to leave the beautiful bow out in the mud and decided finally to take it with him. Maybe someone in Stormwing had lost it (unlikely in his opinion) and the storm had unearthed it again. If not, maybe he could get a string put on it and sell it for some more gold, though that seemed a waste of a beautiful thing. It was bound to be worth a lot by how perfectly it was formed, and he knew little about bows.

The boy started gradually into the woods again, the bow held loosely in one hand and his staff in the other. Mage, sensing the presence of the half-blood, trotted over to him on light feet that splashed in the few puddles he couldn't avoid. The stallion tossed his long mane, nosing Phin's clothes to see if his rider might have brought him something. When he found the apple, he neighed with delight and pressed on Phin's arm to make him give it to him. Phin pulled it out and listened to the horse chomp through it with enjoyment before he hauled himself on as he did each day at sunrise, and he and the stallion rode out to greet the morning.

"Today I plan to leave for my mother's northern village," Phin announced to the large man who stood in the doorway of his room at the inn, the same man who had led him to Mage the first time and had been keeping track of him since then, just to be sure he didn't get robbed or lost. "I could use a guide." Phin weighed his money pouch in his hand. "I can pay him."

"I will guide you," the big man said simply.

Phin continued packing his things into the same pack he had used the first time, ducking under the bed to make sure nothing had gotten kicked under there and unearthed an extra sock.

"Thank you," he said, coughing on the dust. "Now, has anyone claimed the bow yet?"

"No," the man answered, shifting his weight to lean on the door frame. "Looks like you have yourself one."

Phin sighed and slung his pack onto his shoulder.

"That's too bad, really. I know little to nothing about archery, but it *is* a pretty piece of wood." Gently, Phin picked up the bow and tucked it into his pack so the top stuck out of the flap.

"Do you think we could stop somewhere before we leave to get a string on it?" Phin asked.

The large man shrugged and then corrected himself with an "I don't see why not." He grabbed his own bag off the floor where he had dropped it, knowing he would be leading the blind boy out of the city. "I think I know a man who could do it fast," the man added.

Phin nodded, rubbing the tip of his staff against his palm, and then left the room, the large man following a few paces behind. He led Phin down a large street, the people just beginning to get up and do things. Two elves strode along behind them, and Phin could tell their race because of the lightness of their steps. He wondered if he could see if he would have noticed. He realized at that moment that he *could* do a lot of things other people couldn't because he was blind. Too bad his father had never noticed, but maybe he hadn't wanted to.

They passed a young woman standing on a street corner and singing, her voice light and pretty. A felt hat lay at her feet, and as they passed, Phin tossed one of the smallest coins in his pocket toward it. His aim was bad, but he heard her stoop and toss it into the hat, clinking softly against the others. Phin felt good giving to something that didn't take seeing, especially since she was a good singer anyway. The big man he walked with said nothing, but he heard a few more coins clink in from the elves behind them.

The man from the store Phin's guide had talked about looked snidely at Phin's pale eyes, but put a good string on the bow. He seemed to take a long time fingering the bow, but in a moment he gave it back.

"It's a nice piece," the man said. "But what are *you* going to do with it?"

Phin felt his cheeks flush slightly, for he knew what the man was thinking. "Brother," he muttered and took the bow back, feeling self-conscious. Then they collected their horses, Mage from the forest, the large man's from the stable of the inn, and left the city of Stormwing, heading northward.

3

A Kidnapping and a Carpenter

Yaja's long black hair hung in silky waves down her back and around her shoulders. The dress she wore was dark purple, long and velvety, and draped off her arms from her elbows. She was beautiful, perfect, and elegant. Her skin was soft olive and unblemished along her arms and face. Bright eyes peeked out from under the waves of her hair, over a pert nose and smooth lips. She was exactly the elven princess she should be: lovely, intelligent, and poised.

Yaja stood up gracefully. She was light-boned, as all elves are, and had majestic nobility all around her. She swept a fold of cloth away from her arm and looped a bracelet around her wrist. Slowly she fastened another long, silver chain around her neck and looked in the mirror.

Everything was perfect for today, the day her courtier would propose. She was eighteen years old, ready to be married. It had been four years since Piaphin had left, and she had barely thought of him since. She had long since put him out of her mind, and she didn't care. There was no reason to.

But then her eyes fell on the only blemish in her appearance: a thin, scarcely noticeable scar that ran along the bridge of her nose onto her cheek. Yaja hated that scar passionately, not because it marred her complexion or that anyone had ever noticed it, but because whenever she saw it she thought of a time when she was younger.

Phin had moved into the palace with her only a few months earlier. They were on one of their day rides in the forest, as they had continued doing for years. Yaja had decided to race on their horses through the brush and trees, off the trails. She had been ahead when suddenly she hadn't managed to duck for a tree branch. It had cut into her face, leaving the deepest marks across the bridge of her nose. Blood was running down her face and into her eyes as she stopped her mare. Phin, unable to see it, crashed headlong into the same branch but his was more of a glancing blow. The thing that stood out most in her memory was how kindly and tenderly he had led her back to the city. How ironic! The blind boy was leading the bleeding princess, his steps slow and careful and his staff tapping the ground to check for places that might make walking harder.

Yaja turned angrily from the mirror, the smile gone from her face. For all she cared, Phin could be dead, wherever he was. The girl ran her hands over her hair and regained her composure. She forced herself to smile and think about her future husband. He was a tall warrior named Jarian, and he was strong, gallant, wonderful, and loving – the perfect match for a sterling, elven princess.

Princess Yaja slipped on a pair of leather sandals, pushed open the door to her room, and started down the steps, letting the long train of her dress rustle behind her. Her gaze passed over the rich hangings on the walls and flitted to an open window where there was blue sky and green trees and bright yellow sunlight poring in from outside. It was a gorgeous day, and there was no way anything would go wrong.

The young woman slipped outside and stood in the doorway in front of the palace, a breeze rustling her black locks and the folds of her elegant dress. Over the forest on the distant northern horizon, dark storm clouds loomed about.

"As long as they aren't here," Yaja whispered, twirling one of her bracelets with slight apprehension.

Her hair billowed in the wind as she walked out a few paces more, savoring the clear morning and the mutter of voices from the city. Heads turned her way in happiness and excitement, awaiting the celebration that was sure to come. Naturally, the whole city knew about the princess's engagement.

Yaja stopped again, waiting, and tossed her hair over her shoulder in an exaggerated motion. Jewelry glittered and jangled from her arms and neck, the motion making her seem to shimmer herself. She smiled sweetly, prepared to wait, knowing he would be here soon.

That was when she felt it; the city had gone deathly silent. Carts still rolled and horses walked by, tossing their sun-glossed heads, but they seemed to make no sound. Two dogs bayed, springing and playing in a patch of sunlight, without making a noise. The girl could see people talking and children laughing and playing, but their feet should have made a patter of noise on the street. It was as if she had just gone deaf. She shook her head as if that would help, rubbing her ears, but nothing changed. The air around was like that of a tomb, except that things moved and breathed without making a sound, unearthly still as they went about their daily lives.

Suddenly, something screamed like that of a banshee in the old legends, the sound cutting through the silent city like a knife. The princess looked up in mad terror, her ears ringing with the horrible noise, and saw something that she thought could only come from the myths of old or a terrible nightmare. All thought of her perfect day vanished like a candle flame, extinguished by a breath.

The monster had slimy hide – black, yet pale like the rider of death – with strips of dead skin hanging off like the old wrappings of a shroud. A small, snake-like head with deep-set flaming eyes, churning orange and red, stared down at her. Wings with strange holes that seemed to have been torn out by teeth and claws to be left hanging like excess cloth, blotted out the blueness of the sky with darkness and held the demon hovering in midair. Its legs were bony, like they had been broken and healed several times, and ended in feet which each had three cruel, hooked claws that gleamed like pale ivory.

The rest of the town had taken notice and people fled, gripped by frightened madness, unable to think, unable to reason, only able to fear. Well-trained horses screamed and threw their riders; dogs squealed in pain they couldn't fathom and ran. Adults and children alike ran in a uniform terror. But Yaja could not; all she could do was stare at the monster and hear the silence of the terrified people, unable even to scream. The monster dipped low, ignoring everything except the girl standing in terror before it, the flames in its eyes claiming to engulf her. Its spell of fear had woven through the town easily, dragging down the people's innocent, unsuspecting minds, but settling most heavily on the target of its coming to the Eastland: the princess of the Elven People.

The monster drew even lower, its flaming eyes bent unblinkingly on the girl's pale face. Her look was one of petrified horror. She couldn't run. It knew that. The spell it held her with was far too strong. All was going just as planned.

In one motion it swept the princess up into its claws, gently almost, so not to hurt her or cut her, drapes of skin falling over her ashen face. She was far too important to injure, too vital to the plan, too essential to taking over the Eastland, and then all of the lands.

Yaja's mind was in a muddled turmoil, like a clear pool that had suddenly been muddied and splashed. She had a fleeting image of her father, and then of her husband-to-be, and then of a boy with scruffy brown hair, pale blue eyes, and a half-smile. Her mind was too confused for her to remember who he was, or where he was, but she somehow knew him as a friend. She couldn't even remember who she was. Then the princess blacked out completely, her regal body falling limp in the creature's grasp.

The slimy black monster soared above the earth, the great wings slicing through the clear air as it headed toward the Westlands, where all was enchanted and nearly all ruled by darkness. Only a small, weak race opposed the monster's keeper there, but they would soon be destroyed as well. There was no hope for the Four Lands now, no hope for them to escape the Master, not while the creature had the elven princess. She was the key.

Far away in the Northland a crack of thunder sounded, drowning out the sound of the monster's second scream. This time not spellbinding, but victorious.

Phin shook his rather fluffy brown hair, a constant torment to his face. Many years had passed and the Northland (where he had found his mother and settled down with her in the village of Havenstead) had now become his home. Instead of growing up to look more human-like, however, he had grown up to look more elven, his limbs and body growing thin and light-boned and his pointed ears slightly more pronounced. His mother always joked that absence made the heart grow fonder. Phin joked back that absence made the appearance stronger, at least in his case.

A lot had changed since his mother had left the Eastland. For one, she had remarried a man who was a widower, and Phin had found himself with a stepbrother, a boy two years below him, by the name of Benji. Contrary to what Phin had first thought, the boy ended up being one of the best friends he ever had, both being slightly rebellious, strong, and half crazy for adventure and something exciting to do.

Benji was medium height with large bones, dark eyes, dark hair that always looked tangled, and a rather sharp nose. His face was easily lit by a smile, which contrasted the seriousness of his eyebrows and facial bones. A sprinkling of little scars ran along his knuckles and his hands, something he pretended to be proud of, though he wasn't a fighter, and he got scars from often helping his father with carpentry. He wasn't all that careful or perfectly coordinated, though he was good enough in his trade and, with practice, getting steadily better.

Phin's hands were scarred and rough too, but his muscles were lean and not nearly as strong or developed as Benji's. He stood at least five inches above Benji in height – a gangly, skinny tallness that caused him to tower over many people – but could never have beaten his "brother" in a fight. They got along well enough that they fought rarely, so it didn't matter if Phin could beat him or not.

Phin stepped out of the house and could feel the wetness still clinging to the air stubbornly. He thumped his longer, newer staff against the wet ground to get his bearings. Benji followed out behind him.

"Did you hear that odd scream a while ago, before the storm started?" the seventeen-year-old asked, looking out across the Rabba Plains, toward the Eastland.

"Yes, what about it?" Phin asked, leaning on his staff.

"I don't know." Benji said quietly. "It sounded like something from the . . . Westland."

The older brother shivered involuntarily. Anything to do with the Westland was evil and vile, something to be feared, or so all children were taught and all people believed. Phin was amazed that his brother had the spirit to even say it.

"It probably was just a large bird caught in the storm," the young man said without conviction.

Benji snorted.

"Liar," he hissed under his breath. Then louder he said causally. "Strong storm, huh?"

Phin rounded on him, "Uh-huh." He sniffed the air and then started off to his stepfather's carpentry shop. "We should check the roof for lost shingles. You *did* remember to shut the door when you left this morning, didn't you?"

"Of course I did," Benji said, indignant.

"Good, because last time I went in to work on that shelf for that woman down the street, the door was open," Phin said.

"I shut the door," Benji assured him. "What I don't understand is why you, of all people, started to work as a carpenter. You can't even see the wood."

Then he yelped, because Phin had swung his staff and caught the other young man in the leg before he could dodge.

"I do well enough," Phin said, bringing the end of his staff back to the ground so he could continue walking. "Why do you think I leave all the detailed projects to you?"

In truth, he did do remarkably well considering he was blind. His hands were strong and rugged from carefully sanding out flat planks to make shelves or the sides for a cabinet. He left the difficult work of assembling and installing the things he had worked on, but his work was prized because it was smoothed so meticulously. His cuts were also always straight because he lay other boards along the sides to get accurate measurements and made sure it was right three or four times before he actually cut things. Though his stepfather had been dubious at first, he now valued Phin's acute hands.

Phin's staff landed in a puddle as they came up to the doorway of the shop.

"You *did* leave the door open!" he snapped.

"People make mistakes," Benji said apologetically.

"You just make them often," Phin teased. "Clean up here. I'm going into the forest to check on Mage."

Benji brightened slightly. "Are you sure you can find your way . . . 'sightless'?" the young man teased.

From anyone else, Phin would have taken it as an insult. From Benji, well, it was Benji.

The half-blood snarled and leapt at the younger man, his staff swinging for him. But Benji had already ducked into the shop. Phin could hear the slap of his large feet on the wet floor.

"It *is* wet." Phin could hear Benji grunt with annoyance as he stepped into a deeper puddle. He snorted and said something unintelligible under his breath. "That chair I was working on is all warped!"

"Your fault," Phin said casually, smiling to himself. "I'll see you later."

Benji growled and kicked water at his retreating brother, but then turned to the task at hand.

Phin walked casually, grinning because Benji had to take care of the shop by himself. It wasn't just him being mean; his stepfather would have had him do the same thing. The young man contented himself with walking to the forest with the staff warning him of puddles. The village seemed very still, for there were few people about.

All around the landscape was shrouded in the strange, quiet aftermath of a storm, which drained the area of its natural sounds. Water dripped from leaves that had caught the rain like bowls. Phin walked up to the trees, confidently prepared to find his missing horse in the musty gloom of the soggy forest.

A rock dropped suddenly into the pit of his stomach; a cold, sinking dread cloaked his face and shoulders, the kind of feeling a person gets when realizing something horrible has, or is about to happen. The half-elf took one shaky step back and listened fearfully for a sound of the dread that had seized him. Silence, the ally of the storm's aftermath, no longer seemed innocent or harmless. It felt like the silence of death or decay. Why was he so afraid suddenly?

Phin took another shaking step back, his staff slippery beneath his sweaty palms. His hands were quivering around the wood, and sweat slid down his face in cold droplets. The young man felt he had to break the lack of noise.

"Mage!" Phin shrieked, his voice wavering slightly in fear. The word hung in the air, like an icicle hanging on a thin cliff and shattered, falling to the earth in thousands of broken pieces. Everything around him was deathly silent for a moment more, then a bird chirped in a tree, and insects began humming from the grass and undergrowth.

Phin listened still into the forest, searching for the hidden evil, but not succeeding. He heard his Mage's large feet plodding forward and waited.

The white horse emerged, just as content in this forest as he had been in the one in the East. He nosed his rider, sensing the fear in him. Phin reached out a quavering hand and touched the stallion, his smooth, familiar coat a comfort. Phin let his chills of an unseen evil fade away into the safety of his horse. Letting out a deep breath, he rubbed his hand over the spot between Mage's eyes, right where he liked to be rubbed, and the horse sniffed his clothes for a treat.

"Sorry I didn't bring you anything, boy."

Mage snorted, a noise that said that he was disappointed but it wasn't too bad of an offense and he forgave his rider . . . this time. Phin smiled and rubbed the horse's nose as he leaned on his staff again. The unease hadn't quite left him; it hung on him like a thin, nearly invisible cloth that he couldn't shake loose.

Benji trotted up behind him, his thick, dark hair tangled about his neck and ears.

"The shop's cleaned up. The rain really didn't get in too far, it just got that chair and a few chunks of wood we hadn't even started working with yet . . ." He caught sight of his brother's face and stopped, concern written into his eyes. For some odd reason his brother seemed edgy, almost frightened. But Benji had never seen Phin frightened. The older brother was always secure and fearless; something was very wrong.

"Phin, you look like you've seen a ghost or something," Benji ventured.

The other, leaner young man patted Mage once in farewell and strode back toward the village without giving an answer. He could think of nothing to say and didn't want his stepbrother to think him afraid of silence.

4

The Finder of the Bow

The wine sloshed gently back and forth in the glass like small, red waves in a tiny, round ocean. Phin listened to them as he leaned back in his chair at the square wood table he had helped build two years ago. His mind still wandered over his sudden dread in the woods, trying to diagram what had scared him. Had something been strange in the forest that he hadn't seen? No, he would have heard it, and all he'd heard was quiet. That was nothing for a practically grown man to be afraid of, because, like his brother thought, he was rarely frightened, especially by something like a shadow or a feeling.

Benji continued shooting sharp glances in his dazing brother's direction that read simply, "What's with you?" Phin's sightless eyes remained fastened to the back wall as if the answers to his unspoken question would somehow come from there.

His mother, a quickly aging woman from the stress of nearly two grown sons, lowered her eating utensil and looked first at the empty chair where her husband should have been, then at Phin, then almost pleadingly at Benji.

"Father's just late, that's all. And Phin, Phin's going to be all right," Benji reassured her gently.

She smiled, a tense, forced smile, but a smile nonetheless. Benji flashed his teasing, laughing smile back at her. His stepmother looked back at her silent, vacant, expressionless son and sighed.

"Phin, what's wrong?"

The young man started back to reality and sipped his wine slowly, settling the churning red ocean.

"Nothing," he said happily, perhaps too happily. The familiar half-smile played on his lips, but it seemed slightly less easy to come and dropped quickly.

"Well," he said, rising, "I think I'll head to bed. Thank you."

The half-blood set his wineglass down, brushing his shaggy hair behind his ears and went out, leaving his mother more worried and Benji slightly agitated, as if something had crawled under his skin.

He and his stepbrother shared a room with two cots and two identical windows on either side. Phin went to his side across the wooden floor and soft rugs, and threw the cloth drapes aside on the small western facing window. The sun had just set and the sky was darkening. Phin faced the forest where Mage lived, where he had gotten the feeling of impending doom. He could hear the leaves rustling in the breeze and the insects humming. Everything seemed fine. The light-boned man cast off his shirt and tumbled into the softness of his straw bed, cursing things that threw his life off from its regular patterns. He enjoyed normality. Slowly he lay his hands along his lower chest and closed his eyes, willing sleep to come over him. It would not.

Somehow, though he was desperately tired, he couldn't sleep. His eyes flicked open sharply. He knew he would need sleep for tomorrow; there would be a lot for a carpenter to do: fixing broken roofs, sheds, paneling and such as that from the storm damage.

As he lay there on his back, his face toward the ceiling, he wasn't sure why he had chosen carpentry. He could not see; that made things difficult in any field of work or trade, but with Benji there to tell him where things were located, he was good enough. Not grand by any means, but good enough. There were sure to be many trips to the forest to gather and cut wood, but he and Benji . . . .

The forest.

Phin shivered sharply and stopped all thought processes. He rolled over and again shut his eyes and willed sleep to come, concentrating upon how tired he really was. Slowly, sleep did come, and Phin's tenseness finally relaxed.

A man, his hair speckled with gray, paced up and down a marble hallway in the elven palace of Niathorn. He wore rich robes and a thick circlet of gold across his wrinkled forehead and around his head. Dark bags from lack of sleep hung beneath his eyes.

It had been nearly two days since his daughter had been swept away by that . . . that thing. His elders and scribes had been working desperately for hours to find a man who could save her, because somehow they knew that no normal person, even a hero, would be able to save her. It had to be someone that could get past evil magic and monsters, someone a magician chose by his own good magic. Because they all already knew, or guessed, that she had been taken to the Westland, somewhere nearly impassable unless *some* magic was used as a guide. The king chose his own, good, powerful mages for the job, but they had not come yet.

Many books of lore, legend, and myth had been pored over by the king's men just in case it might help them in their search. In one it had been predicted that an attack would come upon the elves at a time like this:

"When the elves of the east thrive, the west shall rise up and desire to smite at their foe in order to take control of all the lands of North, East, and South. A spell weaver shall carry away the only child of the king as a ransom and as a breaking of the line of kings. Only the holder of the vine-bow can be the savior, for it will protect him."

The king had snatched the book away and read over that short paragraph written by the unknown author again. That was all the information there was on the subject.

"How . . . how could he know?" the king asked, his voice quivering.

The scribe shrugged, his white hair hanging limply on his head, and said simply, "He was a magician. Often they are correct."

Now the king waited. Slowly, tensely, stiffly, the long dragging minutes slithered by, taking their own leisurely time. The king's concern was for his daughter and the coming of the mages.

Time plodded on. The king paced, footsteps echoing on the flagstone, his exhaustion one sleep could not cure.

Suddenly the two grand doors flew open to receive two figures robed in silver that walked with slow, sweeping steps. One was a very old man with a bald head and a large medallion on a long chain around his neck. He walked hunched and with a short, gnarled staff. The second, who followed a few paces behind, was a woman with lengthy bronze hair. She carried a light sack and a small white baton tucked into her right sleeve. Both had a strange yellow gleam in their already bright eyes.

Mages were feared and rare; no one dared call them unless it was the only option left. They usually remained in their hidden cottages and dabbled in potions because that was where their real power came from. They were not like sorcerers who worked magic effortlessly. Those had all disappeared, and the mages had remained. The king smiled, knowing this was his only chance, and came to them with his arms open wide to welcome them.

"Welcome, mages. Your timing is perfect. You know our . . . problem." The king choked on the word.

The old mage bowed slightly.

"We know. Please, take us to a round, clear pool of water," the man said, his voice soft and calming.

The king was surprised by the sudden strange command, but, bringing two of his most trusted elders, he led the two mages to the pool in his gardens. One didn't question a mage, just like one didn't try to reason with an attacking wild cat. He was glad they were as urgent as he was.

The old mage conversed briefly with the king about his findings in the book of legends and the way the monster had looked, asking for great details. By this time they were outside in the dark, clear night. Billions of stars twinkled down at them, making the surrounding forest look like a blanket of darkness kissed by silver. There was no moon.

The king and the mages then reached the pool, and he was instructed to draw back. He obeyed, thinking only of his trapped and imprisoned daughter, and his two scribes drew back beside him cautiously, trying to look both comforting and respectful.

The woman, who had not yet spoken, suddenly opened the pouch she carried and drew out a small crystal vial filled with a strange amethyst dust that shimmered like purple stars. After a nod from the elder mage, she let fall a small handful of the dust into the water. It floated along the surface idly, twinkling like the reflection of the many stars in the inky sky. With thin hands, the woman mage held out her white baton, then dipped the tip slowly into the center of the pool and the floating, sparkling dust.

Lavender light burst out of the water, shattering the darkness like a sudden amethyst dawn. The king and his two elders drew back in shock and wonder, their eyes temporarily blinded by the sudden luminescence.

Voice soft as silk, the old mage gestured once and the light sunk into the pool, though it still glowed out and fell on the faces of the two mages. The old mage drew back his sleeves and stared deeply into the purple water.

"Show me the Princess Yajandalay of the elves," he commanded the water. It churned like a wild, spinning whirlpool of violet for a few seconds, then stilled again into a flat glassy pool that glowed with purple light. The old mage nodded at his woman companion, and she stared deeply into it.

"Your daughter remains in a dark castle in the Westland. She is chained to the wall by her neck, arms, and legs in a secret room."

The king gasped, horrified.

"Show me the bearer of the vine-bow," the old mage continued. The water again swirled and calmed. In a light tone, the woman mage again spoke. There was a moment of hesitation, and her brow furrowed. She seemed about to speak and then stopped and then started again, faltering in her silken voice.

"He is a boy of nineteen years who resides in the northern village of Havenstead. A carpenter. Our time with the water is short now. Only one more question will be permitted."

The old mage kneeled beside the pool.

"Tell me the name of the bearer," he said sharply, his voice slightly louder.

The water churned but with less conviction.

"Give me the Kadava," the old mage commanded his younger woman companion.

The woman drew out a strange thing that neither the king nor his elders could identify, and handed it to the older mage. He rubbed it along his palms, filling the air with a strong, pungent smell, and then dropped it into the pool. The water turned black and then red and then green and then back to amethyst, swirling intensely. The mage studied it a moment, looking slightly confused, before deciding to say one word, "Piaphin." Just to assure the king of what he had said, the man reiterated, "The bearer of the vine-bow is Piaphin."

The vine-bow twanged loudly, an arrow soaring away from it, remotely toward a straw bale target. Benji, who watched his brother from a safe-looking side of the clearing, leapt aside as the arrow flew off course and went within a foot of him.

"Why are you doing this?" he barked at his older brother who held the bow. He was running his hands over the carvings again, laying his fingernails into the perfect grooves.

"Yesterday," Phin began, reaching down to pick up a fifth arrow, "we worked hard, just as I had thought the night before. So today, I plan to relax and enjoy myself."

"By killing your brother?" Benji asked sharply.

Phin shot him a look and set the arrow to the string. "Ha ha," he said sarcastically, drawing it back. Benji leapt aside until he was out of range of his blind stepbrother.

"You learned to draw back a bow," Benji stated blandly.

Phin nodded curtly. "I like the arm exercise. Am I pointed at the target?" he asked sharply.

"Generally," the other answered, folding his arms across his chest. "But if you manage to hit it, I'll be surprised."

Phin sighed and let go of the string, hearing it snap loudly. The arrow flew out toward the target and buried itself in the ground a foot from the straw.

Benji stifled a smile and a teasing chuckle. "So why did you take this up again?" he asked seriously.

"Lord help me, I don't know," Phin said in irritation, leaving the last two arrows lying on the ground. "I was delirious or something. You'd think being a carpenter and being blind would be enough, but no, I have to be an archer now too." Benji laughed.

The late summer air was balmy, the heat carrying on the heavy wind. Clouds, thin and wispy, lay, unmoving, across the sky. Benji rubbed his face as it flushed from the glowing sun.

"Should we head back?" Phin said finally, running a hand through his thick, light brown hair.

"Yes, I was thinking about doing that," Benji said, trying to sound apologetic. He leaned against a tree.

"Help me get the arrows, okay?" the elder brother said, but it was more commanding than a question.

"Get them yourself," Benji said testily, already unnerved by the sight of his blind brother with a bow and arrow that could suddenly swerve in his direction.

Phin sent a hateful look and pointed at his eyes. The younger of the two snorted angrily, like an offended horse, but went to the target area and began plucking wooden arrows from the ground beside his brother.

"You really should try to hit the target," he said mockingly. "Or take up something less violent, like sword fighting."

The half-blood said nothing, but merely slung the bow onto his back and accepted the arrows from Benji, but as he did, a taunting half-smile crossed his lips. He retrieved his staff, and they started back.

Two bat creatures the size of large tomcats crawled along the forest floor, their hooked claws tearing into the earth and moss. Both had short, black hair, beady, yellow eyes like amber pebbles, and fangs that dripped with thick, pasty saliva. They had a strange magic that, if radiated, could quail even the most courageous warrior. Yesterday they had sent it out when a young man nearly stumbled upon them, their surprise escaping in the form of an unexplainable fear that struck their victim.

One of the creatures crept a pace ahead of the other, its nostrils flaring in and out as he tested the air. The smell was confused – part man, part elf, and beneath it was a strong scent of something the beast knew only remotely yet recognized. The second hunched, black creature crawled up beside the first. He too sniffed the air. In a snarling, garbled "speech" it reminded the first what they were looking for: a half-blood.

The first creature, nose quivering, claws kneading the forest floor, told the other what he smelled. Teeth bared in almost a wicked, smiling fashion, the second took the lead. It seemed they had found their unsuspecting quarry.

"Follow . . . the scent," it growled throatily, yellow eyes gleaming. "We shall . . . find . . . the half-one." A guttural noise racked its throat.

"It . . . shall not . . . escape us," the other snarled, stretching one arm and the skin wing attached to it. "The plan . . . shall not . . . fail. The Eastland . . . will . . . fall . . . first."

Both cackled like crows and crept deeper into the forest, tracking the strange quarry the Master wanted them to kill, though they didn't know why. The light faded on the third day after Princess Yaja's kidnapping, and the bat creatures continued their search.

5

Summoning

Phin rose an hour and some random amount of minutes after dawn. His hair was sticking up wildly from sweat as heat already swept into the small room, and he quickly scrubbed it down, with varied amounts of success. The young man dragged himself out of his bed and picked up a flimsy shirt with sleeves suitable for the weather. As he turned back to exit the room his foot caught the edge of the bed and he fell. His knee hit the floor hard, bruising and ripping open. Phin knotted up his face and yanked himself to his feet, blood bubbling from the shallow cut. Benji, awaken by the clatter, sat up and looked groggily toward the source of the noise.

"Go back to sleep, Benji, or get up and get away from me," Phin snarled.

Benji rubbed his tired eyes and decided to get up, throwing on a light tunic before leaving. He could feel the edge in his brother's voice and knew that this was one of those mornings.

Phin pressed a palm to his knee to slow the bleeding. In a moment it stopped. Then, limping slightly, he grabbed his staff and moved out into the main dining room, fuming at corners that got in the way of his feet.

He could hear his mother's small feet as they bustled about making breakfast. His stepfather was sitting in one of the chairs and deeply drinking a mug of cider, his position tired. The sound of a lone flute sang sweetly from the front of the house, outside the front door, and welcomed the sun.

Phin strolled past his mother and stepfather, his staff brushing the wall as it dangled from his hand, unneeded in such a familiar place. One hand pushed open the front door, and he walked outside into the open, already warm air.

Benji had a small, wooden flute to his lips and was blowing a sweetly dreamy tune. The town lay before them, just beginning to rise with the sounds of horses snuffling as they woke and dogs whining for scraps. But after Havenstead came the Rabba Plains, a great sprawling prairie that stretched away for miles, rolling and billowing like a horse's well-groomed back. Far away, beyond what an eye could see, lay the city of Stormwing and the Eastern Forest.

"That's nice," Phin said referring to the wood flute's music.

Benji lowered the instrument and held it tightly in one hand, gazing out over the orange-bathed village with dark, warm eyes.

"It's just a simple piece, one of the few my mother managed to teach me before she died," he answered. He chuckled lightly. "Never thought I'd like playing it so much, but it's all I have left of her."

Phin gave a sad smile. "I'm sorry."

Benji looked up at him sharply. "There is nothing to forgive," he said shortly. "You had nothing to do with her death. I've told you that a hundred times, Phin." The blind man nodded apologetically.

They stood in silence a moment, one watching the sunrise, the other listening to the village awaken. Suddenly, a dot of white or gray appeared along the Rabba Plains. It galloped forward, forming into the rough shape of a horse with a rider. Benji watched their approach with fascination.

The gray horse's shadow stretched far across the plains, pointing west, its head dipping and rising as it ran. By his riding position, Benji could tell the man on the horse was an experienced rider for he sat with grace on the running horse's back. But why was he galloping his horse toward Havenstead?

"Horse coming," Phin stated, his fine ears finally picking up the sound, and he leaned casually on his staff.

The rider leaned low on his charger's back. Mane flying, hooves drumming, the horse came, turning clearly into a lean-bodied, lightly burdened messenger's horse. It was nearly to the village now, with little sign of slowing.

The amazement came when it slowed and cantered through the gradually filling streets, weaving expertly around carts and clumps of people, to the very doorstep of the brother's house. The horse slowed, panting and shaking its sweat-soaked neck, and the rider dismounted, tipping his head to the young men.

The man was in his early twenties, elven in appearance by the slope of his smooth bones and facial structures. Pointed ears peeked out from behind golden hair that fell to about his chin. His bright cobalt eyes stared over the brothers, meeting Phin's pale ones and looking down at Benji's brown.

"Is this the residence of Piaphin, half-blood?" the messenger asked.

"I'm Piaphin," Phin said, remembering the elves' honeyed accent.

"A message from the King of the Elves," the messenger said breathlessly. He seemed as winded as his horse. He then pulled a folded and sealed piece of parchment from a pouch at his side and held it out.

Phin's hand groped the air a moment before landing on the letter. The messenger's eyebrows raised.

"Then it *is* true. You *are* blind," he said.

"Yes," Phin said offhandedly.

"I'm . . . sorry," the elf said, lacking anything else to say.

"It doesn't matter," the half-blood said curtly. He handed the letter to Benji. "Read it for us."

The younger brother turned over the note and studied the seal a moment before breaking it. It was a circle with the imprint of a blossoming tree and the sun shining through the many leaves. Then Benji read the tight, looping handwriting, glad he had learned to read when he was small, even if it was a rare skill:

From the King of the Elven People of Niathorn and the surrounding Eastern Forest:

Welcome, Piaphin, son of Galidor. I hope this letter finds you well and contented. Having not seen you in many years I must simply hope this is true. In all urgency please come to the city of Niathorn, your birthplace.

Something terrible has happened that begs me to seek your assistance. The details shall be laid out before you upon your arrival, and I must stress that your assistance is greatly desired. We await your coming at the front door of the Elven Palace. Give my best to your mother and any others of your household. I truly hope to be seeing you soon.

As a final remark, I must ask you to bring your bow and come in all haste.

The group stood in silence for a moment before Phin said angrily, "He didn't even tell me *why* to come. And how did he know I had a bow in the first place?"

"'The details shall be laid out before you upon your arrival'," Benji quoted. "Who knows about the bow, but what do you think he meant by 'something terrible has happened'?"

"I don't know," Phin said blankly, "but he sounded sort of panicked. That's not the way I remember him."

The messenger had gone to his sweat-streaked, panting horse. Benji, seeing the horse was near utter exhaustion, hastened into the house and came back with a bucket of cold water. The rider of the horse shot him a brief, thankful smile as the horse gulped down the cool refreshment, splashing drips of water all over the dry road.

"I know what the king means," the rider said suddenly, his eyes alight with sudden remembrance. A shudder ran through his lean frame. "The Princess Yajandalay was kidnapped four days back or so."

"What!" Phin and Benji both barked, their heads snapping up. "How?" the former asked frightfully. "By who?"

"Some slimy, black flying snake with hideous claws swept her up by some enchantment," the messenger said quietly. "It sent everyone but her into utter terror. She seemed as if she had been petrified. She couldn't even run away."

Benji shivered, knowing something like that could only come from myth or the Westland. But Phin looked cold and morbid.

"Serves the pompous brat right," he hissed under his breath.

The messenger's head snapped up, his eyes burning angrily.

"How dare you, one not even of pure blood and sight. How dare you insult the Princess of the Elves!" he snarled, drawing himself to his full height and build, which was about as tall as Phin and only slightly broader. His hand graced along the hilt of the knife he wore. He was ready to fight for his royal monachy and his race.

Phin, stung by the double insult, clenched his teeth and rose from where he leaned upon his staff. His long hands formed into fists and shook slightly so his staff quivered. No one, NO ONE, insulted him in such a way. He tried to calculate where the rider's head might be so he could hit him with his staff, maybe knocking him out with a good blow to the temple.

Benji, sensing a deadly confrontation, stood between them, trying to remain calm as his stepbrother and the elf faced each other like maddened dogs, bent on ripping each other to pieces. It was amazing that they could get so angry over only a few cheap insults.

"Messenger, my brother has a grudge against the princess, that's all. He didn't mean to insult you or the royal family." Benji continued quickly, now addressing Phin. "Phin, the messenger was only standing for his race and people. Both of you are being fools," he said sharply, turning to each in turn.

The two men drew back, stung slightly by the younger man's last remark. They faced each other a moment more, then turned aside, feeling childish at how easily they had both gotten angry. Phin relaxed his white-knuckled grip on his staff, and the elf let his hand fall from the pommel of his knife. Benji breathed a quiet sigh of relief, watching with amusement the embarrassment of the two men.

"Forgive me," the messenger said awkwardly, reaching out to stroke his sweaty horse. "I let my anger overcome me." He chuckled slightly. "I have a temper problem."

"I apologize as well. I guess I have a temper as well," Phin said, extending a hand. "Forgiven?"

The other man chuckled and took his hand.

"Forgiven. If we meet again, may it be in friendship," the messenger said and mounted his horse. "Thank you for the water for my horse," he said to Benji. "But I am sorry, I don't know your name."

"Benji," the younger man answered, raising his hand in parting.

"And I am Salgo," the elf answered, adjusting the bow on his back. "Goodbye."

"Goodbye, and good riding," said both Phin and Benji. The rider nodded. With that Salgo urged his horse forward, and it started back across the plains, kicking up a cloud of dust, like smoke, behind it.

Phin gave the king's regards to his mother, to her surprise, and went back into his and his brother's room, followed by Benji.

"Packing to leave?" the younger man asked, teasingly.

The elder sat heavily on his bed, dropping the letter beside him.

"I'm not sure if I'm leaving," he said evenly. "If they want my help with saving Yaja, or locating her, I don't want to do it."

"So, you would be sentencing a girl to her death, by torture or by starvation, all over an argument," Benji stated blatantly, his mild temper rising. "Is it just me, or does that seem heartless?"

"Please don't preach to me, Benji. You don't understand how severe the fight was," Phin answered, resting his elbows on his knees and his cheeks on his palms, face down toward the wood-slat floor.

"Then please enlighten my dim, non-understanding mind!" Benji hissed, irritated by his brother's stupid way of taking this.

Phin snapped his face toward the young man, a look of livid betrayal on his face. He pulled his legs onto the bed, swiveled and leaned against the headboard, his unseeing eyes positioned on the opposite wall.

"Fine. Imagine you have a female friend who you have had for . . . ever. Each day you ride into the woods as you've done since you were allowed to leave the city alone. You're fifteen, she's barely fourteen. As you ride along, she starts to talk, telling you all about how she's been thinking more about suitors and courtship. I – you're not really surprised; she's been gradually talking about this stuff a lot. And she does talk a lot."

Phin smiled fleetingly and stopped for a moment to take a breath. Benji seated himself on his own bed, cross-legged.

"But then she turns to you," Phin started again, "and says that her father told her she ought to be looking for a man who's strong, brave, flawless, and wonderful." Phin sighed. "You've started liking this girl, you know, in more than a passing friendliness." He smiled suddenly. "And how could you not? She's wonderful; kind, friendly, delicate, trustworthy . . . too many things to name." The smile dropped again. "She was the only one who liked you for who and what you were. But when she said this it was like someone just dropped a rock on all your happiness. You ask her what she means. She says that she wants a warrior for a husband, someone who will take care of her, of her noble birth. You feel crushed but keep up your composure. That's when it happens. She says that she once liked you . . . a lot, but now knows it would never work and that she's starting to look for someone more, 'worthy' of her. Then you lose it completely and demand of her why she had ever been a friend to someone so 'unworthy' of her standards. She answers, 'It isn't that you aren't an okay friend, but you aren't husband material.'"

Phin growled, his mouth curled up in a scowl, but continued, "You can tell she wants someone unflawed, untainted . . . better than you. She only makes it worse by her next question, 'Why do you care anyway?'" Phin sniffed, sounding rather like a dog. "You finally just tell her how you've felt for the past while: how you think you really like her and how you couldn't stand to not be her friend anymore. There's silence after you say this. You feel your face flushing and her eyes studying you. Finally she says simply: 'I just like you as a friend. That's how I like you. I'm sorry that isn't enough for you.' You don't know what to say. It feels like you just turned into an ant, and she's stepping on you, hard."

Phin's eyes grew hard like pale blue stones as he continued. "You tell her that you're sorry that you aren't good enough for her standards. She says 'you're taking it too hard' and 'I *want* to stay your friend.' In anger you turn your horse away and start back. You tell her you're going home. She yells at you, 'You're acting like a child,' and 'You really *aren't* up to my standards.' Then follows a big yelling fight where you use quite a few words you shouldn't know and she uses just as many back at you. The last words you say to her are that you hope she finds a worthy man and that you feel sorry for his wretched soul. Neither of you speak again and you both hate each other." Then he sneered under his breath, "Stupid, spoiled, noble prig."

They sat in silence following Phin's speech. Benji shifted uncomfortably. Phin dropped his chin to his chest and sighed.

"Phin, I didn't know," Benji whispered.

"How could you? You're the first person I have ever told," the other answered. "But relating it has made my decision. I will go. I owe it to the king and to the Elven People, but not to the princess. Besides, if it's something I won't do, I can always refuse."

"I'm coming too. I've wanted to see the Eastland since I met you," Benji said congenially.

Phin lifted his face and smiled, extending one lean hand. Benji shook it warmly, and the conversation was never spoken of again.

6

A Pair of Travelers

The two bat creatures crawled up to the town, still hidden by the grass and brush and the shadow that fell on their dark pelts. Large ears swiveled back and forth listening while two noses sniffed the ground for the smell of half-blood.

Gold sunlight faded as its provider set slowly over the forest, sending only soft beads of light above the trees. Twilight crept over the slowly sleeping village like cold fingers of darkness, stroking the roofs of houses, twining into cracked doorways, and settling on windows. Candles and lanterns were extinguished as people settle themselves into their beds and began to dose. Beasts of burden ceased chewing on the ropes or bits that held them as dark twilight's fingers touched them, and even untamed beasts in the street grew quiet even if they did not sleep. A nip of the coming autumn stirred in the air.

The two bat creatures rose up quietly, stretching their skin wings. One took to the air first, like a silent, black wraith. Nostrils quivering, the second followed, its wings as silent as an owl's and blending in perfectly with the heady darkness. They were carried on the wind currents over the unsuspecting village.

A man in a cart riding home fantasized about the warm bed and glass of wine that awaited him. A woman shooed her two children into a small house to go to bed. A dog in the street barked once. There was little other movement. Even the fair light of one candle in a carpentry shop where a man worked late stretched far enough to touch the street with its quivering light.

The first bat creature landed on the roof of a house, out of sight from anyone on a road. The second landed beside him, snarling that it was hungry and complaining that they hadn't had man-flesh in days. Its wings folded and it sat birdlike on the rooftop, unlike what his image might imply. The first surveyed the village with its beady eyes and a look of contempt.

"We . . . must . . . find . . . food soon," said one, in its growling, garbled language. It growled something else unintelligibly.

"Hush," said the first as it gazed down at the street.

"Why not . . . a stray . . . person . . . on road?" asked the beast, licking its salivating fangs.

The first scanned the street below with hungry yellow eyes. They fell upon a man, medium height with thick muscles, who was going home after a long day of work. Smiling wickedly and hungrily, the first bat-like creature turned to its companion, white saliva dripping from its jaws. The other saw the man as well.

"Will hunt . . . the half-blood . . . later," it said. "Food is . . . more . . . to our . . . need." Silently, they soared down.

One threw the man to the ground and the other set upon him. He had no time to scream or shout for assistance before poisoned jaws closed on his throat.

Dawn came brightly, covered slightly by thin wispy clouds that looked pink or tawny in the sun's light. A horse stirred in the woods, pure white except for three long scars on his flank. Pink eyes blinked gently in the new light, and he whinnied with triumph. The horse snuffed the ground and started off to look for a favorite patch of sweet grass.

In the village people rose, stretching from their beds and yawning. Curtains and drapes were thrown open to welcome the sunlight and the coming of day. Children sprang from their beds, eager to be outside or to play in the now well-lit house. Hounds stretched and yawned from where they lay at the foot of doors or a crevasse between two buildings, shaking their fur-covered bodies from nose to tail. Horses pawed at the ground, shaking their manes and pulling against the ropes that bound them so they could crop at the grass around their feet. Morning had come.

Two young men woke, one first. He rolled his shoulders, stretching his thin arms and arching his back cat-like. It was a cool morning, unlike the last, more like autumn, and his bare torso shivered slightly with a chill after being nestled in warm blankets all night. The young man shook his light brown hair as it hung into his face, and he again debated cutting it before swinging his legs out of bed. A pack lay at his feet, stuffed full with food, clothing, a warm cloak, and two flint stones for starting a fire.

Benji thrashed in his sleep. He was a light sleeper who dreamed wild things, having more than once rolled completely out of his bed and yelled about something that made no sense at all. Phin walked up to him quietly.

"Benji," he said quickly and took a step back.

One of the young man's hands swept the air, groping for whoever had dared to wake him. Phin had been caught in his firm grasp before and he had learned to step away. "What?" Benji said savagely, burrowing his face into his pillow.

"Get up. It's time to go," Phin said sharply.

Benji rubbed his eyes and said, "Time to go where?"

"To the Eastland, remember? Or is your memory that short?" Phin asked jokingly, stepping back again.

His stepbrother took another swipe at him and missed, nearly dislodging himself from the tangle he'd made of his blankets, but finally sat up.

"All right, I'm coming," he said, sitting up and running his hands through his tangled hair.

"Then let's go! We still have to get the horses going and find our way there," Phin said.

Benji dragged himself out of bed and threw on a clean shirt that was rumpled from lying crumpled against the wall. He looked out at the gathering dawn with satisfaction and tossed his pack onto one shoulder. Phin was fumbling along the wall beside his own bed for a tunic and the belt he had tossed somewhere. He prodded around with both hand and staff. He finally grabbed both, smoothed over the shirt, lay aside his staff, and got fully dressed.

Benji too was rooting around on the floor, this time under his bed. Then he got on his knees and drew something dust-covered and old out from under the wood planks and straw mattress. With tender fingers, as if the thing would shatter from a touch, the young man swept the dust aside to reveal a worn leather scabbard with a black hilt on the far side.

"Phin, come look at this," he said proudly, and Phin walked over, still tightening his belt while he balanced his staff in the crook of his arm.

Benji waited until his brother was over close enough to hear clearly, and then he whipped out the sword. It went wide and clashed against Phin's staff as he brought the stick up to defend himself. The blade would have cut into his arm if he hadn't moved his staff fast enough.

"It's a sword, isn't it – an ancient one," Phin said as Benji took the sword away from the piece of wood. Phin ran his hand over his staff gingerly. "You gashed the finish." He scowled. "I worked hard on this."

"Sorry, but yes, it is a sword. I've been practicing with it, though I'm sure that I'm terrible because I just nearly took off your arm." Benji re-sheathed the sword and hooked it onto his belt. "But at least I'll have some protection." Phin snorted with laughter as he tenderly stroked his staff.

"The king did say in his letter to bring the bow didn't he?" Phin asked, though he knew he had. He took the bow from where it lay on a small table near his bed and tied it slowly to his pack, coiling the string and placing it in a pocket, and added a small quiver of arrows beside it. The other young man made a snide comment about how Phin was more of a hazard to the people he was with than the enemy was.

The older brother didn't answer, but merely led them out the door. His steps were even and his strides were long just as if he could see, though his staff tapped rhythmically on the hard packed ground.

They stopped behind the house first, where a black gelding stood, tethered to a stake in the ground. He grazed. His mane, tail, and coat were glossy smooth, the handy work of Phin's younger brother who toiled over his prized mount. The horse raised his head, looking down his nose at the two young men and gave a short nicker of greeting to his master. Then he went back to the grass at his feet, unconcerned by their presence.

While Benji saddled and bridled the black gelding with care, having to drag it away from its beloved grass, Phin went into the forest to find Mage. He felt no dread or horror, and with renewed confidence, he went deeper through the trees and waited for his stallion to come to him. Mage did.

When all was prepared, the horses ready, the packs checked, their weapons adjusted, the two men mounted up and started onto the Rabba Plains. It was only an hour after dawn.

"We still don't know how to get there," Benji reminded steadily.

Phin said nothing.

Mage and Storm, the black gelding, walked steadily side by side, both well-rested and fed, enjoying the leisurely gait. Storm's heavy hooves thumped the dirt through the tall grass and weeds, his rider holding tightly to the leather reins. Every so often the albino horse beside him dipped his head down to grab bites of the long grass for a breakfast on the go. Neither rider spoke for some time and let their horses walk. As long as they continued going toward the Eastland there was no reason to steer their horses. Phin's staff bumped gently against Mage's flank in rhythm with the stomp of the stallion's hooves.

Out of sight, the Eastern Forest awaited them.

The man, his hair slightly graying, harnessed his two mahogany horses – one a mare, the other a gelding – to his cart. It was filled with bags of grain from the early harvest and two barrels of ripe, late summer apples. He would have to leave for the Eastland soon.

The village around him, if it could be called a village, teemed with other men like himself; there were really very few permanent residents. It was full of inns and shops and trade markets for the cart men or journeyers or messengers to stay and use, along with a variety of taverns and ale houses. The village was even named for what it was used as: Traveler's Stop.

Three men stood beneath the awning of an inn, laughing and talking loudly. One held a half-full bottle of ale, and it was easy to tell that they had been drinking excessively. Too many men came here simply for the cheap beer and clogged up the streets for the decent folk.

The man shook his head. That was the trouble with these kinds of stops: young drunks and rogues. If there weren't drunkards standing all over the roads there were thieves trying to rob your money purse when you weren't looking. He rubbed one fat, rough hand across his mare's withers and walked to his seat in the front of the cart.

That was when he saw them: two young men, nearly as different as night and day. One was broad with dark hair and intense eyes. If he had been standing, the man thought, he would have been medium height. A sword hung in a leather scabbard at his side, giving him a powerful, warrior-like appearance. The horse he rode was large and black, gleaming in the sunlight like the prince of all horses.

The other man had light brown hair, scruffy and unkempt: one could barely see his pale blue eyes under it. He was tall and skinny, light-boned and almost malnourished by the look of him. But there was an elvish, almost noble look about him. A bow and quiver were strapped to his back.

The horse he rode was white but in a strange, gleaming way. It had pink eyes and three scars along its flank, which made it look even more wild and scary. It wore no bridle or saddle, yet the man on his back sat just as comfortably as if it did.

And oddly, both young men seemed to be coming toward him. The man waited, sitting back in his seat, arms crossed. He felt a little wary as the two grand horses and their two young riders drew up next to him.

"Sir," asked the dark one, the younger one by the look of him, "where are you headed? The Eastland?"

"Yes, I go there. Why, pray, do you ask?" the man said politely, but stiffly.

Now the other one spoke, his voice lighter, "We go to Niathorn but do not know the way. We came to ask – beg – for directions if you can give us any."

The dark boy laughed outright, stroking the neck of his black gelding, and turned to the astonished carter.

"I apologize for my brother. He's a bit blunt and honor-less," he said, his dark eyes dancing.

The man in the cart breathed a sigh. They were only young men on a journey to the Eastland. For a moment he thought that they might be two thieves, but even now he wasn't certain.

"What is it that you want from me?" the man asked casually.

The thin man on the white horse heard the slight quiver in the man's voice, so he smiled.

"We aren't thieves or cut-throats. We only want someone to lead us through the Eastland," he said sincerely.

The older man hesitated only a moment before agreeing. For some reason he felt a strange trust for the young men, especially since they looked so lost yet. He nodded politely and smiled, showing slightly crooked teeth.

"Come along. We have a long way to go before we stop for a rest," he said and repositioned himself in his seat. The man picked up the reins and slapped them lightly against the two cart horses' backs as they pawed at the earth. The cart rumbled forward. Two horses fell in behind it with smiling riders upon their backs, Benji looking very pleased with himself for thinking of asking for help at Traveler's Stop.

The afternoon was waning, as summer was, but the graying man in the cart showed no sign of slowing. Benji and the man, whose name was Jack, had become talkative companions, and neither showed any sign of stopping their conversation. Phin contented himself to listen – both to their conversation and the little brook that ran beside the road – which suited him best anyway. But as darkness approached he spoke up, alerted by the chirp of insects.

"When do we stop for the night?" he asked, and Mage jumped slightly at hearing him speak after so long of a silence.

The man turned to look over his shoulder.

"Not until midnight, son, but you and your brother can crawl in the back around the sacks of grain and sleep there. You can harness your horses to the back," he said.

"All right," the two young men said while dismounting. The cart stopped to let them in.

Benji quickly unsaddled Storm and tied his reins to the back of the cart. Phin grabbed a line of rope out of his pack and formed it into a clumsy knot. Mage dodged away from the loop in the young man's hands until Benji was forced to hold Mage still while the rope was fitted around the stallion's neck. Even then Mage fought and pranced, pulling at the rope until it nearly choked him, and the irritated half-blood threatened to hobble the horse's legs and make him hop behind. Though the stallion didn't understand, the tone of Phin's voice was warning enough, and he quieted.

Finally, both tired men crawled into the back of the cart with their packs. Then the carter started off again, gently tapping the mare and gelding that pulled the cart to make them continue. Storm compliantly and Mage reluctantly, followed.

Phin leaned against a sack of grain, resting his head on the side of the cart and holding his staff in his hand. Benji lay back using the sacks as pillows. Night came upon them slowly, as the light from the setting sun faded and all that remained were the shards of brilliance that had once been the sun's rays.

Benji's eyes caught a gleam of light from something around Phin's neck. It was a thin golden chain, the edges rising above the neck of his shirt. The rest was tucked below the fabric and rested on his chest.

"What is that around your neck?" he asked curiously, sitting up.

"Hmmm?" Phin responded groggily, rising from his half-sleep. His hands went to his neck, tracing the chain around and drawing it out. It fell out and showed it was long, ending in a gold pendant, about the size of a man's palm. "Oh, this?"

"What do you mean, 'Oh, this'? I've never seen it before and more often than not you sleep without a shirt," Benji said.

"It's magic or something. Most of the time I don't even feel it or see it. Like it disappears. I don't even know where it came from," Phin said, running his fingers over the strange 'letters' and symbols that made a pattern on the medallion. There was affection in the way he touched it. "I've had it off and on as long as I can remember, as long as I've been blind, but I almost never feel it."

"What do you mean? You've been blind since birth, right?" Benji asked, reaching out to touch it cautiously, as if he feared it might bite him or be poisonous.

Phin shrugged. "There are times when I'm not sure I've always been blind, snatches of things, and whenever this chain appears the thoughts get stronger."

"What do the markings mean?" Benji asked.

Phin shrugged, showing that he neither knew nor cared, though Benji guessed the latter to be false. The necklace suddenly began to fade.

"See. It's disappearing already," Phin said, as it became almost transparent, then vanished. His hand held nothing.

Slowly, Phin tucked the nonexistent medallion into his shirt. He said "good night," curtly, in a way that meant there would be no more discussion about any strange necklace or past lives he might have had and shut his sightless eyes.

Benji stayed awake a while more as the cart rocked and rattled beneath him. The sky was darkening from its dark blue to near black. Flickering stars appeared and the young man in the back of the cart made out a few of the constellations he knew: the Dragon, the Sword, and the Crystal Mountain, something that might have been but had been left to only legend. His eyes landed last of all on the Lightning Star, the brightest flame in the northern sky and something that always told him, if he could see it, home would always be there.

Mage snorted once as he walked, pulling futilely on the rope around his neck. Benji barely heard, for he had drifted off to sleep.

The younger brother woke up as the cart slowed, being the light sleeper that he was. He opened his eyes and saw only pitch darkness and heard only the sound of the gurgling stream beside the road.

Frightfully, he sat up, completely confused by where he was and why he for some reason wasn't in the room he shared with his brother. Then he heard the voice of Jack who drove the cart and saw the flickering of the lantern the man had lit and set on a pole as soon as it had gotten dark. "Steady, Sugar; whoa, Stash," the man was saying as he dropped the reins, climbed out of the cart and rubbed his hands over the backs of the horses as they stopped.

Benji looked up at the sky, just then noticing that the stars had all but vanished.

"What time is it?" he asked suddenly.

The man beside the horses jumped, his shadow shaking in the light of the bobbing lantern.

"'Bout an hour after midnight," he said. "You spooked me, Ben." The man led his two draft horses over to the stream first and let them drink and then let Storm and Mage take a long drink as well. Mage pulled weakly at the rope on his neck but with little enthusiasm

"I'm sorry, sir," Benji said solemnly.

The man nodded, smiled, and stroked the bay mare's back, his face half lit and looking craggy in the lantern light. Benji looked at Mage and Storm, who had fallen asleep almost instantly after they had gotten their drink. The two horses' heads hung down more than normal, their sides expanding and then shrinking with every breath. Storm was little more than a shadow in the flickering lantern light while Mage was like a single star that gleamed brightly in the dark. Benji had never seen a horse "glow" and wondered if Mage might be something *more* than just an equine. If he might have something to do with Phin's mysterious past.

Benji looked once more at the sky, dark and now cloudy. His eyes felt heavy and he sunk back into the grain sacks, knowing he'd have to leave the mystery alone for a while, even if it would most likely annoy him for quite a while. That was one thing he hated about Phin: if something had to do with a subject he didn't like, Benji never got a straight answer from his older brother.

The older man watched the young man until he fell asleep. Then he extinguished the lantern, covering the cart and horses in inky darkness.

Leagues behind the cart flew two black shapes like tattered flags torn free from their masts. Their sensitive noses and large pointed ears traced the air for the scent of the quarry they chased. It was not far; they could tell. On silent, skin-stretched wings they dropped lower.

The creatures had no need for sleep – only blood and food. They would never give up once they had begun hunting until either the death of their prey, or their own death separated the hunter from the hunted. No matter the reason they had begun the hunt, they would finish it. More often than not they didn't even remember the cause of the hunt, but never had their mission failed. The two black shapes swooped lower.

Dawn came slowly, the sun sluggishly dragging its tired body over the horizon from its long night's sleep. It did little good anyway, what with the thick, hazy clouds that hovered on the horizon like a menacing army.

Benji and Phin pulled themselves stiffly out of the back of the cart, their legs tight and their arms cramped. The latter rubbed his hands briskly through his hair and stretched his back where it had been stiffened against the wall of the cart.

"Something," he said, "woke me up," and he groped about for his pack. Mage and Storm, Mage more so, were pulling at the ropes around their necks. These ropes made it harder for them to graze and after walking for a long time and sleeping little, they wanted their fodder.

The two young men dropped out of the cart and untied the horses, ignoring the pins and needles running up their legs. Benji checked the saddle and bridle of Storm for any wear or injury and then put them on his horse again. Mage danced and wandered away from the cart in his joy of being freed until Phin called him back and the horse came, moping. In only minutes they were ready to go.

"You boys have food?" Jack asked. The stepbrothers nodded, opening their packs. "Eat quickly."

Benji and Phin split some dry, salted meat and thick bread before mounting up again. Then they started off, Mage glad for a chance to stretch his long legs.

Hours passed without anything of importance happening. The clouds slowly faded over the endless plains, letting through ribbons of blue sky and saffron sunlight that fell in patches upon the grass. Suddenly the two young men realized they were on a wider dirt road away from the small brook, where the dust billowed in clouds about the horses' legs when they stomped their hooves and swirled around the round, wooden wheels of the cart. Sunlight glittered off the dust, making it look like diamond particles flitted through the air.

The glowing sun continued rising over the heads of the horses and riders, erasing their shadows from beneath them and warming their backs and faces. Then it passed over, stretching their shadows out before them and to their left so that each step made the silhouette waver like a phantom. Slowly, light faded again as the sun dipped below the western horizon to begin its nightly sleep.

The small company continued on for two more days, the horses growing sleek and lean from the pace they went at everyday while the faces and hands of their riders grew bronzy and slightly red from exposure to the sun. Limbs grew used to sitting in the saddle all day and sleeping in the back of a creaking cart all night. Their bodies grew used to travel.

On the afternoon of that second day the town of Stormwing and the far forest of the Eastland came into view, the great boughs of the elven trees billowing in the wind like banners of green.

7

Fight in the Clearing

The smell of the forest was enchanting and earthen, softening the mind and haunting the senses. Trees shaded the mossy, weed-covered ground and cooled the air scented with wild flowers and standing timber. The dirt road the company had followed wound into the thick forest and through the brush and bracken until it was out of sight. Birds and insects filled the otherwise still woods with peeps and buzzing and high-throated cackles.

"The Eastern Forest," Benji breathed in awe, his dark eyes following a tree to the top, at least fifty feet above.

Remembering suddenly all the good times of his childhood, Phin smiled, breathing the sweetly, magically pungent air.

Jack, the cart driver, watched the boys a moment before clearing his throat. "Should we be on? You boys are hardly to your destination," he said curtly.

Benji snapped back with a look like a man that had just awakened from a pleasant dream. He nodded.

It took Piaphin a bit longer. His mind had delved into memories long buried and forgotten, cloaked with bitterness and drenched in anger. But the smell and sound of the old beloved forest with its many winding paths, numerous hideaways, sunny clearings, wild rushing rivers, and bubbling brooks had awakened those thoughts of times so long past. He fondly remembered the rides on Mage, the colt, in the early mornings and the many games of hide and seek with Yaja and other children his age. His mind dug up a faint memory of a secret place where there was one great tree in the center of an almost perfectly circular clearing. He remembered sitting below that tree and dreaming of climbing it. His smile spread with each awakened thought.

"Phin?" Benji asked.

The young man's thoughts shattered.

"What?" he asked absently.

"Do you want to go on?" Benji said with a tone that said, 'Are you stupid?'

"Yes, sorry . . . let's go," Phin said quickly.

The company started onto the road, Mage and Storm pulling at their riders to get at the grass and moss that grew beside the path and around the broad, curling roots of the trees. The air in the woods was cool, a fine repose from the heat of the open plains, and the clear air was a blessing after the haze of dust on the open road.

Instead of the quiet barrenness of the Rabba, the forest was alive with birds and small mammals. As they walked, the world around them erupted with noise and life.

Mage neighed, possibly remembering this forest, or only smelling all the rich vegetation to eat, and stomped his heavy hooves. All there had been on the plains was dry grass and brittle weeds that were not a pleasure to the mouth, especially when it was already filled with dust. Storm shook his long, choppy mane and tugged at the reins that held him in check.

The two bay horses that pulled the cart walked the path as if they had hundreds of times before, without any urge to step off the trail and graze to the point of bursting on the lush vegetation. Jack held the reins with a gentle hand, looking slightly tenser than he had before this. His brow was wrinkled with a strange concern.

Suddenly the path split. The left fork was as wide as the lane they were on. The right was thinner but just as well used, the light imprints of hooves visible in the hard-packed earth.

"This is where we say goodbye," Jack said, stopping the horses and the cart. "Follow the path to the right until it branches. Then take the left fork." He looked ready to leave and then thought better of it. "Phin," the young man's face snapped towards him, "you said you got a summons from the king." Phin nodded. "Then I have only some simple advice for you two: Be careful what you say. Tension is high and tempers can easily flare – tempers of people who have great power."

Phin and Benji nodded somberly. The former was a little confused about the splitting roads. He hadn't even known that the path they followed had forked at all.

Jack waved once, quick and to the point, then slapped the reins across the horses' backs. The cart rumbled forward, leaving the two young men and their horses. Benji watched it a moment before his eyes shifted to the thin path before them.

"Shall we be on then?" he asked, gazing ahead with a light in his dark eyes.

"Yes, let's be off," Phin said. "I have to get this done, but I'm not looking forward to the whispers behind hands when we get to Niathorn. I haven't been seen there in more than five years."

Benji nodded dolefully and started Storm forward onto the thinner path. Phin, slightly confused, followed the sound. Mage yanked at the rider's hands, fighting to keep going, the stallion far more willing to get to the city of Niathorn than his young half-blood master. Phin finally let him have his way and rode in silence.

The two men stopped that night in a grassy clearing. A hill climbed up on the left-hand side and the dense forest loomed on the right. Gurgling contentedly, a stream bubbled along beside the hill, providing water for the thirsty horses and their riders. When Phin drew his head away from the water, where cupped hands had served as a cup, his mouth dripping, a memory appeared in his mind.

A boy – ten – stood at the edge of a wood, calling for his friend. He had heard her come running and dodged her. They chased and rolled for a moment before both lay panting on the ground beside this same stream. Then the girl had asked the boy if he liked being blind, for what seemed the hundredth time. That had been this same clearing.

Phin sighed. He wondered if the princess remembered, and then doubted she would care.

Suddenly, the young man snapped back. That had been the day he had learned that his father was dead. Strange that a good memory should come from that bittersweet day; the same day he had moved into the palace and his mother had left for the Northland. Phin let the rest of the water in his hands slide past his fingers and dribble back into the brook.

The two young men threw their packs down and cleared a space on the ground for a fire. Phin tied Mage and Storm to a tree so they'd be easy to find in the morning, while Benji gathered dry wood from the surrounding timber. Mage tugged at the rope and snorted at his rider with bitter annoyance. Didn't he trust him yet? The stallion struck his rider in the chest with his nose. Phin rubbed the spot between Mage's eyes that he liked to have rubbed in consolation for having to tie him up again.

Benji made a pile of dry sticks on the cleared patch of ground, making sure the grass wouldn't burn and set the whole forest ablaze. The air was already beginning to get cold, and they were willing to attract attention to themselves if they could be warm. It wasn't as if they were being pursued by anyone.

How little they knew.

Phin pulled out his two flint stones and waited for Benji to finish. A hot meal and a warm night sounded heavenly right now. The younger brother arranged the pile to his liking, half stacked in the cleared spot, the other half left as a reserve.

Soon they had a warm fire burning and salty meat on sticks over it, warming the beef until it was sweet and tender. With blankets wrapped around their shoulders and hot food filling their hungry stomachs, they told stories and jokes and bits of gossip from home. Soon they were both laughing and rolling on the ground like two best friends who hadn't seen each other in a year while the meat they had been cooking burned.

When they grew tired they lay back and star-gazed. Phin listened to the nocturnal forest, and Benji told his brother what the constellations he knew looked like, pointing them out more for himself then his blind brother. Then the half-blood told his brother all the things he could hear in the woods that his stepbrother could not: night birds cooing in trees far away, the tread of a light-footed deer, the hoot of a hunting owl. Benji listened, but heard only chirping insects.

After a while they grew too tired even for this. Sleep crept over them, first relaxing their bodies, then closing their eyes. Soon both slept while the fire burned low, slowly turning only to glowing embers that smoked heavily and gave little light against the blue-black shadows that settled around them.

The sound of a sword lashing from its scabbard and Benji screaming, "Light the fire! Light the fire! We're under attack!" cut through the cold air.

It sounded like something from a war zone. Phin leapt from his blanket, bewildered. Benji was still screaming a load of curses and nonsense that raged through the still night like a stampede of panicked horses. The older brother groped about for a dry limb and finally threw it on the fire, wishing he had his staff so he wouldn't stumble around so much. He blew air on the fire until he felt heat again, pulling his hands away from the flared logs. Then his hand went to his dagger.

Benji slashed wildly with his ancient sword at a strange, huge bat-creature. It was the size of a very large cat, with hooked claws on the ends of its feet and fangs that dripped with thick, white saliva. The sword was keeping it from biting or tearing him to shreds, but doing little or no damage to the thing. The monster shrieked and darted about, its skin covered wings kicking up dust off the ground. Still Benji fought with a bloody savageness he himself had never seen before.

Suddenly, another one of the bats soared out of the trees, this time toward Phin. The young man already in the fight hollered at him that another one was coming. The older brother grabbed a burning brand from the fire and stood ready, the flaming stick in one hand, the retrieved dagger in the other.

The bat flew at his face, its claws and teeth extended, and snarled. Phin may possibly have been doomed if not for that snarl. But because he could hear, he swung the flaming branch, starting the monster's right wing on fire. The smell that wafted from it was like that of a rotting, burning corpse and smoldering hair.

The wretched creature rolled in the grass, trying desperately to put out its flaming wing and howling like a banshee. Benji's enemy was still lashing at him, leaping at his throat or darting at his face with claws like hooks of steel. Sweat ran freely down the young man's face, making it shine in the firelight, which gave his dark eyes a flaming glow. His sword still swung wildly through the air, though his arm grew tired, and chopped at the monster that harried him.

The bat hit suddenly, the monster's claws catching him with a bloody, glancing blow across his temple and onto his forehead. Benji screamed, his deep brown eyes clenched shut in pain, but he did not surrender. He did not stop. Blood dripped into his left eye, but suddenly his sword cut across the monster's back, searing apart the skin in a shallow, painful wound.

The bat at Phin's feet came back to life, one wing crumpled and charred black beyond use, crinkled and ashy like burned parchment. But claws and teeth still worked for cutting and ripping. The young man swung at it, but missed. It leaped and razor sharp claws cut into his lower leg. Something between a curse and a yell escaped the man's lips, and he slashed wildly with the dagger and flaming stick. He no longer cared that he couldn't see and that his hearing was muddled with a torrent of sound. Both weapons missed, but the bat creature leapt back, forced to dodge the insane hacking of the young man who seemed to the beast to have completely lost his mind.

Two sets of yellow eyes from the bats made contact, and both knew that the two young men were stronger than they had thought. Benji's enemy soared away towards the woods and the other followed, hobbling and half-flying on an injured wing. They snarled threats and curses in their growling, jumbled language as they retreated, already planning another attack. They were not beaten, just slowed.

The younger brother kept his sword up, his eyes staring into the dark woods, awaiting an attack. Phin panted, balancing his lean body on one leg while the other dripped with blood, his two weapons still held up defensively, though the fire on the stick had mostly gone out.

But after a few long minutes with nothing stirring except the crackling of the wood fire, they lowered their weapons. Benji suddenly collapsed back onto the ground, the sword rolling from his hand with a clatter, and his head gently struck the dirt. He was gasping for breath, one hand pressed against the bloody cuts on his forehead where some of his hair had stuck to the wounds.

Phin tried to walk toward his brother, but when he stepped down on his wounded leg, it buckled under him. Landing painfully on his knee he gave a growled curse that sounded almost like the language of the bats. Slowly, the young man dragged himself toward his brother, feeling foolish and naive. Hadn't he always been told about the evils in the forest outside of Niathorn?

"Well," Benji gasped, "that was interesting."

Phin could only nod breathlessly.

The two young men sat in pain side by side for a moment without moving. They fixed their wounds as best they could, Benji wrapping a strip of cloth around his head and Phin tying up his leg with shaky hands. Both knew they needed rest if they were to heal, but neither slept the rest of the night, their weapons always within arm's reach.

8

A Proposal for a Rescue

When dawn finally did break over the trees it found two men staring into the forest. Benji's eyes were red with fatigue, and lines cut through his usually smooth face. Blood bubbled persistently from the three cuts across his temple, soaking into the hastily-tied cloth, but did not bleed heavily.

The brothers skipped breakfast, so eager were they to reach the city of Niathorn, away from the wildness of the woods, something Phin had always enjoyed. But the happenings of the night had changed both the men's thoughts. If those bat creatures were to attack again . . . they would be ill prepared. Benji's sword hand had served them well and so had the burning brand that Phin had wielded, but how long would they hold? No, it was safer to just get to the city, where there would be other people to help them if the monsters decided to have another go.

The two young men untied the horses, which had remained relatively undisturbed during the fight. Storm was saddled and bridled while Mage grazed, already having chewed through the rope he had been tied with. Phin forgave him for destroying their only rope and picked up his pack with the bow and quiver hooked to the back. He ran his fingers up and down the smooth, engraved wood, the feeling of peace and contentment that he always got from touching it radiating through his fingers. Then he tied the bow back to his pack and found his staff, where it had been cast aside before he went to sleep the night before.

Benji finally announced that he was ready to go. The two young men climbed onto their horses and started off down the worn dirt path at a trot, neither speaking, both from lack of sleep and a wariness of being heard.

The very air around them felt calm. Birds sang as they flew from tree to tree, their wings gleaming with morning light. Sunlight broke warmly through the green leaves that were soon to begin to change color for autumn, throwing slanted paths of light across the road. But neither man would be fooled. They knew the bats were still out there somewhere.

It took little more than ten minutes to reach Niathorn, but the brothers stopped just outside the village to gather their wits. Phin set his face stiffly and turned to his brother. Benji forced a smile, for his own good more than for Phin, since his older brother couldn't see it anyway. Then Phin started Mage forward, the stallion gladly walking the road without a need to be steered, remembering it from ages past.

The Elven City was already alive with movement. Children chased each other through the gravel streets where horses and carts rumbled along, just like Phin had always remembered. Merchants in booths, returned from their travels, shouted out their wares over the road noise to tempt people to see what they had. Bells chimed from the tops of towering cathedrals, ringing over the rumble of wheels and the clatter of hooves and booted feet like the melody of birds had hung over the stomp of Storm and Mage's feet.

Benji and Phin knew they would stick out instantly, either for their race or simply for the sake of what they wore and how they talked. Their clothes were very different from the elven wear, and the saddle and bridle on Storm differed greatly from the others. But, nonetheless, they hoped to blend in and draw as little attention to themselves as possible, which was beginning to seem impossible.

A few people looked up oddly at the brothers and whispered to each other. They were not accustomed to strangers, especially now, while the temper of the king ran high. People guarded their lips and cautioned their steps, avoiding palace guards or royal processions. Ever since the princess had been swept away, the king had been questioning everyone, finding out details about the monster or where people thought it might be headed. But even with all that going on, life went on in the city, though many people were in mourning. Dark clothes hung over windows to symbolize sadness for the loss of the princess, and flowers called tiomias, the sign of sorrow and death for the Elven People, stood in pots everywhere, perfuming the air with their heady scent.

Benji saw the many strange looks. Phin heard the hushed whispers. But they continued on, heads held high, their horses proud.

The castle would have been hard to miss. It stood majestically in the center of town, its spires pointing towards the sky with flags in the elven colors of green and gold fluttering in the breeze. Two huge doors, engraved with lofty oak trees, loomed before them as they approached, making Benji feel small and vulnerable. Guards, clad in mail and bearing spears, stood like statues before the entrance.

"Halt."

Phin and Benji stopped and dismounted, holding their horses beside them.

"Why have you come to the palace of the Elven King?" asked the guard who had commanded them to stop.

The older brother pulled the wrinkled piece of parchment from his pocket, bent and rough from sitting there so long, and handed it to where he guessed the guard was standing.

"I was summoned by your king and was to come urgently," he said with authority.

The guard's eyes skimmed over the note, coming to rest on the first line: the king's title. He looked up at the tall, stick-thin boy before him, then at the younger man beside him.

"You were summoned too?" the guard asked bluntly.

"He is my companion," Phin answered. "The king said to come in all urgency; you are delaying us." His voice was thick with a nobility he didn't really possess.

The guard's eyes widened at the commanding air about the young man before him, who was little more than a boy. But there was something noble about him. With a sigh, the guard handed the parchment letter back to Phin.

"Come," he said and turned toward the giant doors.

Somehow, it seemed almost magically, the doors opened slowly on silent hinges. The room within was stone and marble, gleaming from a recent wash. Tapestries and wall hangings decorated the fair stone with bright scenes of gallant battles and good times, while two grand staircases spiraled widely down from the upper levels, tiomias standing in vases on each step. Their fragrance was overpowering. Phin hadn't realized there were so many of that kind of flowers in all of the Eastland.

A servant came bustling down the stairs to meet them at the doorway, his dark green clothes a sign that he worked in the castle. He was young, his hair all in a flutter and his eyes bright. The man looked as if he was having a very hectic day and them being here hadn't improved it. Without a sound the guard turned and left them to go back to his post.

"Are you Piaphin?" the frantic servant asked quickly.

"Y-yes," Phin answered uncertainly.

The servant sighed as if a great weight had been lifted off his shoulders.

"Oh finally, master! The king has been waiting-er –"

"WHERE IS HE! WHERE IS THE BOY!"

The poor elf jumped along with Phin. Benji looked instantly up at the right-hand stairs.

An elf, broader than most, was running down the stairs. He was graying and on the older side with a few wrinkles on his royal face, especially at the base of the golden crown he had worn for so long. Robes billowing out behind him, he came to the base of the stairs and rushed toward the two young men, arms wide.

"Phin! My good young man! Welcome back to Niathorn," he said and roughly grabbed the half-blood's shoulders in a way he seemed to think was friendly.

Phin coughed uncomfortably and said politely, "It's nice to be back, sir – king."

"Yes, yes, whatever. Now, to business!" the king said. He put an arm tightly around Phin's shoulders and began 'leading' (more so dragging) him away.

The young man stumbled, his weak leg giving way and the sleepless night and long days catching up with him. Benji ran forward and grabbed his brother's arm to support him. With strange shock the king let go of Phin and truly looked at the men.

Both their faces were sunburned and dust-dried. The younger man, whom the king didn't know, had three messy cuts that had been unskillfully 'cleaned' running across his temple. Phin looked half-starved, his ribs sticking slightly out under his shirt, and his hair was even more scruffy than usual. His face was weary, haggard, and fatigued.

Compassion flooded the worried, tense king's heart.

"Talk can wait. You boys need rest and a good meal, it looks like – especially you, Phin," he said and turned to Benji. "I *am* sorry, lad, but I didn't catch your name." He put out his hand in a polite gesture.

Benji took the extended hand and told the king his name and his father's name for formality. The elf felt the calluses and burst blisters that had made the young man's hand rough and stolen away the smoothness of youth too early. He was holding the hand of a man long accustomed to work, not the hand of a boy.

"Now, you two will take rooms and rest for the day. This evening we will talk." It sounded like a command. "Baset!" The servant snapped to attention. "Take these two boys to two good guest rooms with basins for washing and bring them a good meal at noon, or before if they request it."

The servant, Baset, bowed, "My lord."

"Thank you, thank you, sir, for your hospitality," Phin said truthfully. The king nodded and waited until the servant had led them away before he himself left, his forehead furrowed with concern.

Baset led the two weary boys, the younger supporting his limping stepbrother, to two guest rooms.

"There is a bowl of water on the table near the door, and I shall bring your meal later," the servant said, bowing slightly, then turned and rushed away, hurried again by some other pressing matter.

Benji took the room on the left, and Phin limped to the one on the right with the help of his ever-ready staff. The elder brother shut the smooth wood door behind him and turned toward the copper basin of water. He splashed his dry, hot face and worked the coolness into his hands and through his grimy, light brown hair. Phin's stomach murmured softly, but the young man ignored it, going instead to the soft feather mattress, and collapsed into the pillows. His leg hurt, his head swam, and his stomach growled, but still it was his exhaustion that won the fight for most important. The young man's breathing deepened, and he thought no more of the problems around him. Sleep crept over him and was readily welcomed.

He could feel a cart rumbling beneath him, the wood-grains soft beneath his thin fingers. Thunder rolled suddenly and the sound of rain falling upon dirt and grass appeared.

He was riding a horse, its muscles churning beneath him, its glossy coat and mane dancing under his hands. The wind was in his hair, billowing it back around his sun-warmed face and ears. Mage whinnied. He knew the sound well. That was the horse he was on, the hooves pounding the hard earth.

He sat on the ground wrapped in a blanket. The warmth of it and the fire that crackled nearby heated him. Something snarled and he was up, a warm stick in his hand. Then Benji screamed, a sound full of pain and agony.

"Benji!" Phin gasped in his sleep and rolled over, hands flying through the air as if he was trying to catch something. The movement woke him, along with the sudden tightness of the covers around him. Without thinking, the young man's hands rubbed through his fluffy hair erratically to calm himself.

"A dream, just a dream," he whispered to himself stupidly.

The scream had sounded amazingly real. Phin shivered and dragged himself out of the tangle of blankets, happy to be awake. Nonetheless, he was glad to have slept, for most of the fatigue had left him. His mind was clearer, and the weariness was thankfully gone.

Phin crawled from his bed and splashed his face with water from the basin again. Beside it was a tray with a bowl of thick stew (still warm), some bread, and a glass of wine. The young man ate it like someone who hadn't eaten in days, remembering the sweet taste of elven wine. There was no other like it.

Just then did he realize that he had slept in his travel-worn clothes, including his boots, and dozed past noon. Also his leg no longer hurt, nor did he limp. With thin fingers, the young man investigated the leg and found that a long strip of cloth bound the injury. From either medicine, or by magic (most likely the former as magic was scarce and rare and not to be used on simple cuts, no matter how deep), he was nearly healed.

After changing into a clean set of clothes, he walked to the small window. The breeze ruffled his hair and the loose collar of his shirt, and he listened to the gentle sounds of the city. Voices of elves, adults and children, hovered up to his ears along with the noises of horses and other animals. For a moment he could almost imagine he was eleven again and was living in the palace of the Elven King, with his best friend Yaja.

Phin and Benji entered the council room that evening warily, while Baset hovered along behind them, having led them there. Inside sat the king, one of his elders, two strangers dressed in silver, and two other elves. The king rose and welcomed them heartily, leading them to two open seats. Phin and Benji both sat down, and Baset hurried away. Phin wished he could have left with him as his staff scraped the silken wood floor. Then he leaned it beside his chair. The king rose.

"My friends, I know you have all heard of or have seen what happened to my daughter," he said. It was not a question, but still there were many curt, tense nods.

"Then you also know that I would do almost anything to get her back," he continued sternly. More nods. Phin was beginning to feel apprehensive, especially since no one was answering so *he* knew what was going on.

The king went on to explain what he and his elders had found out in the book of prophecies while he paced the floor in front of the table. Then he told them what the mages had found out in the pool.

"What!" Phin yelped, sitting bolt upright. The gathering of people jumped, shaken by the sudden outburst after the long quiet.

"You want *me* to go after the princess," he continued with disbelief, not believing it could possibly be true. "For heaven's sake, your majesty – I'm blind! And she hates me!"

The king folded his hands behind his back and stood his ground, appraising the young man with weary eyes.

"You are the finder of the vine-bow," he said evenly and with diplomatic patience.

"What does that matter? I can give someone else the bow!" Phin snapped and pushed his chair back.

"But you are the one who found it, so rightly you are the only one who can use it," the king answered.

Phin snorted. "I am more a danger to the friends around me than the enemy before me." Benji hid a snort of laughter as he recognized his own words. He thought it would be better to say nothing for the time being. "Most likely your daughter and I both would die with it in my hands," Phin finished.

"You should not jest about such things!" the king thundered with righteous anger.

"I'm not joking!"

The king's eyes glowed with such contempt that he looked ready to slap the young man before him. Hands of the people around the council room were tight upon the arms of their chairs, but no one dared to say anything. Suddenly the old mage rose solemnly from his chair.

"Bridle your anger, king and noble man, and work together to figure something out," he said calmly. "It does nothing for the princess if you two argue."

Phin, instead of being soothed, was angered. He threw himself to his feet, knocking the chair behind him over with a crash, and grabbed his staff both to steady himself, to keep it from falling on the floor, and as something to have in his hands so he didn't just attack someone. He seemed ready to explode at the king like a madman.

Benji grabbed his arm. "Phin, calm down and give me a chance to talk," he said and slowly he rose from his chair. Phin retrieved his own chair and sat down, fist still clenched tightly around his staff.

"Majesty, and . . . other people, I am Benjamin, son of Andrew, Phin's stepbrother. Have him give me the bow, for protection along with my sword, and I can go after the princess so he doesn't have to. We all know the grudge they have against each other, but I can do it, if you think she would come with me." It wasn't much of a speech, but it served the purpose and he sat down, content with it.

The room was quiet. The others in the room waited for the king to answer, but he was simply studying Benji with something like awe. A chair creaked as someone moved, but no one spoke, not even one of the mages. Nobody knew what to say.

"Benji . . ." Phin said quietly, his concern for his brother overriding the anger he held.

"Come on man, I'm seventeen!" Benji snarled, rounding on him. "I'm saving *your* skin."

"My skin doesn't *need* saving. I can do this," Phin said stiffly, his pride slightly wounded by the thought of his younger brother doing the quest he had been asked to do. He got up. "Elven King, I accept."

Benji shot a cunning smile at the king and winked. The Elven King's face broke into a relieved smile, and he instantly respected the young man, though with slight worry at how devious his mind was. Shaking his head, a smile on his face, Benji leaned back in his high-backed chair. He really had had no intention of going on this quest, but it was his brother's responsibility, his calling. The young man couldn't help using a little trickery to get his brother to go. It was for the better, he hoped.

"On a few conditions," Phin added. "One: my brother comes along."

"I wouldn't think of staying behind," Benji shot in, folding his arms across his chest as if this whole adventure was as easy as a walk in the park.

Phin gave a half-smile over his shoulder, which dropped as he faced the assembly again.

"Second: we need a guide to wherever it is we're going."

"Already arranged," the king said, now pleased with how things were progressing. If Phin would go, everything else would go fine. "May I introduce Layen and Salgo."

The two elves rose. Benji then suddenly recognized the second, who stood slightly taller and younger than the other. He was the messenger that had brought Phin the urgent letter from the king. The elf gave Benji a short smile that only slightly breached etiquette before turning his full attention back on the king.

"Layen is a guide better than any other in the East, and Salgo is a messenger who has traveled nearly every part of the Four Lands.," the king said. "They shall guide you to the edge of the Westland, but no farther"

"The Westland!" Benji barked like a wounded dog.

"That is where my daughter has been taken."

Benji slightly wished to back out at that piece of news. Those who went to the Westland either didn't come back or came back profoundly different. He wondered what his dead mother would say if she knew he was embarking on a quest to save a princess in the Westland.

"All right then," Phin said, fairly shaken. He had no idea how serious this journey really would be. "Last: we need provisions."

"That too can be arranged. You leave tomorrow at dawn," the lord elf said in a 'no questions asked' way. Benji and Phin drew back at the sudden command. It seemed the king's patience was gone. He wanted his daughter, and he wanted her now.

"Um . . . all right, I suppose," Phin mumbled. "By the way, where are the horses?"

"In a large open field. Your horse, Piaphin – Mage, I believe you called him – nearly killed one of my grooms when he tried to lead the stallion into a stall."

The young man colored slightly. "My apologies, sir,"

"No, no," the elf said waving his hands dismissively, "All is well. Go get dinner, and the provisions will be dropped in your room later. Be ready to leave at dawn. Salgo, Layen, a quick word."

9

Thunder Storm

Phin shifted the pack on his back. It felt heavy and cumbersome, and pulled on his thin shoulders. He felt somewhat surreal, as if all this was being lived by someone else. Benji yawned and stretched again, his muscles still tired and stiff from sleep. Salgo was running a brush over his gray horse's back tenderly, his gold hair fluttering like the back of the mare in the brisk morning breeze. He didn't seem to want to talk to any of them.

Layen was rather large for an elf. His face was stern and commanding; he was the one who instantly took charge of the group. He loitered beside his horse, a proud gelding that matched the elf's physique.

The air was cool, with a tinge of autumn chill in it. Phin pulled his cloak about him tighter to ward away the nip of cold and smelled the breeze that tickled his ears and face. It was scented with dirt and drying leaves that were beginning to fall softly to the ground, and faintly in the background was the smell of tiomias, the flowers still scenting many rooms and houses.

The young man wondered suddenly why recently he had been interested in smells. Before the storm, so many years earlier, he had smelled the rain before it had come. This seemed to be happening often for some odd reason.

Benji cleared his throat, looking up at the sky above the treetops. "Not to be impatient or anything, but what *are* we waiting for?" Storm fidgeted.

Salgo chuckled in a light elven voice. He had wide-ranging emotions and an easygoing face to go with it. His body was light, with long, thin legs and strong hands. By far he was the best on horseback, used to galloping across wide spaces and traveling for days at a time to deliver his messages.

"I don't know," Layen answered, looking back at the silent castle and the sleeping, shadow-cloaked city. "I thought the king might send us his blessing, but . . ."

"The good king is a bit preoccupied with worrying about his daughter and would be far happier if we just got out of here and did the job," Salgo finished seriously and stepped nimbly onto his gray horse's back.

Then the bald mage appeared suddenly, as if he had sprung out of the earth. They all gasped, but Salgo's jaw dropped.

"Honorable mage, forgive me if you heard what I just said," he gasped, coloring as much as a fair elf could.

The mage smiled faintly. "There is nothing to forgive. You spoke your mind. But I do have some parting words for all of you," he said. "Benjamin, you forgot this in your room." The mage held out the young man's treasured flute.

"Oh, thank you, sir," Benji said taking it, trying not to sound too relieved and panicky. He stowed it quickly away in his pack.

"Always remember the things you have read," the mage said suddenly, laying a wrinkled hand on the young man's shoulder. "You are a noble . . . stepbrother to Piaphin." Benji wondered vaguely what had caused the delay. "Your knowledge will serve your group well."

"Salgo," the mage continued, turning to the messenger, "run before danger comes, and you will not have to flee after. Your following this advice may save your company one day." Salgo looked at him in confusion, but the mage had already turned away. "Layen, do not always trust to logic as you do now." The mage regarded the older elf with a kind of severity. "It may one day save your life."

The mage turned last to Phin, his eyes warm and compassionate. "Phin, your past, and your sight, will return to you when you take your other form." He smiled suddenly as he faced the young man. "You have a very interesting time ahead of you, but it will all make sense later."

The odd mage's last remark instantly made no sense to anyone. Other form? My past? wondered Phin. *What* will make sense later? No one knew what to say. Then, beaming at all of them like a prideful father, the old mage clapped his crinkled hands once and disappeared again, gone so suddenly it seemed as if he had been sucked into the ground again.

Phin shook his head as he clambered shakily onto Mage's back. He had coaxed the wild, free-willed stallion into taking two saddlebags thrown across his back with a strap, but it made mounting difficult.

"That old elf's half-mad – he must be," Benji said, sitting stiffly on Storm's back.

"I agree," Phin said, grabbing the white stallion's mane.

"Don't say that!" Salgo warned. "Mages are strange people, but need to be shown respect. They know things: things no one but mages know."

The ears of the stallion called Mage perked up at hearing his name used so many times.

Phin shook his head, still baffled by the mage's odd comments. "Shall we be off?"

"Yes, the morning is nearly all the way up," Layen said, throwing his leg over his broad gelding's back. With barely a touch the horse started forward, trotting briskly in the morning air.

Salgo's mare, which was much lighter and quicker, was soon beside him, followed by Storm and Mage. Their riders shook off the weariness of the night in hopes of a new adventure.

The air remained cool even as the sun rose above the horizon. Clouds stretched like long fingers across its mighty face, causing some parts of the land below to be hidden in shadow and others bathed in lemon-colored sunlight.

The four horsemen rode on in the Eastern Forest. Salgo took the lead, Layen close on his right flank. Benji and Phin, side by side, followed behind. The younger brother was still stiff and tired, but his eyes were alight with adventure-seeking. Phin was still trying to find a comfortable position for the pack on his shoulders and his legs around the cumbersome saddlebags.

"There must be enough food in here for a year of travels!" he snapped finally.

Salgo laughed and looked over his shoulder at him. "Maybe if we all ate like you," he said, referring to how baggy the shirt Phin wore was, when it would have been tight on anyone else.

Phin snorted. "If we all ate like me, it would be gone in a week."

They laughed, not believing him.

"It's true!" Benji shot in. "He eats like a starved horse and still is as skinny as a stick with his ribs jutting out."

"Thanks, Ben," Phin said sardonically. The two elves ahead laughed loudly. It was as if they were all old friends.

Large branches had been cut from the trees to make room for the path. Rocks and logs had been rolled or thrown aside by some strong hands and the trail was amazingly smooth as it cut through the dense forest. The horses enjoyed the brisk walks and slow trots, their hooves stamping the packed earth in a drumming rhythm. Echoing loudly through the forest came the sound of men laughing and talking. It was as if a joyful party was going home, not embarking upon a possibly dangerous journey to the dark and dreaded Westland.

Many miles behind crawled a large, bat-like creature. Its feet gripped the ground in an almost uncertain motion, its body hunched and creeping like a beast afraid of being discovered. The coarse fur along its neck was standing up like the hackles of an angered hound, its nose sniffing the ground as it crawled.

The monster didn't dare creep along in the center of the path; there was far too great a risk of being seen. No, it crept instead about a foot from the trail, covered safely by the brush at the feet of the tree. Dense underbrush and tangled bushes concealed it from the eyes of anyone that might look back.

Its companion had gone to get another 'friend' to help them succeed. It wasn't that they had failed, only that they needed help, though the monsters loathed the help of any creature besides their own kind. But the prey was stronger than they had expected, and guarded by others like it that cut with cold iron and attacked with strength that should not have been found in a weak "human". As much as the beast hated to admit it, they needed assistance. The wing of the crawling bat-creature was evidence of that. It was still crumpled and unsuitable for long distance flying.

The monster suddenly smiled, or what was meant to be a smile. It looked more like a snarl, its sharp teeth dripping. Nonetheless, it was pleased. The smell of his quarry was here, only an hour old and moving slowly. There were others with it, yes there were others, but the assistance would take care of them. It smiled its bared-teeth smile again.

The bat didn't speed up its slow careful steps. It was in no shape to take on four men or run down four horses, not yet. Baring its long fangs in frustration, the monster knew it had to wait for the return of the other and their reinforcement. What it was that would help them, it didn't know. But it would be fast and lethal.

This time they would not be eluded. This time they would savor the taste of the elven blood and man blood in their mouths. The quarry, the half-blood, would be killed slowly, deliberately. He was the only one who really mattered; the others were only added bonuses – blood to tantalize them and to make them want more.

The Master knew his servants well.

At the same time, around noon, the small group stopped to eat and stretch their legs, giving the horses a few minutes to graze and rest. Then they started back off down the trail. Layen, who was obviously the leader, said they could just walk the horses casually because they were making good time.

The party continued on at their leisurely pace. Phin and Benji continued on a merry conversation, Salgo putting in a word or phrase once in a while. Layen spoke little, content on watching the road ahead or consulting an old parchment map he kept folded and stuffed away in his pocked when he wasn't using it. The sunlight deepened, warming the forest as late afternoon crept upon them. But late afternoon turned to twilight, and twilight to evening, and the sky darkened to a mystic blue.

As the darkness fell about them, the group drew off the trail and into a glade of lush sumac trees, their leaves only slightly red along the tips with the coming of autumn. A thin, ribbon-like stream that had dug itself into the ground wound through the sumacs like a thread of silver. The four men let their horses drink their fill before tethering them loosely to the trees. Sumac leaves provided a thick canopy, much like a roof, and the group dropped their packs there.

"Shall we have a fire?" Layen asked, holding up a dry branch.

"No!" both Phin and Benji yelped in fright, sounding rather like scared children.

Salgo and Layen starred at them oddly until one of them asked bluntly, "Why?"

Then the two young men told their companions about the bats and the terrible fight in the night.

"That's why you came in to Niathorn all bloodied," Salgo said, as if that was the missing piece in an essential riddle.

The two young men nodded solemnly, and no more was asked. They all slept well that night and were awakened early by Salgo, who shook them in a not-too-gentle manner. Layen suggested they eat quickly and then start off to make better time. The two young men nodded sluggishly, their eyes heavy and their limbs loose-jointed.

They all ate a bit of the bread and meat that they had packed and spread a little bit of the fruit between them. The horses again drank from the stream, this time joined by their riders.

Phin choked. The water was ice cold and woke him up easily. He pulled his water carrier from his pack and filled it the rest of the way with the stream water, knowing he might want a good drink on the road. Then the four of them started off again, in the same order as before.

The day was cloudy and cool, cool like rain and a wet fall. Phin and Benji pulled their warm cloaks from their packs and wrapped themselves in them. Phin's thin frame still shivered slightly in the cold, and a clamminess refused to be kept out by the thick cloth. He wished it would rain and be done with this cold, drab waiting.

His wish was granted.

The cloudy sky above suddenly rumbled, as if insulted by his anger at the cold. A drop of icy rain fell to the ground. Another soon followed it.

Layen and Salgo dug into their own packs hastily and both drew out two grayish-green cloaks. By then the rain was falling in steady drops. All the men, at almost the same moment, pulled up their hoods, shading their heads in the tunnel of cloth.

Great drops continued falling, clattering down on the trunks of trees and the earth below. Streams bubbled and rippled with the new water, rushing along more quickly in their frenzy to get where they needed to go. It had been a dry summer, nearly a drought in the Eastland and the rain was welcomed, but not by these four travelers. Phin now regretted wishing for something as foolish as rain when there was no dry shelter for them in sight.

The horses shook their manes and coats, displeased at the sudden wetness that fell into their fur. Hooves sunk deep into new mud as it formed in the path, and the saddlebags failed to keep the water from the things inside. Still no one suggested stopping. They awaited Layen's word because he was leading them, though only Salgo and his mare seemed to not be bothered by the rainfall.

But the leading elf, riding upon his broad gelding, showed no sign of stopping. He seemed to be either stubbornly acting like the rain wasn't there, or just too plain stubborn to stop at all. The horses plodded along without spirit and with ears back, only going for the sake of their masters, Mage especially.

Still the rain pattered on like the nimble steps of a cat, leaping and bounding from leaves, to tree trunks, to the backs of the rain-sloshed mounts. The thunder was its low purr, the lightning the flip of its gossamer tail.

There was a clap of thunder, like the rain cat's snarl, and three of the horses whinnied and spooked in fright. Salgo, who rode the only horse who hadn't, tried to settle the others and soothe them back to walking peacefully. With Storm he succeeded, for he was the tamest, but the other two failed to relax.

The thunder persisted, rolling and crashing again, as if the cat was hissing and spitting, fighting with the clouds for domination. Phin gripped tightly to Mage, one hand under his neck, the other on his mane. The young man was suddenly reminded of his first trip out of the Eastland. Then too there had been thunder and a spooked Mage who had tried to flee. There had also been the sound of dogs barking . . .

Again, over the thunder, he heard hounds yelping and again other noises were mingled in, though he couldn't distinguish what they were. It was all a jumble of thunder, dogs, and forest.

"Steady, steady boy," he soothed, unsure why he said it. Something deep within the depths of his soul cried for him to follow the sound of the beasts and the storm. Some part of him was screaming that that was where he belonged and that he had to follow it. His heart felt as if it might just leap from his chest and chase the receding thunder. But the young man shook his head, dismissing such foolish thoughts.

Mage reared and gave a war whinny that echoed in the trunks of the trees. His dripping tail lashed wildly and his pink eyes flared with ferocity as he bared his square teeth. The rest of the group drew back. Phin touched Mage along his jawbone, speaking calming words into the stallion's sodden mane, but it seemed Mage heard the beasts above the thunder as well, and he would not be soothed.

But the storm was lessening. Rain still fell heavily, but the cat's rumbling purr was drifting away. Phin's heart yearned for him to follow, to spur his horse forward into a run. He swallowed, forcing these feelings down into the pit of his stomach. What was wrong with him?

Salgo grabbed Mage's mane and brought him about, his mare's wet mane slapping against Phin's arm. The elf's sharp blue eyes were staring at the half-blood with concern.

"Phin, are you all right?" he asked.

"Of course, I'm fine," Phin answered quickly, pulling Mage in check. The stallion snorted, dipping his wet head and shaking his dangling forelock out of his pink eyes. His ears remained mulishly back.

Salgo patted the white horse's neck and swung his mare away. Layen had gained mastery over his gelding and was again in control.

"Everyone set?" he said, more from habit than anything else. Without waiting for an answer he said, "Good. Let's go. It's just rain, after all."

Phin rubbed his sightless eyes and found he was sweating. He pulled his hood closer around his head, obscuring his chalky face from view, and started the albino stallion forward, settling into brooding thoughts. The cat's last purr murmured through the trees as the feline padded away on his wet, leaping paws and lashed his gauzy, lightning tail one last time in an elusive parting.

10

A Different Path

The rain finally cleared, leaving behind a wet forest, but the clouds stubbornly refused to let the sun shine through. Four men on four horses rode grudgingly through the woods, their spirits dampened with moisture like the forest around them. Benji's unfaltering optimism had wavered. They were wet and uncomfortable, jolting as their horses stumbled along the wet path, picking through puddles and mud bogs that had appeared before their feet.

Suddenly, Layen turned them off the large road onto a sketchy, less traveled road to the left. It was sharply cut with rocks and logs that had fallen across the path and no one had bothered to cast aside. Tree branches stuck out over the path at exactly the right height to take off a tall rider's head – someone like Phin or Salgo.

"Lovely, this should be loads of fun for the four of us and our soaked horses," Salgo snorted malevolently. His mood had changed dramatically from the laughing, merry elf, to this angry, short-tempered one. Even his horse looked sullen and annoyed, her tail flicking with agitation.

"Right," Layen said, completely unemotional and even-tempered as always. "We'll go in single file."

"Not that we can do anything else," Benji pointed out.

Layen had finally had it. He did have emotions, but they didn't come off as strongly as a normal person's did. "All right! Salgo, Benji, neither of you are being forced to be here! Go back to your comfortable rooms at Niathorn if you wish. I mean it. Go!"

Neither Salgo nor Benji moved. The latter ran his hand over the scabs on his temple and dropped his eyes. The former just continued looking into the woods as if deep in thought, his eyes narrowed slightly.

"No," he said finally. "Let's go. You aren't wrong about these kinds of things, Layen. But I don't hear our all-essential member talking."

They looked back at Phin. He was stroking Mage and muttering to the wet stallion in a calming voice like a child talking to his pet dog when it was afraid of thunder storms. When they stopped he looked up suddenly.

"Sorry. Did you men make a decision yet? I thought I'd wait until you stopped arguing," he said calmly, with a bit of sarcasm in his voice though his face was unreadable under his long hood.

"If only you were all like him," Layen said wistfully, shaking his head.

They chuckled and Salgo explained to Phin the trail. The young man wrinkled his nose at the sound of it, especially of branches jutting out at him that he couldn't see.

"If we have to go, we shall," he said finally. What they could see of his face looked unhappy.

So it was decided. Layen went in first with Salgo taking the rear.

As little as Phin would have liked to admit it, he enjoyed Salgo's little stream of warnings and commentary. The thin elf told him when to dodge tree branches or swerve his horse around rocks, using his smooth gentle voice like he was talking to a spooked horse. Phin followed those directions and by doing so saved himself a lot of pain and bruises, but Mage soon grew annoyed with turning and stepping around both mud and brambles.

Layen led the way like a brigand in his own territory. He knew the turns and twists of the trail as if they were lazy paths in a garden. When Benji finally asked him about it, he responded shortly that this was his life: tracking and guiding. Benji sunk down and ducked a heavy, dripping branch. Phin followed suit soon after because of Salgo's careful guidance.

He realized that a staff would have done no good here had he been on foot, and he would have badly hurt himself.

Everything dripped with the rain. Benji and Phin were extremely grateful for the warmth and protection of their elven-made cloaks. The horses, with no such protection, were soaked with water, their manes hanging limply along their necks, the forelocks hanging damply in the horses' eyes. Storm and Layen's gelding were the most unhappy. They were accustomed to warm, dry stalls when it was cold and wet outside. Both plodded along, stamping their hooves in the mud and snorting with displeasure.

The day dragged on, still damp and chilly. A cold breeze rippled through the trees, cutting like a knife into the very bones of the men, even through the warm, thick cloaks. Noon came without a change. There was nowhere to stop to eat, so the group ate as they rode, the horses grumbling to themselves because they didn't have a chance to graze.

It was quite difficult. They were forced to duck and dodge tree branches and saplings while staying on the back of a horse that was often stumbling or stepping upon rocks or logs in the way. If that wasn't enough, the young men had to try to eat while balancing in this act. More often than not they choked on a piece of salted pork or stuffed a chunk of bread into their eyes. This didn't improve anyone's tempers.

At about mid-afternoon the clouds began thinning and letting bits of blue sky through like shards of azure glass. The sun cut sharply through the remaining clouds and rained down its warm yellow light to dry the wet, cold land.

The four men looked up at the leaves that were green and dripping still with the small, escaping beads. The youngest, Benji, threw back his green hood and felt again the sun's rays on his weary face and tussled brown hair. Phin pushed back his clammy tunnel as well and breathed.

"We can get in a few good hours of brisk walks and long trots when it dries. We'll be coming to a larger way again," Layen said, dragging his waterlogged hood away from his stern face.

The horses continued on, lifting their hooves higher than usual, almost in a prance to keep from getting stuck in the muck of the woods. A few moments later, Layen stopped them.

"This is the new path," he said, pointing to two very thick and fierce looking bushes.

Salgo cocked his eyebrows and shot a look at Benji, but said nothing, remembering their prior experience with Layen's odd paths. Phin wondered at the awkward silence and the stop, but decided not to ask questions. Someone was bound to tell him what was going on sooner or later. Mage and the other horses took the break to crop a few mouthfuls of the dank grass.

"Guardian shrubs!" the group's guide snapped by way of explanation. Then addressing the bushes, "I know the path lies there. Let us enter!"

To Benji's amazement the bushes shuttered, sharp needles and leaves quivering. Then, almost grudgingly it seemed, the two bushes pulled apart to reveal a well kept, smooth path with a few wet leaves along the trail. The crisscrossing branches above made a thick roof that had let only a little of the rain through.

Layen turned his gelding sharply and went at a bouncing trot down the road. Benji spurred Storm in behind him with Phin beside him, Mage sniffing the gnarled bushes with interest.

The shrubs quivered angrily as if they longed to stab and scratch the horses that trotted by. Their needles clacked together in a kind of growl. Salgo leapt his horse quickly forward as they snapped shut, missing the mare's tail by only inches.

"Feisty bushes, guardian shrubs," Salgo said as he turned and looked over his shoulder, as if he was regarding the weather.

"But good guardians," Layen said brusquely.

The four horses leapt forward at a strong canter, enjoying the freedom of the wide, well-kept road. Their hooves drummed deeply on the hard-packed dirt so that one could almost imagine a song traveling with them.

11

A Stronger Attacker

By the next day, late morning, the group stood at the edge of the forest. Salgo was in the lead, his golden hair fanning back in the wind. The great middle grasslands, called simply the Great Plains, billowed before them like a sea of stationary green.

Layen pulled up beside the elf's stopped horse. The messenger's forehead was furrowed slightly, and he looked with questionable eyes out over the plain.

"Something wrong?" the leader asked.

Salgo's eyes continued to gaze intently out over the plains.

"I can't tell. Something tells me there is, but I don't see it," he answered. The worry dropped, and his good-natured attitude came back. "I'm probably just suspicious. Let's be on."

Salgo's mare stepped lightly ahead, his soft ears pricked forward. She suddenly whinnied shrilly, her front legs coming up in a tiny kick that her elven master would permit. Her rider moved with her and stared again into the open plains quietly.

"What's wrong?" Benji asked, urging Storm forward.

The mare by now had quieted, looking like she always did. One dainty hoof pawed the ground, and her nostrils still quavered.

"Must have caught the smell of a wolf or something in the wind," Salgo said calmly, worry and uncertainty still written in his eyes. "Let's get some running in, shall we?"

Without an answer, he galloped the mare forward, her tail soaring behind in her smooth gait, and down the slope of the hill leading into the Great Plains. Phin, having heard the tone in the elf's voice, knew he had lied. It was odd. Salgo and his mare were not like this, and the messenger had never concealed something if it was important. Phin wished he knew what it was.

The group galloped on, enjoying again the feeling of the wind in their hair and the unhindered sun on their faces. Grass whispered and sang beneath their horse's legs as they sailed down the gradual hill, their steps so long it almost seemed as if they were flying. Phin leaned low on Mage's neck and urged him on mentally, loving the feeling of freedom that he got when he rode Mage in the open. His hands loosened slightly on the stallion's lashing mane, and he allowed himself to cling almost wholly with his legs, the white stallion's mane brushing at his face with teasing strokes.

Benji's Storm raced along beside him, swinging his broad, black body in the wind and fighting for his head so he could stretch out and beat the white stallion. The big gelding's hooves stomped the ground, shaking the earth and crushing the weeds beneath him. Benji clung on tightly, half with wild panic, the other half with wild joy. The horses were covering ground as easy as walking, and when Benji glanced back, the Eastern forest was leagues behind. They raced up the next hill, the sun on their faces.

Salgo was still in the lead, his mare accustomed to fast gallops. The gray horse galloped into a valley, tearing up the earth beneath her supple legs. Her rider was standing slightly in the stirrups, guiding more by mane than reins. Then the mare screamed, her kind eyes white with panic. She reared, nearly throwing her accomplished rider, his head snapping forward so it slammed into her neck with bone breaking ferocity.

The elf on her back, who was an expert rider, recovered, grabbed on, and held, his nose dripping with blood. Dark gray mane blinded his eyes, got in his mouth, and tangled with his own golden hair. The mare dropped and then reared again. She was mad with fear, her eyes rolling, and her ears clamped against her skull.

The others ran down into the valley to her, their own eyes wide with dismay. She was nearly having her exposed stomach ripped out by a giant, two-headed snake! It was tan with broad, scarlet bands that looked like bloody gashes. Sharp gleaming fangs that dripped with poison were in a gaping snarl. A red, forked tongue was lashing out like a dagger, tasting the air for the mare's scent. With its heads in a raised up position, it was taller than Salgo's terrified mare.

The two heads, large as human torsos, were winding back and forth, seeking for an open spot to strike. Sharp, needle-like barbs traced its spinal cord, down both necks and to the tip of its tail.

"What on earth is that?" Benji shouted. "Where did it come from? Why didn't' anyone see it?"

"What *is* it then? Someone describe it!" Phin bellowed back.

"It's a giant, two-headed snake," Layen said with his usual diplomatic calmness.

"Oh, what fun," Phin muttered darkly, holding Mage's mane firmly in his hands. "Just what we needed." He had no doubt that it was connected, however remotely, with the large bats that had attacked him and Benji in the night. Mage's muscles surged under his legs as he launched forward.

Layen grabbed his short, thick sword and leapt from his gelding's back. The horse was more than happy to flee, and it ran, reins flying in the wind. Benji, though shaking with fear, his insides like ice water, did the same, unsheathing his ancient sword in one shaky motion. Phin pulled Mage up, praying his stallion was brave enough to stay still. He could hear the murmur of the serpent's body as it pulled itself across the grass, breaking stems and leaves with each movement of its scaly belly.

Layen and Benji rushed in, the latter rather shakily, and began hacking at the monster's necks and body with their small-seeming weapons to buy Salgo time to get away. It snapped its jaws down toward the two stabbing sword points, giant eyes glaring at the two people who dared to attack it. The scales along its body were far too thick and hard for the swords to pierce. Still, the two brave warriors attacked the snake's snarling heads, stabbing for any opening they could get while darting away from its snapping jaws.

Phin summoned his courage and cantered Mage toward the frightened gray mare. Salgo would not be able to hold on long, and the gray mare showed no sign of trying to run – not while the snake-heads toyed with her and covered her escape routes.

"Salgo!" the young man hollered, forcing Mage toward the panicked mare.

It wasn't a good move. One of the snake's heads turned in his direction and stretched its neck to take him.

Mage was brave, but rather stupid in his gallantry. The stallion screamed a war cry and attacked, bucking like a crazed horse. He whinnied again and reared, striking the head in the jaw with one strong hoof.

Phin, having put all his concentration on Salgo and the mare, fell, landing in the grass, with the saddlebags beside him. The snake's head snapped at where Mage had been, only a step from where the young man lay, gasping for lost breath. Phin dropped his heavy pack and bow and got up, long dagger in hand. It was wholly guesswork. All he had to go by were the snake's sounds, and it made few. Mage, having been nearly bitten, had finally run.

Meanwhile, Benji and Layen were still chopping at the snake erratically, like children battling a "fake monster" with sticks. Benji's muscles were numb, straining to their breaking point and screaming in an unheard language. Sweat ran down his face making it look polished. The scabs on his temple burned.

Salgo finally slipped, losing his hold, and fell from his crazed mare's back. The snake's other head dragged its body forward, pinpointing its cruel black eyes upon the elf on the ground.

Phin's mind was swirling. Strong memories he had never heard before flashed wildly through his head. The young man shook his head and went into a crouch. He had heard the snake move. It was near him, so close . . . right by where Salgo had fallen.

Phin tightened his grip on his dagger's hilt, felt the muscles knot in his legs. He leapt toward where he thought the monster was, like a great (insane) cat.

And missed. His jump was too high, and he raked open his stomach on the snake's barbs. It had lowered itself toward Salgo, and Phin's jump had been too strong, his thin frame flying above the monster's back. The young man landed on the grass, blood welling through his ripped shirt – and ripped skin – and soaking the grass red. But it had succeeded his purpose. The snake turned its dark eyes upon him and away from Salgo. It could smell the blood; it could almost taste it. That was what it wanted.

The snake's second head was still biting at Benji and Layen. One of its eyes had been punctured, and strange, dark blood frothed from it.

"Is there . . . any way . . . to beat this thing?" Benji gasped. He was still frightened as anything, but what else could he do? That was when he saw Phin on the ground, drenched in blood.

"No!" he yelled in disbelief, and ran behind the tail of the two-headed serpent, dodging the whipping spikes.

The second head followed him, tangling itself with the other. That's what gave Layen the idea.

"Hey! Benji, Salgo, if you can hear me! Make the snakes fight themselves! It's the only way," he shouted, lashing at the snake continually though his sword was going dull on its thick scales.

Benji heard as he kneeled over his wounded brother. Phin's arms were crossed over his stomach, but he forced himself into a sitting position. Pain washed over his tight face, lashing through his pale, vacant eyes as sweat flowed down his face.

"I'll go," he gasped, yanking himself to his feet. Blood had clotted the wounds, but still a little of the warm fluid seeped through.

"Phin, you can't," Benji started.

"I have to . . . I'm the one . . . the snake wants. I'll be bait . . . so one will . . . bite the other. You keep that one busy," Phin said pointing toward the sound of the second head which Salgo was now shooting at, having pulled himself off the ground after his mare had run away. "I'll lead the other . . . toward me . . . just watch."

"But-"

"Do as I say!" Phin snarled, his face contorted in anger and pain. "I am still your elder brother by two years."

Benji was taken aback. He nodded curtly.

Phin, of course, didn't see his nod, but started off anyway. His right hand was still closed on his long dagger, the other clamped over his slightly bleeding torso and what was left of his shirt. Benji hollered at the head nearest him, drawing it toward him. Layen still fought the other.

"Hey! Hey snake! To me!" Phin gasped for a deep breath. This was taking all his strength and bravery. He was calling a monster toward him with only a knife to defend himself. "Come here, snaky-snaky. You can smell my fresh blood. I knov you can. Come! I challenge you!"

The snake swiveled its head, slapping Layen away with its tail. Slowly, it advanced with jaws gaping and tongue flicking lightly out to taste the air. Benji still held the other at bay, watching his brother with anxiety.

Phin backed up, his knife hand behind him, waiting for the feeling of the other's neck. He felt it suddenly, cold and hard as steel under his fingertips, with each scale like the edge of a dagger. It flinched at his touch, but continued keeping at Benji, who harried the monster with his sword. Phin waited, realizing how foolish this was. He couldn't see, and he was going to try to leap aside at the right moment.

Salgo saw it. He saw a thin, bloody young man standing unflinchingly before the head of a great snake monster. All Phin had was a dagger and two blind eyes. Yet he stood like a warrior in battle, weapon up, even if it was only bravado.

The elf knew what he was going to do. He stood still, watching and waiting. The snake barred its teeth, a look of hate and hunger in its dark eyes. It pulled itself forward slowly, coils of flesh cutting through the grass. Then its huge head struck forward.

"Jump!" Salgo yelled suddenly.

Phin followed orders without even thinking and dodged, sprawling flat and getting a mouth-full of grass. There was an inhuman scream as one head's fangs burrowed into the other's neck, cutting through the metallic scales as if they were soft clay. The creature thrashed and writhed, its own poison bubbling through it. Both heads burst into flames – black, foul smelling clouds of smoke billowing up from the burning corpses. Then it disappeared in an eruption of smoke, either dead or gone.

Phin passed out from pain and exertion and blood loss, the ground spinning a moment before he lost all thought.

12

Time of Recovery

Someone was fanning his face, while two thin hands wrapped his stomach with tight cloth. Phin groaned. His head felt like it was filled with fluid that was being stirred wildly. All the muscles in his body were tight, wound cords that refused to move or break. He groaned again, slightly louder.

"He's coming around," came a voice. "Are they wrapped yet, Salgo?"

"Yes, just got done," said another voice, lighter than the last. "They weren't as deep as they looked at first. I don't think any organs were injured."

Phin opened his eyes, but they dropped again. He wet his mouth, trying to speak. It was too dry to even move, as dry as a desert, but willing the little strength he still possessed, he said, "W . . . water."

"I got it," said the second voice, which Phin now placed as Salgo.

Cool liquid flowed between his slightly parted lips. It filled his mouth, and the young man willed his throat to swallow. Life danced through him like snowflakes as the water filled his thirst. He sputtered as he got too much, and the excess slid out the corners of his mouth.

Now Phin felt the pain in his stomach and lower chest. The cuts hadn't been deep, as Salgo said, but they had been long and had bled heavily, sapping him of strength he desperately needed. The young man breathed deeply, which hurt, and drowned himself in the air. This time his eyes stayed open. His head stilled again.

"Is the monster dead?" he asked apprehensively, ashamed at how quivery and frail his voice sounded. The last thing he remembered was a lot of grass, shrieking noises, and his head spinning.

"Gone. We don't know if it is dead, but it's certainly gone," the first voice said. Benji. Phin now knew it was Benji.

"You're quite a brave man, Phin. Someday the elves will sing ballads and songs about you as you stood before the great two-headed snake," Salgo said, laughing lightly.

Phin smiled faintly. He wiggled his hand slightly just to see if it would move, and it did. Then he breathed deeply again and shut his eyes.

"Where's Layen?" he asked. His stomach still throbbed and hurt. At the moment it felt like he would never move again, except in small motions.

"He went to find the horses. He's got a nasty welt on his legs where the snake's tail got him, but he wouldn't just sit back and let the horses run wild," Salgo answered.

"Mage will," Phin said softly. "If Layen comes back and I'm . . . out, then tell him that." It was too much work to talk. Phin sighed and allowed himself to sleep again.

The company stayed a long time in that place, waiting for the wounds to heal. Layen came back in the late evening leading Storm and his own brown gelding. The dark stallion had red, irritated patches along his saddle line, ripped reins, and a tangle of briar and weed for a mane and a tail. Layen's gelding was far better off, the leather of his saddle and bridle much stronger and softer than human-made.

Four days they spent by the grass that had been torn by the monster snake's tail. The days dragged on, but still they waited. Phin slept often, barely moving or speaking when he was awake. Under Salgo's and now Layen's rather mediocre wound-healing knowledge, the cuts mended into scraggily scars. But still Phin didn't get well. Benji, while he groomed and healed his horse, hoped his sudden thoughts were wrong: poison on the snake's barbs.

Salgo was worried, often pacing or sitting sullenly, chin on his knees, staring off into the plains. There had been no sighting of his mare, and he was bothered by her absence. Layen went out daily to hunt for the two lost horses, with none to little success. He sometimes saw sightings of Mage, but he held true to what Phin had first said; the stallion would come back on his own.

On the third day there was still no sight of Salgo's mare or a change in Phin's condition.

Light shone above the horizon, the first signs of morning on the fourth day. The whole group slept, most fitfully. Two horses stood dozing, ropes around their necks that kept them fastened to the ground, shoulder to shoulder. Their heads hung down by their ankles as the breeze rustled their manes and tails like grass in a well-trimmed meadow.

Phin shuddered, his arms prickling from the cold wind. He felt the tickle of fur against his face so he raised his hands. Mage nickered kindly. Phin rubbed his chilled arms and sat up, remembering nothing about the two-headed serpent or his injuries. But he felt as weak as a kitten, which he found appalling.

The young man groped about for his pack, but it wasn't there. He stretched, his fingers feeling the air and the coolness of morning wrapped around him. That was when he remembered.

A stab of pain cut into his stomach. Phin reeled and fell back into the grass, gripping his stomach, and a gasp escaped his clenched jaws. Mage nosed him with worry, standing behind him like a protective mother. Benji sat bolt upright. He had been sleeping even lighter than usual, and the sudden gasp had awakened him.

"Phin?" he said, rubbing sleep from his eyes.

"Yes, Benji. It's me," the older brother said tightly. "I'm just in pain, you know. Nothing serious."

Slowly the agony subsided again. Phin let out a breath he hadn't realized he'd been holding and reclined back on his elbow.

"So are you better then?" Benji asked tensely. "You've been unconscious off and on for days."

"Yes. I think I'm all right now. I'm tired of wasting time." He used Mage as an anchor to get up, his hands shaky as he clung to the stallion's neck for support. His legs shook, unused to holding his unsubstantial weight. Mage pushed at him with his velvety nose, trying to help him up higher. Slowly, he gained his feet and stood still, gripping Mage with white-knuckled hands, and wished not for the first time – and not the last time – that he had a staff and had never left home.

Phin was well enough to ride Mage again, his silky coat soft beneath the young man's hands, and he now hung at the back of the company as they started off. Salgo's mare had been found not long after Mage had returned and Phin had gotten well, and the messenger had only said with gratitude, "Phin, you must be our good luck charm."

Now the group rode forward again, bags packed, wounds (for the most part) mended. Layen led now; Salgo's mare still needed to regain her confidence. Storm and Mage walked side by side as they usually did. Their riders conversed lightly, but Phin held his scarred stomach without thinking about much of anything.

Their pace was slow, but they crept on with few rests between long walks. The open grasslands seemed deserted, save the birds and the weeds. Once Salgo saw a herd of deer, so distant that neither Benji nor Layen could see them. Phin rode in calm, patient silence. His mind was set upon moving so his healing wounds would hurt less. He had felt it once; he didn't wish to feel it again.

Mage seemed to understand, picking his steps carefully to avoid stumbling or jostling his rider, and often turned back to look at him with his wild, violent eyes. Benji was amazed at this, swearing to himself that Phin's steed was magic. Phin didn't seem to notice that his horse was any different than another, but was more grateful than usual that Mage took care of him.

The day passed. Then another. Still they traveled on, without a change in the ever-rolling grasslands. It was as if the horses were standing still and the earth below was spinning like a child's ball. The gentle pace was soothing on Phin's still tender stomach.

Night fell on the second day. The sliver moon rose, thin as a thread, the horizon orange and trailing after the setting sun. The blue sky darkened.

"I think I see a grove of trees ahead," Benji said suddenly, pointing. "Or else it's a trick of the light."

"No, I think you're right," Salgo said, "A little to the right?"

"Yes."

"Then we'll make for that," Layen decided. "It sounds like a safer place than open plains." As if in defense that the open plains *were* dangerous, a wolf howled.

The horses veered toward the trees, their hooves hitting the hard-packed-ground in a rhythm rather like drums. Trees, soft and whip-like – saplings by their bark's greenish tint – waved in the breeze. The four horses were strapped to the trees, stripped of saddles and bags, and left to graze on the soft grass that grew around and between the narrow saplings. Their riders set up a makeshift camp, eating a cold dinner of meat and fruit.

"We really could use some fresh meat and a fire to cook it over," Layen said stiffly.

The two young men sighed in unison.

"You know," Benji said, "I think that two-headed snake was sent from the Westland to stop us. Like the bats were."

"Have you just been thinking over this for a long time or something?" Phin snapped, settling himself against a tree with the same kind of attitude. The ache of his torso was worse than usual, and his disposition reflected it.

Benji shrugged, dropping it.

"I'm so sick of this whole 'quest' thing," Phin said suddenly. "We're going off, being injured, and attacked, for what? A girl. A girl I hate and who hates me. Why did the king send *us* on this suicide mission? And don't tell me about the vine-bow, I don't' want to hear it."

Layen put a restraining hand on Salgo and shook his head.

"When she sees," Phin said, "that it's *me* who's saving her she probably won't come anyway, not with someone so 'below her status.'" The words came out in a sneer. "This is so meaningless. I don't know why I ever agreed to this."

Phin, having said his piece, leaned back and listened to the wind in the trees and the night birds' crooning. He felt very annoyed and slightly whiny. Mage nuzzled his neck in sympathy, almost as if he understood, and Phin raised a hand and stoked his face. Now Layen and Salgo understood. They had known that the princess and Phin had been friends.

Now they guessed that the fight had had something to do with Phin's "disabilities."

Benji was startled by his brother's sudden explosion. He wished suddenly that they were both home and that he was listening to Phin gripe about some work they had to do or laughing at a funny story. He could almost see them both wandering the forest and hear Phin's staff tapping the ground. Then he remembered Phin's grumpy face in the morning as he was forced to drag himself out of bed to join Benji. The younger brother could see his friend leaping onto Mage's gleaming back and charging literally blindly down an undefined path, forcing Benji and Storm to follow. Benji sighed and let his head fall back and hit the bark of the tree behind him. He felt like he was losing his stepbrother, the brother who was his best friend.

The bat creature was fuming and needed some way to vent its untamable wrath. Its claws tore into the fertile earth, tearing out chunks of grass and other clumps of foliage. The monster ripped them apart and scattered what remained all over the ground, spitting and hissing as it did so. The anger and indignation was too much to be appeased by simple grass and dirt, but it continued hacking at the weeds and ground until there were large chunks missing from around where it stood, and the plants that remained were broken and hanging on bent stems.

How? *How* was it possible that a few weak, stupid two-leggeds and their large, kicking horses had managed to escape a craite, the fiercest snake and killing beast in the whole of the evil Westland? Two skinny elves – the creature spat as the word passed through his thoughts – and two *boys* had destroyed a feared monster for the most part unscathed! If only, *if only*, the wretched prey had died from the crate's spine barbs. If only the yellow-haired elf had been eaten by the great snake – he *and* his nasty kicking horse – and had his bones coughed up later by the mighty craite, right in front of the Master. Wouldn't the Master be pleased then! But the bat creature knew he'd be more pleased to hear that the prey had been killed, he and the foolish two-legged that had decided to help him. Then the bats would feast on their horrid kicking horses and gorge themselves nearly to death on the blood of elves and men. And the two-legged *would* die; the bat creature and whatever assistance it took would destroy them.

The monster, fully tired of attacking thoughtless grass, heard the squeak of a field mouse. It snatched up the rodent and began to crush it beneath its claws. The mouse squealed and fought to get away as its bones were crushed, but the bat only continued to kill it, relishing the thought of when the creature being crushed beneath its grasp would be the hapless prey.

13

Goblins

The group left that morning early. For some strange reason, Phin seemed a lot happier, as if the sleep had helped his attitude. Really, his stomach hurt less.

"We can pick up the pace," he said simply, throwing the saddlebags on Mage, who had been left untied in the night. The wild stallion snorted and pawed the ground.

So they did. Their horses easily picked up to a trot, and the grass was soon whisking beneath their feet. A blue sky splashed with cotton-puff clouds, like foam in the ocean, seemed to smile down at their steady progression.

Benji kept Storm reined in as the horse strained to run again, having not done so in many days. There was a wish to hurry in the air that each horse felt and each rider responded to. No one knew exactly what it was, whether it had something to do with the bats or the two-headed snake, but they all felt it.

The days blended into one rolling movement, each one the same as the one before it and the one after. Travel was quick and calm; only rarely were they forced to go around a hill or old structure from a time long past, which Benji always had to inspect. The only times of excitement were when Benji found some rats that had made his blanket their home and ran about shouting and shaking the offending cloth, or when Salgo fell off his horse and they all had a good time poking fun at him about it, though they'd all done it at one time or another. Phin's nerves were soothed by the simple companionship and the lack of duty he felt. No longer was he hauling wood back and forth from the forest or doing simple carpentry projects for five hours of the day. Benji too was thriving off the constant riding and the chance to chat with the two elves about the Eastland. The journey had again become a leisurely ride over hills and grasslands, with only occasional stops at villages and towns for supplies, and there they were respected as brave travelers, though no one was told their real duty. Only they would know that, but for now, going into the Westland seemed like something every far away from where they were now.

Until Salgo saw the smoke wafting along the horizon.

"That's coming from where the village of Dimming should be," Layen said with concern. "I was going to stop there for some more provisions."

"A bonfire?" Benji asked nervously.

"Too much black smoke," Salgo said. "Come on."

He whistled lightly to his mare, and she leapt forward, starting across the grass in a ground-covering gallop. Mage, at Phin's bidding, was next to follow. Storm and the brown gelding were close behind, neck-and-neck.

As they drew closer, the cloud of smoke got thick. Phin suddenly sneezed as they slowed to a trot.

"I can smell it," he croaked.

"You what?" Benji asked.

"You must have a very heightened sense of smell then," Layen said. Phin sneezed again, nodding through his watering eyes.

Layen tapped the gelding lightly with his heels and started forward, closely followed by the other three who studied the cloud of dark smoke with growing unease.

Again they started over the plains, jogging toward the black gloom that wafted up into the peaceful, blue sky. Layen, though worried, seemed anxious to get to the source of the smoke and know what had caused it. Benji, though more apprehensive, was close beside him.

The group began climbing a rise, urging on their mounts as the grass and weeds brushed their legs. The sun stretched their shadows behind them, long and wavering. With a snort, the first horse topped the small hill.

Surprisingly close before them rested a village, or what had once been a village. Fires burned in the streets and on the crippled skeletons of houses, eating away wood and framework. As the group drew closer they saw that doors were smashed in and windows shattered, lying in scattered, glistening pieces on the ground. The bodies of men, women, and children – even livestock and hounds – littered the ground in bloody, mangled heaps. Some were on fire; others had spears or arrows driven into their backs or chests, and still others were cut with what looked like knife wounds. A torn and battered red flag, which hung limply from its pole with deep rips in it, was the small company's only form of welcome aside from the smell of blood, death, and fire as they came toward the front entrance.

Phin choked on a smell and taste in the air that filled his nose and mouth; it dripped with heat and an unidentified, hideous feeling. Benji could say and do nothing. His eyes were locked upon the bodies and pools of scarlet blood, staining the dirty cobbles of the streets. This was his first account with hideous, innocent death. He couldn't even turn away.

"Dimming has fallen," Layen said quietly.

Salgo pulled his horse up short. "I can't go in there," he croaked, his voice sharp and raspy, coated with a strange, thick sickness.

Layen looked into the elf's blue eyes and nodded curtly. The messenger turned his horse away, staring instead at the grasslands as the gray mare galloped forward. In a strangled silence, the other three turned toward the village. Layen dismounted. The two young men followed on shaky legs. They sent the horses back to Salgo, and the three remaining people started forward on foot. Smoke burned their eyes.

"Wh . . . what could have done this?" Benji said, swallowing to open his tight throat. "What *would* do this?"

Phin, holding a hand over his nose and mouth, was glad, for once, that he couldn't see. He had never heard that indescribable emotion in Benji's voice. The blind young man wished fleetingly for a staff to guide his steps.

Layen kneeled beside a body, gently pulling an arrow from the blood-soaked back. He studied it a moment before growling, "Goblins. Hideous scum of the earth!" Layen snarled, throwing the arrow into the dust and standing up sharply. "They've no need for knives. The claws on their spider-like hands serve just as well. They run about in bands, pillaging and killing, destroying tiny villages like this and taking everything from them that's of any worth until there is nothing left for even the birds."

"Please," Benji said shortly. "Stop. I can see it. I don't need it verbalized."

"Deathly archers they are, and terrible killers – only fit to be thieves and rogues," Layen continued, as if he hadn't heard the young man's plea. He looked to the fallen arrow, then to the surrounding houses. "We should not linger here," he said. "There could be some still around."

"How right you are, *elf*," said a low, guttural voice, heavily accented. He said the last word like it was something vile he wanted to get off his tongue.

The three men spun around. Before them stood a tall 'man.' He had tall, sharp hound's ears, a spiked nose, and tiny black eyes deeply set into his gray-skinned face. Thin as a branch, with arms and legs like gray tree limbs, he stood before them, half-foot long claws unfurled and a wicked smile on his narrow, lipless mouth.

Layen whipped his sword free. Benji, beside him, was already holding his ancient blade forward. Phin pulled at his long hunting knife, dropping the hand from his nose and mouth though the stench was almost unbearable. He had no idea what the creature was, what it looked like, or why they were even going to attack it, but its voice made him think of one thing – evil. He gripped his knife and faced the growling voice.

The goblin laughed, high and shrill in contrast to his deep, guttural voice, as if three children were brandishing sticks at him while hiding behind their mothers' skirts. He whistled between his pointed teeth and four more goblins, same body shape and skin color as the first, leapt out of the houses and from the roofs where they had been crouching like insects.

The first goblin whistled again. Thirteen long-clawed goblins surrounded the three men, each looking exactly the same as the others.

Each wore a grubby hide around their waists as their only clothing, but each also had long, knifelike claws and skin as thick as the bark of a tree. Benji looked wistfully to where Salgo had been waiting, but there was no sign of him or the horses. The messenger had left them to fight alone.

Five goblins leapt upon them, claws cutting and ripping through clothes and skin. The two men and the elf fought, hacking wildly at the fleet gray bodies that moved with the agility of wraiths. One fell, his stomach gorged through by either Layen's or Benji's sword. But it was a useless fight. For every goblin that fell there was another there to take its place. The lead goblin whistled.

The fray ended, leaving a bleeding, panting trio still standing in the center. In a harsh language the lead goblin commanded his followers, "Bind the scum. Take their weapons and bring them to the camp." The group fought, but it was futile as the coarse ropes bound their wrists.

They were marching, marching heavily along, watching drops of their own blood drip to the ground, mingled with their sweat.

Phin couldn't help being slightly angry with Salgo. He had thought the valiant messenger might leap in at exactly the right moment and save them all from certain death. But, no, here they were: marching most likely to a slow and painful death at the hands of the goblins.

The young man swore bitterly under his breath as he stumbled. A hand on his shoulder led him none too gently, but didn't seem to have grasped that the man he led had sight problems. With his hands tied behind his back, every muscle in his body exhausted, and his mind completely muddled, he managed to hit every uneven patch of ground.

Benji plodded along beside him, sweat dripping down the side of his face. His breathing was slow and ragged with fatigue and anger. Phin could hear his heavy steps and the sharp steps of his driver behind him.

Suddenly, there came the sounds of a camp. Growling voices yelled and squabbled, conversing or fighting in their guttural language that afflicted Phin's well-tuned ears. Strange mule-like creatures brayed and kicked as goblin drivers loaded things onto their backs or flayed them with leather whips for refusing to move. Goblin hounds with sharp tails and ears growled and fought over meager scraps and bones at the foot of pitched tents. The three prisoners had entered the camp of goblin raiders, Phin only hearing the frightful sounds.

Goblin men and women alike jeered and laughed at the three bleeding captives, pointing and hoping for a good spectacle. Children grabbed handfuls of grass and rocks and threw them at the elf and the two young men, while they laughed and cheered when one struck its mark. Benji was nearly half-blinded as one barely missed his eye, rapping instead against his cheekbone. The masters of hounds didn't bother to hold back the great black dogs as they ran – teeth bared, ears back – toward the company. Phin and Benji's drivers cuffed and kicked those beasts away, though the monsters still managed to sink their teeth into the captive's legs.

The slow procession came to a halt at the opening of one great, black tent. Two well-armed goblins clothed in crude armor, unlike the light cloth around the waists of the commoners, questioned the drivers before letting them in, shoving their prisoners inside in front of them.

A goblin with the same build as all the others sat in a chair adorned with strange marks upon a mound of earth, a thing meant to be a goblin's throne. Robes the color of dried blood draped over his stick-like frame, and an old, crudely made crown sat upon his head, circling his tall, hound-like ears.

"Who and what are *these*?" the king asked in his own growling language, clicking his spindly fingers, claws sheathed, against the arm of the throne.

The lead goblin in the party bowed deeply and said, "We found them in the destroyed village. The one elf-kind was cursing our race. They might be spies, or something useful to the Master of the Westland." His voice was like brittle leaves in the winter, edged with frost.

The king, who was the goblin on the throne, growled, stroking his sharp chin with two spidery fingers.

"They dare stand before me? The great, powerful king of the Khenen Clan?" he snarled, slamming his fist down on the arm of the chair. The wood quivered.

The two young men had no idea what was going on. They knew nothing of the goblin language; they hadn't even known goblins existed until now! If it had been under other conditions, Benji most likely would have been enthralled. As it was, both young men could only listen to the growling, garbled language and pray they survived the outcome.

Upon hearing what the king said, the three drivers kicked, pushed, and dragged the captives to their knees with their heads bowed and their bound arms held behind them.

"That's better," the king said. "If they are what you say they might be, why did you not kill them?"

"They could be useful, your Eminence. Why else would an elf and two men be wandering the plains, except to spy upon the work of the Khenen Clan, or the great Master?" the lead goblin said smoothly, if anything sounded smooth in the goblin language.

"What!" the goblin king bellowed, leaping from his throne. "Take them away and put two in a tent, legs and arms bound so they cannot get away. Gag them. Bring the third to me. If he will not talk, bring one of the other two, but he *will* talk." The goblin king stared down at the three captives with eyes like black flint.

"And if none of them will speak?" the lead goblin hissed slyly.

"They will be left in a tent, bound, gagged, and without food, to starve slowly to death," the king sneered. "Did you get their packs?"

"Yes, your Eminence."

The goblin king took the three sacks and held them in his skinny hands, surveying their make. Then he turned each over in turn and let the contents spill out, clothes unfolding and food scattering all over the hard earth. Benji swore, but his driver kicked him until he became silent again. Phin fixedly faced the floor, listening to the goblins scrape through their things.

The goblin king suddenly seemed to realize they were there. "Take those maggots away!" he snarled.

The leading goblin directed his followers to drag the captives out. Their sentence had been declared. As they left, Layen bent toward his companions and whispered, "Say nothing about the princess or our journey to the Westland. Goblins always know what's going on – they'll know about the kidnapping. All will be lost." Then his driver yanked him aside, but the elf mouthed quickly, "Don't tell."

"Who are you?" the goblin king asked through the lead goblin, who seemed to be the only one who was able to speak anything but his own language.

Benji looked up from his bent position, dark eyes burning with hate like a caged animal. He was the one they had brought before the king.

"My name is Benjamin," the young man spat. Two goblins held his bound arms and shoulders so he had no chance to run, or move for that matter.

"Why are you on the plains?" the king goblin asked.

Benji clamped his mouth tightly shut. He believed Layen when he said they shouldn't tell about going to save the princess, fearing that they were in on the attack and would set upon the elves. He remained rigid, refusing to speak even when the king asked again.

A blow crashed into his jaw. His teeth hit together and the hot salty taste of blood filled his mouth as he bit his tongue. The young man fell to his left knee.

"Answer!" the king snarled, his small black eyes narrowed.

Benji tried to speak and all that came out was a croaking growl.

"Speak, you stupid human!" the translator snapped, unbidden. He grabbed hold of Benji's chin, tilting it up until the young man's eyes met his own. A trickle of blood seeped from the corner of Benji's mouth.

"I will say only that our journeying has nothing to do with your band of cutthroats," Benji said.

The translator's claws were let loose from his fingers, each only inches from the young man's face. Benji yelped but kept his straight, piercing face, denying them the chance to see his fear. One claw was close enough to his eye that if he blinked, his eyelashes would touch it. The young man swallowed and tried to look nonchalant, his eyes bright. It was bravado.

"Be careful what you say, dog. I have the power to take your very life," the goblin said, pointed teeth gleaming.

Benji lifted his chin, exposing his throat.

"Take it then," he hissed with more gallantry than he thought he could possibly possess.

"What is this? Take your hands from my captive. You shall only attack him when he refuses to speak," the king said harshly.

The translator curled his claws in again and turned to the king, "Yes, your Eminence," he said, bowing sharply, in a rather forced way.

"Now, Benjamin . . . where are you from?" the king said through his servant in a fake, calm tone. Benji hated the way he said his name.

"The north," Benji said, coughing on a little of his own blood.

"Good," the king said after hearing his answer. "That's a fine boy. What brings you to the plains?"

"A journey," Benji said, pulling against his bonds again, to no avail.

"Now we *are* making progress," the king breathed. Then raising his voice and lowering his face toward Benji's, he asked, "What kind of a journey?"

Benji again shut his mouth and refused to speak. After a moment the guard pulled back his shoulder until it was nearly dislocated. Blinded by pain, the young man fell to the ground.

"If you answer, the pain will end," the king said lightly, gracing his spindly fingertips along the back of Benji's neck. A shiver ran down the young man's spine.

The young man considered telling them. He considered just letting everything out and being free. But he knew the pain wouldn't end. If he told, they would all probably be tortured to death for being "spies" against the Westland, and the princess would die.

"We are not spies," he said finally. The king and his servants could get nothing else out of him, no matter how much they injured him. He forced his face to remain calm.

"Take him away!" the king finally commanded. "Bring another in an hour. Let them see what has happened to *Benjamin*. We shall get the truth out of them."

14

A Hopeful Thought and a Moving Camp

Benji lay on the dirt floor, his body throbbing with pain. Phin tried to comfort him, to tell him he had done well. But gags and binds kept him from doing so. After a moment of wrestling and fighting with teeth and shoulders, Phin did finally pull the gag away from his mouth.

"Benji?" he asked, resting his cheek against the dirt.

There was a muffled groan and the sound of a large form rolling in the dirt. Then Benji spoke. The voice wasn't muffled like Phin had expected.

"We're going to die. If not by endless beatings, then by starvation," he said bitterly.

"We could escape," Phin suggested without much conviction.

Benji forced himself into a sitting position. "How?" he snarled. "We haven't got weapons, tools, or even free arms and legs. How do you propose we get out?"

"Salgo's still out there," Phin said lightly.

"A curse on Salgo and his descendants!" Benji nearly yelled.

"Don't curse Salgo because he is free. Curse us because we're trapped," Layen said gruffly. He too had been able to remove the gag. "It seems you two have switched. Benji is now the pessimist and Phin the optimist. Maybe if you stop being opposite forces, maybe we'll survive."

The two stepbrothers quieted. Benji winced in pain as dirt got into his open cuts.

"Thank you. Now," Layen said, "Benji, tell us what you were asked."

The young man shivered, hating to face the pain-filled thoughts.

"They wanted to know my name. I gave it to them. They wanted to know why we came out here, and I wouldn't speak. I know now that they shouldn't know about where we were headed. I'm afraid they might be a part of the plot against the Eastland," Benji said. "I was hit in the jaw when I didn't answer." He could still feel the throbbing and bruising in his cheek.

"Good. Good for you, Benji," Layen said proudly. "Even though this group is only a band of thieves, they are in connection with goblins from the Westland. Anything we say against their plan *will* go to the Westland."

"Then it's agreed. We will not tell them our mission," Phin said firmly.

"You shall find it far harder to stick to that when they're beating you," Benji whispered, recalling how close he had come to telling.

Phin sighed and turned to his brother. "I know," he said dryly.

Benji nodded sharply and collapsed to his side in the dirt. He closed his eyes and breathed deeply. Lack of sleep and lack of strength overcame him and soon the young man was asleep. Layen soon followed.

But Phin couldn't relax. Something picked at him, prodding him to stay awake. He dragged himself to his knees and crawled toward the entrance. Pressing his ear to the door he heard the dying of the camp. It was dark, and the few people awake were drunk goblins sitting around a fire and a few patrols on the edge of the camp. A song – if it could be called a song – suddenly rang out. It was unmusical and horrible sounding, in the rasping, growling language of the goblins.

Then suddenly there was another sound – the sound of light footsteps and quick breathing. Phin leaned even more toward the door. The sound came closer, and suddenly a knife stabbed through the crack between the tent curtains, bringing a flicker of reflected light into the prison.

A long phrase of words sounded in an elvish voice. The smell of grass and horse and trees came in with the words.

"Salgo?" Phin whispered. "Salgo, is that you?"

"The messenger hears," the voice said. "Phin, keep heart; I'm coming back as soon as I can to save you."

"Hurry. We don't have much time. We've got no food and water, and Benji's got no spirit left," Phin said in a desperate whisper.

"Tomorrow if I can," the messenger promised. "Keep heart, but someone's coming. I have to go." There was a jerk, and the sound was gone. Phin strained to hear him, leaning into the tent. The knifepoint was gone as well.

The young man fell back into the dirt, relieved and safe feeling. Even the earth felt soft beneath him. Salgo was going to save them, but why couldn't he now?

Suddenly there was another set of footsteps coming toward the tent, these ones sharp and sounding as if claws gouged the earth. Phin drew back just as the tent parted. Something grabbed him with rough hands and hauled him to his feet.

"Time to meet the king," the goblin sneered with a coarse laugh as he dragged the captive from the tent. "He's been wanting to see you."

The goblin king tapped his spindly fingers on one of the arms of the throne, feeling a bit bored. Then he saw the guard dragging Phin into the tent, and his spirits lifted slightly. He found it truly enjoyable to interrogate prisoners, and as his translator came to his side, he felt very secure about it too.

The two guards held Phin in the same position as they had Benji, and the king stepped from his throne mound, pleased. "Ah yes, the skinny one."

Phin listened to the goblin king's sharp steps as he came up to him, but he remained with his head facing the floor. The thought that Salgo was going to save them made him feel strong.

"What is your name?" the king asked instantly, the goblin beside him translating.

"Piaphin, son of Galidor," Phin answered, remembering exactly who he was giving him added strength. He kept his face toward the floor.

The goblin smiled, thinking Phin's bowed head and calm answer a sign that he was weaker than the last one. The interrogation continued, the king asking the same questions he had asked of Benji, and Phin balked just as his stepbrother had. The goblin king and his translator grew angry, and he was kicked and scratched. The second goblin grabbed Phin by the jaw and made him 'look' into his face, and he noticed the paleness of Phin's eyes and his distant look. A cruel smile crossed his narrow face.

"Your Eminence, this idiot captive is blind," the goblin said.

The king looked at the translator coldly. "Why would that matter in this?" he asked shortly.

"Only that blinds are dull and usually have no idea what's going on in their own lives. He's completely useless." The translator unsheathed the claw of his index finger and lay it against Phin's throat. The half-blood swallowed, feeling the cold, steel-like claw against his skin. "I could simply dispose of him . . ." he trailed off meaningfully as he drew a line of shallow blood across the half-blood's gullet.

The king looked sharply at the other goblin. "Don't kill the stupid fool. Throw him back in the tent. Slitting his throat would be too quick, too simple." He snapped his spidery fingers. "Bring the last."

For some reason, early the next morning the goblins decided to move their camp. Guards came in early, dragging the three beaten sleeping captives to their feet. Ropes around their legs were cut and new ones tied around their necks so they could be led like beasts.

Tents were taken down and packed up. The mule-like creatures called khcalks or literally "ghost-feet" were piled high with baggage and tent pieces. Hounds were muzzled and chained to the khcalks whiles families of goblins waited beside their beasts.

Last of all, the king came before his people. He had five khcalks to himself, each so over laden with goods that their legs wobbled from the weight. After speaking to the crowd, he mounted one tall khcalk about the size of a pony and led the caravan forward.

The prisoner's stomachs growled and churned from hunger. The translator came to them lightly, a smile on his thin, sharp mouth. Three faces, bruised and dirty, snarled at him.

"And how are our prisoners doing?" he asked mockingly.

Benji, half mad with pain and anger, leapt at him, nearly choking himself on the rope about his neck. How the young man had planned to attack him, with his arms secured behind his back, was unknown to any of them.

"Temper, temper, little captive," the translator said shaking his head. "I believe you're going mad, but after a beating like each of you experienced, I wouldn't be surprised."

Benji subsided, being forced to stop if he wished to breathe. The three guards laughed.

With a mocking, torturous smile the goblin turned and strolled away, chuckling to himself. Then they were forced forward by the jab of a finger in their backs. One long, hideous day began.

15

Escape

Salgo sat on his horse, looking like some hero of ancient legends as he stared down from the top of a hill at the caravan of goblins, his golden hair billowing in the breeze. He sighed and knew he would have to follow. Behind him, grazing serenely were Storm, Mage, and the brown gelding. The man sighed again, running a hand through his flaxen hair.

Why had he told Phin soon? Could he possibly get to them by tonight and set them free? Would the camp even stop 'soon'?

Salgo growled at all the forces that had opposed him. Then with a whistle, he started down the hill, leading the three other horses behind him. He wrapped left, staying to the side and behind the caravan.

All the long day the elf tracked the troop of goblins. They never stopped or rested, and so neither did the stubborn elf. Salgo feared most for his friends who were most likely chained and forced to trot along without food or water or rest.

Sweat dripped into his bright eyes as the day wore on, and he swept it away with the back of his hand. He would have to sneak in soon or be prepared to find the three dead bodies of an elf and two young men. They wouldn't last long in this end-of-summer heat without food, water, or rest. He realized that if he wanted them alive, he'd have to save them tonight, just like Phin had asked him.

But Salgo knew he looked nothing like a goblin. He was fair with blue eyes and gold hair – a horse rider with a soft, light voice and smooth bones – everything except sharp and angular. If anything he was the opposite of a goblin.

For long hours the messenger stalked the caravan, forced to wait until nightfall to rescue the captives. He ate little, too anxious to do anything but lie low, weaving back and forth behind the goblins on North Wind's patient back. Finally the sun began to drift toward the western horizon, and the light faded. Salgo prayed the goblins would camp for the night or at least stop. Thankfully, his prayer was answered.

Right after dark, when the sky was a dusky blue and still slightly orange across the horizon, the caravan stopped. Khcalks slowed and were released from their burdens, while small tents (not the house-like ones that were in the camp) were set up for the night. Fires were lit, springing up in the darkness with violent sparks. Drinks were pulled out and sacks of food spilled open. It was the night of no moon, the clan's monthly celebration.

Phin, Benji, and Layen could drag their weary legs only a step more. Their whole bodies shook with hunger and strain. Then they collapsed.

"Drag them to the edge of the camp. The spirits or their own needs will rid us of them," the translator said. "The king has lost interest in captives that won't talk. If anything, we're doing the world a favor by ridding it of an elf and two men, especially the blind one."

Three great hands grabbed hold of each of the prisoners, hauling them to their feet and dragging them to the edge of the camp. Before they could even struggle, ropes bound their legs. Then, without a word, the guards turned back to join the festivities, laughing that they didn't have to lead the ugly captives anymore.

Benji spat grass out of his mouth and lay on his side. Layen forced himself into a sitting position and stared up at the stars. Phin lay where he was, trying to forget his weak, throbbing body, and his unquenchable hunger. They hadn't eaten for at least a full day, and he was already skinnier than the rest of them. They stayed in their positions to wait for either death, or something better.

Salgo left the horses behind in a clump of brush and trees, leaving them untied. Slowly, counting on the camouflage magic of the elves to keep him hidden, he crept toward the camp, using both his hands and feet to maneuver the vegetation without making a sound. He knew that with the magic none of the goblins could see him unless he wanted them to – which he didn't – but if he made a wrong move, they would still be able to hear him and catch a glimpse of him. Sometimes he could run upright, but at the sound of a goblin, he threw himself full on the ground, sounding to his ears like a pile of bricks hitting wood planking. He remained on his belly in the grass and knew he had no idea where the prisoners were located. But he planned to threaten a guard. He had never done anything like this; he was a messenger, not a warrior, and this was not usually a part of delivering blasted letters! The elf struck the ground with a silent fist, hoping what he planned would work. Slowly and with elven grace, he pulled himself off the dewy ground and continued, keeping to the shadows.

Trusting his light steps and slow breathing, Salgo drew near to a guard who looked only a foot or two to the elf's left side. Running on the balls of his feet, Salgo flipped out his knife and ran behind the sentry. The sound of the knife leaving the sheath caused the goblin to turn, rusted sword out in a gesture of defense. But he saw no enemy.

Salgo was already upon him. He kicked the sword from the goblin's hand, leapt around and grabbed hold of the guard. One fair hand passed over the gray man's mouth, a knife pressed to his throat.

"Speak even a sound more than I bid you and your blood will be on the ground," the elf breathed sharply in the goblin's ear. "You will obey." It wasn't a question.

The guard nodded, but his clawed hands were inching toward the elf's arm. In one sharp movement, Salgo pinned his arms behind his back.

"Lead me to the prisoners," he commanded, knowing there was no way he could escape if the treacherous goblin planned to lie.

"I . . . I don't know. They were taken to the edge of the camp and left to d-" The blade of Salgo's knife pressed into his neck. "All right!" the goblin hissed. "I will lead you there."

"Away from the fires and the guards, or I will slit your throat and run," Salgo said, with more conviction than he felt. He wasn't even sure he could kill a man, even a goblin, but the words sounded truthful coming from his mouth.

The fearful guard nodded, feeling cold sweat slip down his face, because, like all goblins, he valued his own skin over anything else. He had never encountered elves before, but had always considered them meek and soft. Now one was possibly going to cut open his neck and leave him to die!

"Walk," the elf commanded.

Slowly, tripping over pebbles and grass in his fear, the goblin sentry led him toward the camp. Salgo made little sound behind him, but there was a consistent pressure at his throat and a strong hand holding his arms tightly behind his back. The two fleeting figures ducked behind tents and into the shadows of goblins and beasts, though occasionally one of the hounds raised its head at their scent. All the while the goblin led silently. He was young and didn't know what else to do.

They wound through the camp, always on the outskirts and away from the fires. The sound of drunken men laughing and hollering dinned to an undistinguishable moan. Only a few khcalks knew of their passing as they raised their heads from grazing, shaggy forelocks in their eyes, and wondered vaguely if they would be loaded. When the two figures passed, the small group of beasts continued chomping the grass, their dark shaggy coats protecting them from the autumn night chill.

The goblin stopped and nodded shortly. Three forms lay or huddled in the grass only a few paces away. Their positions were awkward, showing that their arms and legs were bound. Salgo's pace quickened.

One face looked up as they drew near. It saw only the tall thin body of a goblin that looked even more angry and sharp than usual. The face shrunk away, feeling that this goblin had been sent to kill them.

"Kneel," the voice in the goblin's ear commanded, when they were right beside the group. "Untie them."

Salgo let go of the goblin's hands but pressed the knife firmer into the goblin's throat.

"I'm surprised you know my language," Salgo whispered suddenly.

"As a guard, I was forced to," he said, as his shaking hands reached for the first captive's legs.

Salgo took one crawling step away from the goblin so the captives could see him, letting the elfin magic fall away.

"I must be delirious. I'm seeing Salgo behind him, but that can't be, can it?" Benji said, rubbing his eye into his shoulder.

"Hello, Benji. Are you all right?" Salgo said tightly.

The goblin had cut open Layen's bindings, and the elf was rubbing and flexing his legs, looking with wide, surprised eyes at the goblin and the elf. The guard started on Phin, and the young man was soon free.

"I knew you'd come back," he said, "ever since last night."

Salgo nodded. "I followed you all day, hoping you'd be all right when I got here. Are you?"

"I don't think you'd call this 'all right'," Phin whispered wryly. "But we're alive, which is more than I hoped for."

By now all three prisoners were free.

"Where are our packs?" Layen asked.

"How'd you capture *him*?" Benji asked at the same time.

Salgo put up a hand. "The packs first. Take us there," he commanded, reaching for the goblin's hands.

"Never!" the goblin cried and leapt at Salgo, unleashing all of his claws. The elf sprang aside, his knife up. But goblins were even to elves in speed and balance, and he struck the messenger with the weight of his body. Salgo rolled backwards but landed on his feet, cat-like, one side of his shirt torn open by the goblin's claws. Before the gray-skinned monster could cut him again, Salgo launched himself at the goblin, burying his knife in the being's chest. The goblin fell with a shriek.

The three freed captives stared at Salgo with amazement as he extracted his knife from the monster's heart, looking in disgust at the gore-covered blade. He wiped it on the grass and didn't look at them but back at the camp, sliding the useful knife into its scabbard again. Lights were flickering, and the shouts of angry goblins carried through the still air like a distant earthquake.

"We've been found out," the messenger said with surprisingly little emotion.

On the back of one black, knobby-kneed, ghost-foot sat three packs and a few scattered weapons. His mane was tangled and thick and fell down almost to his knee. A long tail dragged on the ground, sometimes fluttering about his small hind hooves.

Suddenly, three men came jogging toward him. He lifted his head from grazing and looked at them with soft, caramel eyes. The goblins cared little for things that weren't made by other goblins, so they had left almost everything in tact. Even their weapons, well made in the elves and men's eyes, were hated by the goblin kind and considered near to useless. All they had taken was the food, though the goblin king had planned to trade what they didn't want for things they did.

"Can you men get the packs off the donkey-beast quickly? I think they know something's happened, but they don't know what," Salgo said, watching the camp.

At that moment a goblin came out of the clump of tents, away from the fires and other goblins. He had heard a guard scream, and though the rest of the camp was willing to just go back to their festivities, he wasn't. The goblin came to the dead sentry's body and the ropes carelessly left behind. Anger boiled in the black eyes.

"The prisoners are escaping!" he bellowed in his garbled language.

"They know for sure now!" Layen snapped, understanding enough of the goblin speech to know what had been shouted. Benji dropped the pack he had just untied.

"Grab the donkey's rope and run for those distant trees!" Salgo yelled, thrusting the khcalk's lead rope into Phin's shaky hands.

The half-blood held the khcalk and ran on weary, tight-muscled legs. Twice he fell to one knee and was forced to drag himself forward. The khcalk brayed and ran beside the young man, the packs on his back rattling and thumping his sides where the group had loosened the bindings.

Benji and Layen toiled on before him, keeping their eyes focused on the trees ahead. The sound of the goblin's yells and snarled threats rang in their ears. Phin ran faster, feeling the khcalk suddenly pull against him. He turned and pulled on the halter around its mouth, forcing the khcalk to follow him.

Goblins stopped their celebrating at the other goblin's cry. Many grabbed swords and spears and ran toward his voice. Others lit torches and screamed curses on the elf-kind and man-blood. All of them left behind their festivities to chase down and destroy the fleeing captives.

Salgo dashed ahead of the group, having much more strength than the others, and whistled. His mare raised her head from within the trees and sprang out into the open, leaping toward her fleeing master. The three other horses, after only a moment's hesitation, followed readily, each looking to their riders.

"Get to the horses!" Salgo was shouting, dragging Benji's tired and battered form forward. "Run! Run!"

A few narrow, cruel arrows flew toward them. It was frightening, running through the dark toward some horses while irate goblins chased after them and arrows rained down around them. The two tired men and the weary elf forced themselves on, feeling the whistled down among them like falling stars.

Salgo was the first to grab his horse and swing on. Benji clambered onto Storm's back next, followed by Layen onto his gelding. An arrow grazed Phin's leg, tearing through cloth and skin. The young man fell, losing the strength he had, and wrenching hard on the khcalk's head so it bucked and snorted.

Mage ran to him, nosing his master and pushing him so hard he got to his knees. But the stallion was too tall for the injured young man to mount. The khcalk brayed and spooked, shaking and kicking again. Salgo spun his horse around and rode to Phin. Adrenaline was purely moving him.

"Come on, half-breed, to your feet!" he yelled, tumbling from his horse's back in a rather un-elf-like way.

"I can't. Leave me behind," the young man gasped.

"Without you this mission is pointless," Salgo said, grabbing hold of Phin's arm. "Put your foot in North Wind's stirrup, and I'll push you up. Go!"

Phin obeyed, and Salgo pushed him fully into the saddle. After tying Phin's hands to the reins, he slapped the horse's flank. Phin clung to the mare as she sprang forward. She could tell the rider on her back was weak and rode differently than Salgo. Her strides were smooth and even as she followed the other two horses before her. One was only a fleeting shadow in the dark.

The goblins were so near, Salgo could hear their steps and the clatter of their weapons. He was stuck with a wild stallion he didn't know and a pack-laden donkey. Still the elf hooked the khcalk's long lead rope to his wrist and threw himself on the albino stallion's tall back.

The horse reared and bolted forward, dragging the galloping khcalk behind him, nearly tearing off Salgo's arm. He clung like a sack to Mage's back unlike the amazing horseman he really was, gripping the stallion's mane and around his neck while his body bounced. Like wraiths in the night, running recklessly through the plains, the four horses and the strange goblin pack animal galloped, fleeing the goblin army that slowly fell behind.

"Whoa, stallion, steady," Salgo said, pulling gently on the mane. His wrist was getting burned from the rope that was slowly strangling the beast behind them. Mage's only response was to flick his head and keep on. Salgo growled. This night had been stressful enough without Mage being stubborn and blatantly disobedient.

Phin clung to the glorious mare beneath him. He was regaining his senses, but his strength was gone, drained away like water into the ground. All he could do was hold desperately to Salgo's mare as her feet drummed the ground beneath him. The young man could hear her snorting breath, the wind in her coat, and feel the ripple of her muscles beneath his thin body. Her coat was as soft as velvet under his quivering hands.

Benji and Layen were slightly better off. The former was only feet behind Layen, his black stallion easily covering the ground. Their eyes were usually focused ahead on the dark open grasslands, praying there wasn't a log or tree ahead that would break their horse's leg. Sometimes, though, the young man's eyes ventured back over his shoulder at the small points of light far behind them which showed that the goblins were still after them. He turned back, his heart pounding in rhythm with the hooves, and urged the gelding on. The black horse snorted and took an extra jump.

Layen leaned low on his gelding's back. He was numb, holding tight to the horse's mane, its reins flying in the wind. The horse had its full head and was bounding over the grass like a fleeing deer, not caring at all about the rider on its back.

It was so quiet now the group was stunned. They were now so far from the group of goblins that they couldn't even hear them. That most likely meant that the goblins couldn't see them.

"Veer left!" Salgo yelled, finally having gotten the stallion to a bouncy canter, though it hurt his ribs and his backside. "Left!" Benji yanked his stallion right. "Your other left, Benji!"

The embarrassed young man pulled Storm left and followed Layen closely. Phin wasn't sure how to turn. He pulled the reins, just barely left, and amazingly the mare turned and leapt after the other two. Salgo followed on a stubbornly jolting Mage.

After about one half-hour of fleeing at a breakneck speed, the horses were frothing and snorting. Their steps slowed as they shook their heads, fanning their sweat-streaked manes. Layen was the first to pull his horse to a stop. Storm stopped beside him, dipping his head in an attitude of defeat as Benji staggered off, standing beside him on shaking legs. A moment later the gray mare, North Wind, pulled to a stop too. Mage and the khcalk were the last to slow.

Phin untied his hands and stumbled off the mare, landing on his back on the turf and refusing to get up again. The grass felt like a feather bed beneath his worn out body. Salgo threw himself off Mage, standing shakily and rubbing his lower back.

"How in the name of all," he cursed, "do you ride that rock with legs?"

Benji was leaning heavily on Storm and dragging the saddle off because, though he was tired, he couldn't neglect his horse. It fell with a thud to the ground. The young man rooted through one of the saddlebags until he found food, then ate ravenously. Both the other once-been-captives followed his example while Salgo watched them, glancing once over his shoulder. There was no sign of the goblins. They were free again.

16

Return to the Journey

The sky went from black, to dark blue, then to gray, and finally to pink and strips of gold. Falling over the four sleeping men, the first rays of sunshine shone their yellow light over the grassy plains. Phin rolled over in his sleep as something rubbed at his face. He swatted at it, but it stepped aside only a moment before returning to him again, persistently nosing at his clothes.

"What?" he asked groggily, waking up. He grabbed hold of the something and ran his hands over it. "Mage? No, too small and shaggy. I know, you're that little horse I was dragging behind me last night!" He shivered involuntarily at the memory, touching his newly cut leg and then the thin cut on his throat. He was happy to feel that they had scabbed over.

Phin rubbed his hand over the shaggy little pony, feeling where the imprints of the packs had been. The khcalk nuzzled his face, making a contented noise, somewhere between a bray and a whinny. The young man was startled by this sudden display of affection.

"What are you?" Phin asked absently, running his hand up one mulish ear.

"It's a ghost-foot," Layen said sleepily.

"Excuse me?" the young man said quietly, turning slightly toward the voice.

"A ghost-foot. A little pack mule, named for its tiny feet," the elf said going back to sleep with a sigh.

"Ghost-foot, I like that," Phin whispered a moment later.

The way the khcalk nuzzled him made him feel rather like he was petting a large equestrian dog. Phin had always liked dogs, but had never had one. For some reason they had always seemed to like him too, except, of course, though goblin hounds.

The ghost-foot finally got bored with investigating the young man and went back to grazing on the foliage. Phin lay back in the grass, enjoying his ability to stretch his arms and legs, though the cuts from his interrogation grated at him. A strange coldness settled on him whenever his thoughts wandered even remotely toward goblins – his mind still filled with their icy, tormenting voices – and he quickly thought of better things.

Benji shrieked suddenly and sat up, his dark eyes wide, cold droplets of sweat rolling down his face. His breathing was sharp and ragged as he clutched his chest and wiped the moisture from his forehead with the back of his arm.

The other two men woke up in a flash, and Phin snapped into a sitting position. Ghost-foot, as Phin had unofficially named the khcalk, whinnied shrilly and kicked. It seemed he was easily spooked. The four horses' ears snapped about, then relaxed, and their mouths never stopped cropping the grass and weeds.

"What is it?" Salgo said, on his feet instantly.

Benji held his forehead. "A dream," he whispered to himself. "Only a dream." The young man breathed deeply and relaxed.

"Good Lord, you gave us quite a fright," Layen said, clutching his chest.

"Well, shall we go?" Salgo said calmly.

"Yes," Phin answered, getting up. Even the taste of coarse bread and dried meat tasted wonderful after not eating for a day.

The horses were re-saddled, the khcalk packed again, and then they started off. Tied to Mage's saddlebags was a rope that went down to Ghost-foot's neck.

"Are we just keeping the donkey?" Benji asked finally.

"I suppose so. Phin, you don't mind do you?" Salgo asked.

"No. Actually I rather like the little Ghost-foot," he said. Then something else occurred to him. "Salgo! We haven't even thanked you!

We owe you our lives!" Benji and Layen joined him in his exclamation of gratitude.

Salgo colored slightly, but was smiling. He raked a hand through his golden hair. "I must admit. I was scared out of my mind. It was one of those things you always hear about in tales around warm fires in the winter, when men tell their wild stories of adventure and magic to gullible children who will listen," Salgo said. "When I'm an old man I'll be telling my children's children about this, and they won't believe it."

The other three laughed, and the tense mood was broken.

Slowly the days passed. Salgo took care as best he could of the wounds his three companions had gotten from the goblins – Benji's shoulder and Phin's cut leg from the arrow being the most serious. Most of the injuries were shallow and had been given only to cause pain. After that day of recuperation, Layen steered them back onto the path they had started on, with the help of his old map, which all the while had remained folded in his breast pocket. The band of goblins had taken them a good deal northwest and out of their way.

"Heavens, we're behind schedule," Layen snapped with exasperation the next morning. "We *should* be to the Westlands in two days."

Salgo, who was looking over his shoulder, laughed. He pointed to a spot three quarters of the way to the Westlands. "If we're here," he said seriously, "then we would have to run all day and all night until the horses' legs fell off."

Layen snorted and folded up his map. "Let's go, but we won't run. The princess can wait a week or more," he said.

Salgo sobered, "Let's hope so."

Phin shook his head. He still didn't know what to do when they got to the Westland, and the very thought of it made him feel small and defenseless. He had seen what the Westland could do: giant bats, two-headed snakes, and the young man had no fortification against it. It was just him – a blind man with a well-carved bow that he hadn't even fired in all their trials.

Phin eased Mage forward, feeling more hopeless than ever. His mind cast about a moment for anything and landed on a stupid question with no relativity. He thought, "How had Salgo known to run away?" Then a strange voice sounded in his head, a voice that had been spoken to them, what felt like ages ago.

"Run before danger, and you shall not have to flee after it," the voice whispered.

"The mage," Phin muttered to himself. His horse turned its ears back toward him at the sound of his name. The other things that the mage had said fluttered through his mind, like winged insects with no apparent purpose. Strange that one should come true and save their lives now. Was it just coincidence?

"– mountains, did you say?"

Phin fell back into the real world at Benji's question.

"No, not mountains. They're only eroded hills, not that tall either. The whole place is barren and rocky with dusty, pointed slopes we have to maneuver through," Layen answered curtly.

"Can't we go around? *I've* heard they're haunted . . . children tell wild tales of them in the Northland. They call them the Death Backs," Benji said in a ghostly, haunted manner.

Salgo laughed. "The only thing haunted about them, or so *I've* heard, is getting lost."

"And we won't," Layen said firmly, slapping his trusty map with the back of his fingers. "And no we can't. We're behind schedule as it is already; we don't have time for more delays. Besides, you're getting a little old for ghost stories."

Benji raised an eyebrow and drew back besides Phin. His brother sat silently on his horse, waiting. Mage flicked back his ears.

"I know they are," Benji hissed through his teeth.

Phin shot a 'look' at him. "Really," he said dryly.

"Do you remember that old farmer who lived on the east side of town? The one who went on that long trip once?" Benji prodded.

Phin's eyebrows creased with questions, but he nodded shortly.

"He went through the Death Backs. I was only eleven, but when he came back he told us about it. His skin was all pale and clammy, his eyes wide and hollow looking as he spoke," Benji said quietly.

"You weave quite a tale. You should give up carpentry and become a bard," Phin said, shaking his head. Benji went on, acting as if he hadn't heard him.

"The man said that it was full night when a monster appeared by the side of one of the mountains. He said it fanned two huge bat-like wings and took to the air, blotting out the stars with its body and wings. Then it turned toward him and soared down, its great wings finally blotting out the moon. Great yellow, cat-like eyes turned on him. He said his horses went mad, and he barely escaped with his life."

Phin finally could hold it back no more. A laugh escaped his tight lips, and he stifled it with a cough that rasped in his throat. Benji looked toward him sharply. "All right then! Maybe it *is* just a story," he said, laughing.

More likely it probably is, Phin thought, but he said, "Benji, you have more imagination than all the rest of us put together."

17

The Death Backs

"Those *are* mountains," Benji said.

"They're just eroded hills," Layen said again, throwing up his hands in exasperation. "Come on, you suspicious fools. Let's go in before you cast judgment. It's just some bloody dirt!"

Benji, though he had tried to dismiss the old story, felt a sudden apprehension hold him. He ran his hand tensely over his hair. Even Salgo, who trusted Layen like a father, was beginning to feel dubious about these supposed 'non-mountains'. Phin could only smell the dryness in the air.

When the small fellowship stepped into the Death Backs, a dusty, barren feeling clung to them, and they couldn't get it to go away. The grass was brittle and brown, if there were patches of it at all. Between the awkward clumps of dwarfed vegetation there was only hard-packed earth with long jagged cracks that ran through it. Rocks littered the ground before and around them, jagged and sharp-edged like the 'eroded hills' in front of them and rising up on either side. It seemed as if all the life had just forgotten this barren piece of ground.

The wind stirred the drying leaves of the few stunted trees, blowing up swirling clouds of dust. It blew into the riders' faces, stinging their eyes and choking their throats. Mage, who had gone in white, was colored a dirty brown in only minutes. Cloaks were retrieved and hoods pulled over the faces of the men to keep the dirt off. Amazingly, it wasn't hot – only dry and barren.

"How on earth did it get like this?" Salgo asked. "It looks like all rains and rivers forgot this place!"

"Some say magic," Layen said. Benji perked up. "I think that's a load of rubbish." Benji slumped down again. "It must just be where it's located on the plains."

"But the air is so dry," said Phin. "Did it just suddenly get so dusty and hard right off the plains or was it gradual?"

"Gradual. The grass just sort of slacks off, and the earth hardens. I can't explain it, but it's like that."

Nobody spoke again, for fear of getting strangled by dust and the gusting wind that carried it. The horses toiled on, heads down, feet constantly stumbling over the cracks and stones. Ghost-foot didn't seem to mind nearly as much as the regular horses and their riders. He had again been tied to Phin's saddlebags, and he was contently walking, his long, thick forelock keeping the dust from his eyes and his small hooves easily avoiding the rocks and ruts.

Slowly, as day gave way to night, the wind stilled and the clouds faded. The place was silent as a tomb and eerie as one as well. A thin slice of moon shone out, overly bright in the open gloom, and stretched their shadows out to their sides. The shadows of the mountains looked like black holes that light would never get into. Trees, withered and dying, were only skeletons in the silver light.

"Shall we stop?" Salgo asked, throwing back his hood. His gold hair looked flecked with gray in the moon's shine. Only his youthful face and bright eyes would have kept people from thinking he was old.

"Yes," the other three answered.

"Besides, tomorrow the moon will be bigger. We can travel then and get at least a little more ahead," Layen said. Salgo and Phin nodded readily. Benji did as well, but less easily.

Under a tree, the group set up camp. Four horses and a khcalk were harnessed to the sorry plant. Their riders settled in below, still wary of starting a fire and not really needing one anyway. They ate in turn, curled up in their cloaks, and went to sleep. The dry earth around them shuttered at the thought of another night, when the winged monster would again prowl the skies.

Dust billowed around the horses and riders. The air was dry and dead, the hills around them cracked and tan like old bones dried in the sun. The tree behind them quivered, scattering down the few more patched and crumbling leaves it had to show on its shabby branches.

Phin awoke as dirt blew into his half-open eyes. He had been dreaming of a waterfall that crashed down out of the mountains and into a clear, bubbling lake. He could hear it, but how he could tell it was clear, he didn't know. His mouth was parched with dirt that had somehow slipped in, making the dream of water even more unbearable.

The young man pulled his cloak tighter around him, the hood falling over his face, and struggled to his feet. He tapped a body lightly with the tip of his boot to wake whoever it was who slept near him, wishing for the hundredth time that he had a good, smooth staff. He now couldn't even remember where he had lost it or if he had brought it at all. His old life seemed ages ago, lost in a torrent of mythical monsters that weren't suppose to exist and endless days of riding.

Layen murmured something and sat up, sleep still clinging to the elf's eyes. He yawned and awoke the other two, leaving Phin to stand alone, feeling useless. Mage nickered at him kindly in sympathy, rubbing at his neck where a chain had appeared over the narrow scab where the goblin had cut him, the sore itching from the ever-present dust.

One of the young man's hands came up, and he snatched at the chain, his slim fingers following it down to the round pendant at the end. This was the second time during his journey that it had appeared. He rubbed the tip of his forefinger over the markings that he would have liked to study while he idly scratched at the cut along his throat.

"What do you have to do with me?" he muttered to it gently.

As if in answer, the necklace faded between his fingers until all he held was air.

He grunted softly at the bizarreness of the necklace, then dismissed it. It didn't really matter . . . did it?

Benji dragged himself from the hard ground, stiff, with pins and needles pricking up his legs. He went instantly to his horse. The pure blackness of Storm was now dirty and mottled.

"Grab some food, men, and let's be off. We've got a lot of ground to cover before we stop tonight," Layen said.

"Yes, captain!" Salgo said, snapping his legs together and mocking a salute, his hood bobbing over his eyes, creating a well needed moment of comic relief. Benji and Phin chuckled lightly.

"Ha, ha," Layen said unhappily. "Get on your horse. I am still your elder, or I'll start calling you 'lad.'"

Salgo snorted and stepped lightly into his mare's saddle, some food having already made its way into his mouth. Phin untied Mage and pulled himself on, still buried in his long cloak and hood. From the saddlebags he grabbed some meat and cheese and a flask of water, glad he hadn't carried most of his food in his pack. All the excitement of the food had worn off, and he again wrinkled his nose at the dry, boring rations that now consisted of only crusty bread and stale meat. And it all tasted like dirt. What he wouldn't have given for a slab of warm steak, a slice of thick bread, slathered with butter, a bowl of fruit, and wine sloshing freshly in a glass. The thoughts depressed him and made him salivate. Mage, his ears back, seemed just as unhappy about Phin's rations as the half-blood was because, with the way things were, there were no spare apples for him to filch from his rider.

The day felt long, dry, and dusty, just like the day before. All around them the air hung like cobwebs from an ancient tomb, stale and bitter from age, and too long spent draping stiffly. Eroded hills wove together and around one another with what seemed no order or reason. The team of horses followed around them, their riders' directions muddled and twisted, lost in the endless erratic range. Only Layen seemed to know the way and the others could only follow, trusting his map, praying he was right. Benji and Salgo saw the look of confusion he once exhibited as he studied his map, but they both pretended they hadn't.

The clouds of dust rose up again like miniature sandstorms, sometimes engulfing the parched crew.

"Drink your water sparingly," Layen advised, facing away from the wind. "We won't get more until we escape this place."

"You can see why people think this place is haunted," Phin murmured to his brother and Salgo. "We'd be utterly lost without a map and a guide. The very air around makes my sense of direction feel . . . broken."

"The air reeks of magic," Salgo said seriously.

Benji's head snapped up from the depths of his hood. A puff of dust splashed into his face and choked him for a moment. When he had gotten his breath back he said, "Did you say '*magic*'?"

"I did. This seems like just how it always is before something horrible happens: a monster attacks, a specter emerges from the ground . . . that kind of thing," Salgo said.

"So you believe in magic?" Phin said accusingly.

Salgo shrugged apologetically, "So I'm a believer in legends as well, but only to a certain degree. This just feels like the kind of place, for no normal place could be so unnaturally dry."

Suddenly, North Wind lurched, tripping over cracks and rising ridges. Salgo fell forward, hitting his face into the horse's sleek neck.

"That's it!" Salgo snarled and slipped out of the saddle. "I'd rather walk than keep nearly breaking my nose." The elf grabbed the mare's reins and led her, though she nosed at him gently to make sure he wasn't really angry at her. "It was bad enough bloodying it in front of the giant snake; I don't need it when I can hardly breathe anyway."

Benji and Phin were startled but realized the wisdom in his rather sharp statement. They too dropped from their saddles and led the horses, Phin holding also the rope to the small khcalk. They walked with Phin in the middle so he could hear both men beside him. The blind man now longed for a staff, but Mage, sensing his master's discomfort, walked carefully and away from large cuts in the ground or clumps of broken ground, his chin an ever-present guide on Phin's shoulder.

Layen led tirelessly, driving his horse around the tall hills and down through dry ditches – long cracks that may once have been creek beds and some that looked as if they'd been torn by giant claws. His horse picked his way carefully through as if he was accustomed to all terrains and grounds. The two seemed a good match for each other.

The group stopped only once for a quick meal, and then they were back off. Phin's legs ached and told him to stop, but he refused. He would prove he was just as strong as the others were.

The next day came, and they did the same thing, all the riders clothed in dusty cloaks while all their horses were a musty brown. They drank their water only in sips, finding no appetite in stale food, and all but Layen feeling lost in the endless labyrinth of rock-incrusted hills. They weren't even sure Layen knew exactly where they were, for he studied his map with perplexity more often than usual. The horses walked with dragging feet and low spirits, their ears back, and snapped at each other over the few tasteless bits of grass that had survived the dryness.

"What was so bad about open grassland?" Salgo asked with grit blowing into his face, and all the rest agreed. Benji almost never spoke because the dust choked him whenever he tried, and Phin had begun keeping his blind eyes permanently closed.

Another day started with the rise of a pale sun on the rocky horizon, signaling the third day in their excursion to the Death Backs. The group woke morosely and with short tempers. The horses grudgingly began their walking again, though dust rubbed against their tack, causing uncomfortable sores on their skin. No one felt like going on again in the dry, unchanging landscape of rugged hills and craggy earth. The sun even seemed feeble against the sheets of dust that coated the land. The day wore on the same as the last two, though the travelers bickered with each other more and acted more sullen. Of all the land they'd passed through, the Death Backs were beginning to feel like the worst. And, as Salgo said, the feel of evil magic was intensifying.

18

A Dragon's Lair

As the sky darkened, the group watched the rising of the moon without really caring. All around, the air was falling still again, the dust clouds settling again to their beds to rise again tomorrow. The stillness that followed was dark and almost made one feel cold, though the night was pleasantly cool. It was as if the evening was trying to lull them into a sense of security, when really it was planning an attack. Soft silver moonlight exposed the earth in a different way.

Salgo suddenly made a noise like that of a frightened animal and stopped dead on his feet. His breath was caught in his throat. The other three in the fellowship circled about, their eyes slowly adjusting to the settling gloom as they tried to make out what the messenger had seen.

Lying on the ground, slightly buried, was a corpse. It was decayed, nearly all the flesh and skin missing from the skeleton, but what remained lay in strips over the lifeless carcass. The marks on its body looked like huge claws had torn through it, leaving the remains nearly mangled beyond recognition. One of the eyes was still in the skinless, bloodstained face, and the mouth was still shaped into a scream of fear and agony. Beside it on the ground was a destroyed heap of cloth that may have once been a saddlebag or pack. Another skeleton, the flesh picked clean, the rib bones crushed, lay on the ground: the sprawled body of what once may have been a mighty horse.

Salgo reeled back, dizzy and sick from the gore of the broken bodies. He leaned heavily on North Wind and forced himself to breathe.

The mare nickered gently, nuzzling his neck. The others had to rip their eyes away from the gory scene and stagger back.

"It *is* haunted," Benji gasped.

"It's like when I saw my family die." Salgo choked on something more than dust. "Please," he was pleading now. "We should leave this place."

Layen and Benji nodded shortly, stepping away again. Phin could smell the decay and death, the dried blood that still clung to the dusty ground. He could feel the stale sting of death and almost sense the pain that hung in the air over what he supposed to be a dead body. The air around it seemed icy and poisoned. He clung tightly to Mage's mane.

Salgo grabbed the mare and steered well clear of the skeletons, walking with a stiff, jerky gait. Phin kept hold of Mage's neck and mane in his hands and followed the elf's trail, nearly stepping into the remains of the horse, but his stallion led him far enough away. The other two followed, silently and slowly. The accursed Death Backs had lost all sound.

The messenger was leading now, tugging his mount along behind him. Phin walked close beside him, his steps quiet but sounding like drums in the eerie silence of the dark. He had no doubts now that the unnatural dryness of the place was caused by some kind of black magic, as skeptical as he was about that kind of thing.

There was a scream, but not a human scream, a scream like that which would rise from the depths of hell if it could. The world plunged into total darkness for a moment and then back alight with moonlight as if they had blinked. Beneath them the earth seemed to shake like great hooves were galloping upon it, nearly yanking the travelers off their feet. The four real horses screamed, ripping free from their master's control and galloping into the night, Mage pulling the little khcalk behind him.

"The Death Back's Wraith! The Death Back's Wraith!" Benji was screaming over the throbbing of the earth. He pointed up toward the moon, his finger shaking.

A great shape sailed over, its head as long as a man's body, with eyes like orange and yellow flames. Then it landed before them on the ground, claws chopping deep gorges into the packed ground, which explained a few of the ruts they had seen. The earthquake stopped. The air stilled. The monster only watched them with glowing eyes and a mouth agape with rows of gleaming teeth, each as long as a sword. It seemed to be looking them over, waiting for something. Three of the men could not move but were held spellbound by the creature's eyes. Only Phin stepped back, feeling he might be able to get away . . .

"Sleep . . ." the creature said softly, its voice like the wind of the mountains, raindrops on trees, thunder over the grassland, fire crackling in a conflagration. It was lulling and terrifying all at once.

"Breathe deeply, my guests, and do not fear. Sleep . . ." the creature said again. "You shall come home and stay with me . . . sleeps . . . peace . . . stillness. You are tired and weary . . ." There was a long intake of cold breath. "Sleep . . ."

A cool, silver mist fluttered from the creature's mouth, twinkling in the moonlight. It engulfed Layen first, who was closest to the monster. He dropped to the ground in an instant sleep. Salgo and Phin felt next the touch of the mist's cool, restful fingers, and they collapsed together to the hard earth. Benji still stared deeply into the creature's flame-filled, cat-like eyes.

"You're a dragon," he breathed in awe and wonder with only a touch of fear. "A real dragon."

The dragon smiled a toothy smile and breathed thicker mist upon him. The young man tumbled softly to the ground. In one breath the serpent swallowed the mist, grabbed Benji and Layen in its two claws and wrapped Salgo and Phin in its prehensile-ending tail. It chuckled to itself and beat its giant wings, which lifted the coiled, serpentine body off the ground and into the air, once again blotting out the moon.

Layen yawned and barely lifted his head, brown hair tussled. His vision was blurred with sleep. The four men had been sleeping slightly in a pile, like a litter of puppies. Salgo and Phin, still asleep, were leaning against each other and a wall, with Benji's head against Phin's shoulder, his mouth slightly agape. Layen had been sprawled against the wall with one leg over Phin's. The elf's head dropped back again, heavy as if he had drunk too much wine or had taken a strong sleeping elixir. His eyelids felt weighted.

Salgo and Phin shifted at about the same moment. Their heads hit against each other as they lifted them, and they groaned. Their heads also felt heavy and they soon fell again to their chests.

"I had the strangest dream," Phin mumbled absently. "Some monster with a soothing voice swooped down on us."

"Mine too. Except that the horses ran away in mine," Layen said. "But it's foggy, and I remember feeling rather deaf."

Benji groaned and lifted his head. He yawned widely and let it fall back again. "I had a really vivid dream just now," he said softly.

"Yes, we all did," Layen and Phin said together. The sleep was wearing off, but very slowly.

Salgo fought the heaviness, forcing the sleepiness away from him. He lifted one hand, which felt like a weight, and rubbed his face. The dust and grime of the Death Backs still clung to him. Then he opened his eyes.

They were in a dirt cave, like a rabbit hole that had been built into a hill, except that it was the size of a cathedral. The floor was packed and hard, and the walls rose up to a domed ceiling that seemed a mile above. Sunlight shone feebly in through the only entrance or exit – an upward sloping tunnel fit for a monstrous serpent that led to a wide hole that was so far up it couldn't be seen. Salgo didn't see any of this; he was staring at the enormous hoard of gold, silver, jewels, and other precious things and the monster that sat upon it.

She was snake-like, with long coils of body and tail that wrapped around her treasure, except for the two short legs and four-clawed feet at her front. Her head was large and reptilian with ridges above her eyes and nostrils, horns escaping from beside her small, pointy ears. Every inch of her body, tail, and head was covered in great teardrop-shaped scales. By first glance she was flame colored, a mix of orange and deep burning scarlet, but when one looked closer you could see scattered scales of cobalt, emerald, amethyst, and gold. Black wings, thin and gauzy like the sail of a ship (as large as one as well) were folded neatly across her heavily armored back. But it was her eyes that unnerved the elf.

They were large, like yellow glass, with dark slit pupils. Fire, or so it seemed, burned behind them, ever dancing and churning. The orbs were large and glowed above her long, thick, wedge-shaped muzzle – ever staring, never blinking.

Salgo yelped and pushed against the wall. She was as long as ten horses even when coiled and must have been as long as thirty when she stretched out. Benji, Phin, and Layen had fully awakened now and were also staring at the gleaming dragon.

"I don't think we were dreaming," the messenger breathed.

The dragon lifted her horned head, and crossed her two front feet rather like when a person crosses his or her arms. Her jeweled hoard reflected off her polished scales so that she glittered.

"Hello, my guests. I am indeed pleased to see you awake," she said soothingly. The voice was the same but less enchanting than the night before.

Benji staggered to his feet, in complete awe of the serpent. Though he was afraid, she was extremely beautiful.

"Why do you stare, young one?" the dragon said, growling in the back of her throat like low thunder. A bit of fire snapped between her long, charcoal-stained teeth.

The young man stared deeply into the eye of the creature and said truthfully, "I have read a lot about dragons, but all fall short of the real thing."

A ripple of deep blue swirled along her back, and she closed her eyes like a cat being stroked, one clawed foot curling around a clump of her treasure.

"Then it's true!" Benji blurted. "Dragons do change color with emotion."

"Yes, and I enjoy your inquisitiveness. Continue," the dragon breathed, and her last sentence was not optional. She was as vain as all dragons were, and her favorite topic of conversation was herself.

So Benji did, swallowing first to clear away the fear he felt at addressing a monster that could kill him with a swipe of her claw. He asked all the questions he had wanted to know about dragons and whatever else came into his mind. A person had to obey a dragon if he wanted to keep his life as long as he could, which Benji did. Even the dragon seemed to enjoy answering his constant stream of inquiry and she proudly told him of how she had ruled the Death Backs for centuries.

"What are you called?" he asked finally, feeling timid.

The dragon lifted herself higher so she looked down on the company even more, her giant head with its flaming eyes staring over them. There was an intake of breath as she stretched to the full height her short legs and serpentine neck allowed.

"I am Firebreather, Great Serpent, Winged Snake, Scarlet One, Death Bringer. My names are many: Murder, Death, Kingdom Killer . . . I am Saraphain to the elves" (Salgo and Layen jumped involuntarily) "and Basilin to the dwarves in the mountains before. The goblins, who I see the most of and prey the most upon, call me Halkat. But for you and your language, child, I am Varisi," she said.

Phin choked. Benji's eyes widened, and his jaw dropped. "N-not *the* Varisi? The-the one . . . that destroyed Kern?" he stuttered.

"The same," Varisi said, flushing yellow with pride. "The kingdom fell in barely a day."

"Enough talk!" the dragon Varisi snapped suddenly. "Think deeply, while I am away, on how to keep me interested. Your survival depends completely on how well you keep me enticed. Escape is futile."

She pulled herself out of her hoard and crawled/slithered to the entryway. As soon as her long, red tail had passed, there was a burst of flame, and the entire entrance was engulfed in fire that kept its shape so that it looked like a wall. Through the blaze she said, "Steal a single coin from my hoard, and you will die. Trust me, I will know." Then she disappeared completely, leaving the fire wall crackling, an impassible door that held them entombed.

Phin pulled his knees up to his chest and pressed down his forehead. This is bad, he though weakly. There was no food or water, and their only escape was covered by a door of fire. Never had he felt so utterly the pain of prison, not even when he had been chained in the goblin's camp. He wondered numbly if this feeling was a side effect of being in a dragon's lair. Never had he felt such a lack of hope. It wasn't natural, but though he tried to tell himself that, the feeling wouldn't go away.

Layen and Salgo got up slowly. The latter turned and kicked the wall in sheer frustration.

"I will NOT entertain the vile snake! I say we grab up some of the weapons from the pile and be ready to attack her as soon as she comes back. I don't care if the monster is female!" he snarled.

"It won't work," Benji said. "You heard what she said. Don't you think that would apply to weapons? We'll be roasted alive."

Salgo, who had already grabbed an old sword from the pile, threw it back in disgust. "Then what do you say we do?" he said.

"These walls are dirt, aren't they?" Layen asked, fingering one. "Maybe we could dig out. There are cups and bowls in the dragon's hoard," he seemed to be thinking out loud. "If we dug far enough we would reach the edge of the hill."

"Still wouldn't work," Benji said. "It's –"

"Then what do you propose we do?" Salgo and Layen bellowed together.

Benji threw up his hands in exasperation. "I don't know!" he yelled shrilly. "I – don't – know!"

Salgo began pacing wildly back and forth around the wide, dragon-sized chamber, his forehead wrinkled, his hands folded behind his back. He muttered angrily under his breath and scuffed the ground with the heels of his boots. A few times the group tried to call him back, but he seemed immersed in his own dark thoughts.

Benji sat heavily back next to a pile of treasure and began fingering pieces under his hands, lips pressed tightly together in thought. Layen sighed and leaned against the opposite wall, still thinking of escape. Phin was in his first position, rubbing his forehead. He was so confused by all of this. His mind felt muddled, but he could tell that the tensions developed in traveling the Death Backs had not lessoned in the dragon's lair.

The group waited tightly the whole time Varisi was gone, pondering escape and at the edge of their thoughts, a way to entertain a murderous dragon. It seemed impossible to do. They weren't entertainers; they were just simple men with simple talents. Was Phin going to do juggling tricks with swords and golden goblets while Benji played his flute, Salgo sang, and Layen danced a jig? The thought was comical, and idiotic.

The young man felt a tug on his neck and lifted his hood. A pendant jangled lightly on the inside of his shirt. He lifted it out and rubbed his fingers over it as he had done so many times. "What am I to do?" he thought to it. "What can we do?"

"– Use your mind –"

Phin's fingers dropped the necklace in shock.

"– Follow what you believe –"

"What on earth do you mean?" he thought desperately. He still couldn't believe a necklace was *talking* to him. This kind of thing didn't even happen in tales! He snatched up the medallion again.

"– You must trust yourself. There is always hope. Trust yourself –"

It began to fade.

"No, please. I still don't understand!" Phin yelled in his head. He clutched the pendant, but still he felt it disappear.

It was as if someone had struck a light in his mind. Ideas raced through unchecked like wild horses. A new hope, like warmth and healing, flowed through his body, and he found himself on his feet.

Without thinking he went to the 'door' of flame and stood before it, the heat intense on his face. Ideas still blazed through his head, some daring and foolish, while others seemed almost possible. The rest of the group had stopped what they were doing and watched the young man.

"Somebody get me something out of her pile. Something long," Phin commanded suddenly. In a moment, the hilt of an old rusted sword was set into his outstretched hand.

Slowly, he put the tip of it through the fire, counted to ten slowly, then drew it out. Almost timidly he touched the metal and yelped. It was searing hot, hotter than he had ever felt. He put his burned fingers to his lips. They felt raw and burned from even that small of an encounter.

"I could have told you dragon fi –" Benji started.

"Benji, please shut up. Just this once," Phin said harshly, and the younger man fell silent.

A thought suddenly reared in Phin's head, stamping and making a ruckus, saying it had the best idea. The idea said simply that he should change how he thinks. Then it went back to galloping recklessly with its fellows, keeping Phin from being able to think clearly.

Phin chewed on the idea a moment, before slipping the rusted sword back into the fire, his burned fingers still to his lips.

"It's a warm fire, like the sun on your back. Comfortable and soft. It's gentle and warm, nothing else. It isn't 'dragon fire' or even fire. Just warmth," Phin whispered, feeling it in his mind, the gentle sunshine of fair summers when he was on the outskirts of the Rabba Plains with Mage and Benji. The imaged was enhanced by his lack of sight, to his satisfaction.

When he drew the sword and touched it again, it was exactly as he had envisioned it: warm and comforting. He dropped the sword in surprise with a clatter on the packed ground. Before he lost his nerve or started questioning what he felt, he imagined the warmth and thrust his hand through, praying quietly that he'd still have a hand after this.

There was a warm tingling sensation that remained as long as Phin continued to think of it. The half-blood smiled, and to the horror and astonishment of the other three, he stepped through. The fire licked at him, but only in a warm, almost playful manner, but as soon as he let the thought of warm sunlight slip away it grew hot again. He concentrated fully, and then he was through, his clothes hot like they had lain in the sun to dry.

The air on the other side felt clean and cool. Was it possible the dragon lived on the edge of the Death Backs? Phin hoped so. He had never felt so happy or proud of himself. The young man could have yelled with joy and fought the strongest monster he could have found, brandished a stick at Varisi, tossed a handful of pebbles at the two-headed snake, thrown a leaf at the bat-creatures. For once, he, the blind, useless one, had fixed a problem first.

"We're coming, Yaja. We're coming for you," he said boldly.

But his confidence was slightly treaded by the sound of great wings approaching. His smile faded, and he stepped back through the fire, nearly getting burned because he couldn't hold the thought of the warmth.

"How . . . how, it can't be . . . but," Layen stuttered, grabbing hold of him roughly.

"I promise to explain later, but she's coming back," Phin said, struggling away. "Trust me. We are as good as free." He hopped it was true, but if dragons knew things as well as Varisi seemed to, they might just be dead.

For laborious hours the captives listened to the dragon eat the two deer carcasses. Varisi had looked at them all with hate and anger when she had returned, as if she guessed one of them had found something out and had sniffed at all of them with her great, scaled nose. The dragon settled protectively over her hoard and ate the deer, blood and gore splattering the ground, but not anywhere on her treasure.

After devouring the beasts she spit the bones into a pile of other ones that stood off to the side of her true hoard and turned sharp cat's eyes upon the group huddled against the wall.

"All of your names, now!" she snarled, fire crackling warningly in her voice. Her scales flushed black along her neck and beside her claws.

Benji stood up shakily, remembering how he had read that dragons enjoyed riddle talk and you should never tell one your name, or they would make quick guests – or meals – of your friends and relatives as well. Swallowing, he began, "I am Storm Rider, half-blood's brother, believer of legends, worker of wood. My friends shorten my name, though people of height keep its length." The dragon had settled in, enjoying puzzling through his words, though her eyes still glowed with agitation. He continued, "Music from a wooden flute I play. I have seen death and survived, seen life and nearly died. I am the youngest." He bit his lip, awaiting her answer.

"Very interesting. You shall find it difficult to endure the Westland though," Varisi said quietly, craning her neck until her wedge-shaped head was only inches from him. Benji stiffened, frightened. "You are called Storm Rider." The dragon shook the spines on her neck with a clatter before looking sharply at the others.

Phin felt her gaze and stood up. He wasn't sure what to say but the words flowed as if he had rehearsed them before. "I am man, yet not man; elf and yet not elf. I have eyes but do not see, ears but hear better than many. There is nothing hanging about my neck, but I know it's there, as I know the Mage I have tamed. My name is 'sightless' in the ancient tongue of the woodland people, though few call me by it," he said and held his breath. There seemed to be a long moment of worrisome, ponderous silence.

"You intrigue me, thin one, more than any guest I have had. Your smell I have felt from centuries back, before I haunted these dry lands, and none have stood before me so fearlessly," she breathed, flicking her long tail. She contemplated him a moment before saying, "Next."

Salgo stood up and ran a hand through his golden hair, deciding to follow the other's suit.

"I am a messenger, and I ride the North Wind. I lost all family when I was young, but still I survive and travel the world on Wind." He spoke less figuratively and told more about who he was. "My horse and weapon are my greatest tools," Salgo finished, feeling stupid.

Varisi moved slightly toward him, staring deeply at him with her eyes. "I sense a very dark past behind you, elven one. Your thoughts are cold, and one day the pain will take you and there will be none then to avenge," Varisi said softly. Salgo looked suddenly very pale at her words, as if a spell in her voice promised what she said.

"Salgo can handle it," Layen said firmly, not allowing fear to quiver in his voice. "He is a stronger man than you make him out to be. I know; I have seen him. You have not."

Salgo snapped back and smiled appreciatively at him, a pallor still hinting at his face. But the dragon turned with hate in her eyes. "And you are?" she growled, containing her wrath, but not in her scales. Most of them had flushed black in her anger.

Layen shrugged, trying to look ill concerned by the huge dragon before him with smoke fluttering out of her nostrils. "I am only their guide and in some ways their protector. There is nothing special about me, except that I am one of the few to have ever seen a dragon," Layen said, finally dropping his eyes from her hot, oppressive gaze. His knees, though he pretended it wasn't true, shook with fear.

The dragon coiled back against her hoard at the compliment. Her vanity overrode her anger.

"Tell me now why you entered my barren lands. Do not leave anything out or lie. I will know, and I will find out in the end," Varisi said, teeth gleaming like ivory as she smiled.

Phin swallowed. The giant room suddenly seemed repressively hot. Did they dare tell her? Did they dare refuse? She seemed to know a great deal about them already by the hints she had given them when they stated their 'names.' The others seemed to be waiting for him to speak because this *was* his quest. So he began, ignoring the tightness in his throat and the dragon heat clinging to his skin and clothes.

He told her of the message from the Elven King concerning his daughter, of the attack from the bats, of the trip out of the eastern forest. Phin left out whatever he could to protect any innocent people involved, but he told the dragon everything he dared. She listened passively, occasionally commenting, her tail flicking casually. She scoffed at the fight with the two-headed snake, saying that ought to have know that the only way to kill a craite was to make it attack itself. Then she clicked her teeth together when he told her about the goblins, which was not a very comforting sight.

"They are my usual guests, though surly and very boring," she said casually. "I tire of them easily and often eat them after only a few days. I am often lonely, even with them as company. You, my guests, will be much more interesting and last much longer, though I fear in the end I will tire of you as well." Her tail lashed irritably at the prospect.

Phin found it difficult to speak after hearing that he and his companions would all be eaten as soon as they weren't *entertaining* any more.

"Enough. I know you have left things out of your story, but it was long in the telling, and I forgive you for it. You have been most interesting, and you need not worry. I shall sleep now, but the door shall remain," she said, curling herself around her treasure. "There is a stream near the back, for even dragons need water, though too much quenches our flame." She gave a laugh like distant thunder. "There is also a chest of food. Use sparingly." Then the serpent's great orbs closed, and she slept, her great chest rising and falling so that her scales rustled slightly. Occasionally one eye opened a crack to watch them like an untrusting guard dog might.

The small group moved to the back of the cave and drank deeply from the water and ate a little of the food she had kept, more to get away from the monster than for the sake of hunger.

"Avoid the meat," Layen said, wrinkling his nose. "Varisi would think it funny if she fed us some of her prior guests, and I don't think eating goblin sounds that appetizing."

Benji dropped the piece he had been holding with a look of revulsion. "At least she is giving us *some* food and water," he said. "Maybe there's a little kindness in her?"

"She just wants us to last longer," Phin said with disgust, wanting suddenly to hit the brute with something. It was far worse to be toyed with by a dragon than anything they had endured so far, at least in Phin's opinion.

"Now, tell us about you stepping through the flames!" Layen blurted out as if he'd been holding the question in for quite a while. Varisi growled in her sleep and switched positions, causing the group to stop in silence for a moment.

They all dropped their voices even lower and huddled together. "First I want to know Salgo's past," Phin said. "What the dragon was talking about."

Salgo sighed and leaned heavily against the wall.

"Tell them, Salgo," Layen said quietly. "They deserve to know too."

The elf ran his hand over his eyes and sighed. "If you must know. I was the oldest in my family; eleven I was at the time," he began. "I had two younger brothers and a sister. My whole life I'd been captivated by horses, but that day one saved my life. The things that attacked my village that day look slightly like men, but more wild and untamed, with shorter legs and longer arms. They ran in, lashing through the houses and attacking people. A group of men tried to shoot them down, but something stayed their arrows and they were killed – all of them. My father grabbed the horse we had and threw me on it with my sister, who was only three years younger than I."

"'Ride!' he commanded. 'Make for the city of Niathorn and warn them.' So we did. I spurred the horse forward, and we rode to the top of a hill that looked down on my home. To this day I wish we hadn't looked back. The wild men tore into the house and slaughtered the rest of my family. It was horrible. Then we turned and ran away, my sister clinging around my waist." Salgo finished softly.

"But what happened to her?" Benji ventured quietly.

"Five years after we came to Niathorn, she died . . . winter fever. That's why I became a messenger, so I would never have a permanent home to worry about, and because I love the open plains," the elf said shaking his head. "Now, Phin tell us what you found. My past is behind us, but we still have a future."

Phin shied at the words, slightly shaken by Salgo's tale, but slowly he related his findings with the wall of fire.

"So," Layen said, "you're saying that if you imagine that it isn't hot, it won't be hot?"

Phin nodded firmly.

To his amazement their guide laughed, throwing back his head. "That's completely illogical!" he said, wiping his eyes. "It couldn't be possible."

"Not everything *is* logical," Benji snorted. "Who here guessed we'd end up in the lair of a dragon, *logically* I mean. Who even truly believed dragons existed outside of legends?" That sobered their guide. "I believe Phin."

"Benji's right," Salgo said, looking as if he had never told his story. "The mage said that I should run before danger and not flee after it, which saved our lives. Benji probably saved us too by remembering what he'd read about this blasted dragon." Varisi again growled in her sleep, tail unsettling a few gold bars and a silver cup. "Now it's your turn, Layen. Don't always trust to logic."

19

A Way Through the Fire and Varisi's Wrath

The three stood before the flaming doorway, looking at the crackling, glowing fire. Benji shuttered. It seemed hot indeed. He took one hesitant look back at the sleeping dragon. She had been sleeping a long time, long enough for the company to have eaten, slept fitfully, and refined their plan for escape, scarcely hoping that she would still be sleeping when they were ready to try. Time was impossible to decipher in the monster's lair, though it seemed as if days or weeks or ages had stretched past.

Varisi's eyes squinted tight and relaxed, her claws flexing over pieces of her treasure. She bared her teeth and scratched into the hard ground with one great foot, her tail lashing irritably like a cat's. It was as if she knew something was wrong.

"Hurry, Salgo! Find what you can, and let's go!" Layen hissed, also eyeing the dragon warily.

The younger elf was digging along the edge of the dragon's pile for weapons, trying hard to ignore the huge monster only feet from him. He knew they needed the vine-bow to save the princess and other weapons to defend themselves. Again he reached into the pile, carefully and quietly setting aside golden coins and jewel-encrusted armor in search of usable objects. Varisi growled, as if she could sense the defilement of her precious hoard, and Salgo ducked her thrashing tail.

Finally he pulled forth a sword, its hilt dappled with sapphires and rubies, but the blade was sleek and sharp, slightly rusted in one place, but still strong. Salgo set it on the floor beside him and dug again.

After only a while more he pulled out a worn bow, still bearing a string. Salgo drew it back, pleased with finding a weapon *he* could use. If he found North Wind, he'd have an extra quiver. The elf then pulled forth Benji's ancient sword and the vine-bow. Amazingly they had stayed together.

"All right," Salgo said and took his findings to them. He looked fearfully up at the mighty dragon as he spoke and stepped toward his companions. Varisi moaned, rolling violently.

"Now," Phin instructed quietly, "think of something other than heat: warmth, cold, whatever. I think I'll go first."

Again he summoned the thought of warm sunlight and stepped through, hoping it would work again. There was a warm whoosh, the fire licking at his hands and hair, and then he was through.

Benji looked fearfully back at the dragon, set his thoughts, and then followed Phin. The fire felt like the time he had stepped under an icy cold waterfall. He could almost feel the droplets sliding down his arms and face.

Phin smiled toward his brother as he stepped out, rubbing his arms and quivering.

"'Suppose I shouldn't have thought of cold water," the young man said, raking his fingers through his dark, rather overgrown hair.

Salgo swallowed and breathed out. He didn't feel nearly as brave as those two, especially after revealing his past, which always made him feel slightly exposed. The elf shut his eyes and imagined one of the mornings in a forest, right after dawn when he was riding his mare. He could perceive the cool air and the almost magical feel about it. Concentrating on this picture, Salgo stepped through, the briskness of morning tickling his arms. He couldn't believe this was really happening.

Layen was the only one left.

"Come on; step through," Benji insisted, worried again by the dragon's aggravated movements.

"I can't," the elf admitted harshly. "It's fire – burning, searing fire."

It took a great amount of time for the other three men to convince him. They each took turns speaking, urging him to at least try. But he stayed sternly set that he could not and would not. Benji finally grew too exasperated and yelled an unbridled curse.

Varisi's small ears twitched, and she opened one great, flaming eye, easily taking in the situation. Her scales blazed black-scarlet, and her great head reared up, both eyes shining like bowls of fire.

Benji's dark eyes widened in horror, and he bellowed some un-enunciated curse. Layen whirled around, looking as if he would evaporate into a puddle.

"Through the fire! Through the fire!" Phin was screaming. The ground around was shaking and thundering again. He could tell the dragon had awakened, even without eyes that saw. The earth was shaking under his feet, and he found it hard to keep straight.

Layen obeyed without question and literally dove through the wall of flame. He had no time to think about hot or cold. The elf had never felt so afraid in his life than he was at that time with the dragon behind him, blazing black as storm clouds and streaked with deathly crimson. That fear seemed to be enough.

At that moment, Varisi belched forth a great engulfing spew of fire. Salgo grabbed Benji and Phin (who had a hold of Layen) and pulled them into a niche in the wall. The fire billowed passed, hotter than a roaring fire. This was no magical fire meant to stay in one place like a wall, but true, burning flames.

"Run!" Phin screamed as soon as he was to his feet. "Run like the wind, you idiots!"

The blind young man launched himself forward and tripped and fell over a chunk of the roof above, which had fallen. He got up, with the dragging support of Benji's yanking hold, and galloped forward again, lost in a thunder of the crashing tunnel and the dragon's roars.

Salgo ran upon his thin legs like a fleeing deer, dragging Layen behind him. They had mounted the slope toward the door when another cloud of fire roared toward them. The two elves pressed themselves to the wall, the fire singeing a bit of Salgo's hair and the tips of Layen's boots. Benji and Phin threw themselves face-first to the ground, feeling the heat rush over their backs and necks as if they were about to be cooked for someone's meal. It was a very unpleasant thought, considering they were trying to outrun a dragon. As soon as the fire diminished, they were up again, running as fast as their legs would carry them and falling all over themselves because of the collapsing ceiling and cracking floor. Clods of dirt and rocks showered down on them.

The tunnel sloped upward very sharply, and the four travelers were forced to half-climb, using their hands to grip the uneven ground and dodge around the falling pieces of rock and dirt. Phin could hear Varisi's huge feet and snake-like bulk rushing toward them as he stumbled along, the vine-bow clenched in one hand.

"Faster," he panted, gripping his brother's shirt. "She's coming." He choked on the dust, his lungs heaving in his chest with the exertion and the earthen debris.

"I know," Benji gasped, wiping dirty sweat off his face. "Keep running. Just – keep – running!"

The thought of an enraged dragon behind them spurred them all on. Her anger was shaking the rocks and dirt from tightly packed holes, filling the tunnel with dust and the smoke from her mouth and nostrils so that it was difficult to breath. Phin had lost all sense of direction except forward.

Suddenly, they reached the great hole of an entrance. The sky blazed with late afternoon sunlight, the grass rippling about as the dryness of the Death Backs gradually thinned back into the grasslands. But before the four men could get to the haven of freedom, there was a horrible quake in the earth that threw their feet out from under them, and they toppled to the ground. The entrance was slowly being filled with rock and rubble! Their one escape was closing as they tumbled about on the heaving floor, grabbing for any handhold that might help them to their feet again.

Varisi suddenly came into view. She was fearsome, and her eyes blazed with scarlet fire while her whole body was black, spines flared out like the feathers of an angry bird. The dragon shrieked in victory when she saw her prey cornered and hurdled herself forward, sail-like wings kicking up more dust as they thrashed in the cramped space. They had to do something quickly, or she would have them.

Phin was actually the one who found the cavern in the wall. He stumbled in his haste and hit the cracked barrier, his arm going into the hole. There were two choices – the darkness or the dragon. Varisi bugled, gathering her breath for a burst of fire. It was the darkness then.

"In here!" the young man yelled, throwing Benji inside with a yank of his arms. Salgo dove next, dragging Layen in beside him. The finder ducked in last, falling face first into the cavern because he fell over a rock. He rolled when he hit the ground, crashed into someone's legs, and found himself being pulled to the back of the hole. Dirt was in his face, clogging his mouth, and he could hear the raspy breath of his fellows. Outside came the roar of the great monster, Varisi.

Only seconds after, the dragon's hatred drove her to do something foolish. She screamed and forced her head in after them, the spines along the back of her head lodging in the dirt and rock. Only her snout and one eye fit inside. Smoke from her nostrils filled the hole with a cloud that reeked of dragon, but she couldn't flame.

Benji wasted no time. His hand closed on the familiar hilt of his ancient sword, and he drew it forth. With a vengeful smile on his face, he raised it toward the monster's head.

"Have a taste of your own vengeance, evil worm!" he bellowed, stabbing the muzzle. "That was for Kern!" He jabbed at her again, across the flap of her nostril. "That was for anyone else abused by you."

But his courage was failing. Her eye had lightened in color and now looked sad and betrayed, like a dog whose master had just struck for disobeying. It wove a tight spell around the three men in sight as the scales on her face went into a cheerless, pale gray. The fire of her eye danced, mesmerizing.

Phin could not see. He didn't understand why Benji had stopped striking the monster before them. In only moments he understood, sensing the dragon's spell in the air, but because she wasn't speaking, it had no hold on him. The young man grabbed the jewel-hilted sword that Layen had let carelessly fall from his hand to the ground and slipped along the wall to a place where he stood near the section of Varisi's wedge-shaped head. Holding it in two hands, he raised it. Varisi was too intent upon Benji and the other two to notice one thin, blind man holding a sword above his head, his face smudged with dirt.

"Guide my blade," Phin prayed, closing his eyes and seeking any high power who would listen. He took another shaky step forward, prepared to stab the sword downward. Blood pounded in his ears and his heart beat in his chest like a hammer against his ribs. This was his only chance. He had to at least injure her so they could escape. He had to use his blindness for the advantage of his friends.

Downward the blade sailed, stabbing into the mesmerizing eye. Benji and the others awoke from their trance as the dragon screamed and threw back her head, shattering the tunnel wall. Great chunks hurdled into the air and rained down on the group. The two men and the two elves dodged the falling bits of wall and clumps of rocks, ducking into holes and corners that seemed safe from the descending debris. It seemed as if Varisi was going to destroy her whole eroded hill – lair, hoard, and all.

The sword was still forced into one gleaming eye as Varisi screamed and writhed in pain. Her tail lashed into the wall, breaking more holes into it in her pain and fury. Her great claws tore into the ground as she spasmed, the blade having stabbed through into her brain. Then she fell with an ear-shattering, thunderous roar. Then all lay still, the dust settling again onto the uneven, torn open ground. It was suddenly deathly silent.

The men crawled out of their hole in the wall and away from the body, all except Benji and Phin. Salgo and Layen moved back toward the main room. Benji sighed sadly and made the sign for mourning.

The dragon's unbloodied eye fluttered and opened weakly. It was still like yellow glass, but the fire behind was only dying embers that burned feebly. Her voice rattled, the death rattle, but still she spoke.

"You would mourn me, Storm Rider?" she whispered in a barely audible voice.

"You may be the only dragon left," the young man whispered, laying a hand upon her hot, armored neck. "I would mourn for such a magnificent beast, evil as you are."

The dragon gave a low, distant roll of thunder. "I have never met one like you, young one," she said. "I too would have mourned you, when I killed you."

Benji took his hand from her neck.

"A scale and weapons you shall have when I depart," she whispered. Her yellow eye turned to Phin. "None have dared attack me before."

"Until now," Phin said softly.

"You still intrigue me, thin one. I respect a brave warrior . . . though I hate you for cutting short . . . my long life. You shall have a weapon as . . . well. You will use it one day for something of great . . . importance." Her tail twitched slightly. A claw curled tightly. "Mourn for me . . . both of you," Varisi said in her final breaths. "My spirit shall be with you . . ."

Then the fire in her eye died, and Varisi, killer of Kern and terrorizer of the Death Backs for more than a century, lay still, the color fading from her glittering scales.

20

Treasure

Phin and Benji kneeled beside the dragon's body a moment more, their heads bent. The former lifted his first and turned slightly to his brother.

"Do you think her last words were a curse? That she'll haunt us the rest of our lives?" he asked.

Benji shrugged and said, "I don't know." He sighed softly. "I don't know what she means by weapons, either."

At that moment, two of Varisi's longest spines fell from where they lay nestled within her dying scales and rolled down her serpentine back to land before the two young men. Each was nearly as long as Benji's leg and deathly sharp at the tip. They were pure black except for two bands of scarlet in the middle and a tip of shining blue.

"These must be the weapons," said Benji as he reached down to coil his fingers around the base of the spine. Then he held it up like one would hold a sword.

"It's so light," Phin said, also holding his aloft. "Yet it seems sharper than any sword or knife." He ran his hand along it, trying to decipher exactly how it looked.

"If you're through with the dead body, you must see the treasure!" Salgo yelled excitedly.

Phin got up to join him and so did Benji, but he first took with him one scarlet scale, still hot and burning with life, from Varisi's interlacing covering and put it gently in his pocket.

The hoard was tall and sparkled, with all the gold and diamonds anyone could want. Without the dragon upon it to draw the attention of one's eyes, they fell upon the great mound of treasure. Golden coins and chains glistened beside jewels, diamond-encrusted weaponry, crystal statues, gleaming silver shafts, and bricks of precious metal. Some of the beautiful treasure was so rare that they couldn't even place what it was.

"We can't leave all this as a monument to a dead monster," Layen said calmly, though his eyes gleamed.

"Of course not . . . but it would take fifty horses to carry all this, and at the moment we have none," Salgo said. He picked up a mirror lined with sapphires and then a spear, the shaft made of ebony and ringed with gold.

"It must have taken a thousand years to gather all this," Benji said, lifting up a handful of jewels and rings. "Who knew there was so much wealth in the world?"

"It's the riches of a hundred kings of the old tales," Salgo said, slipping a gold and emerald arm ring over his hand.

"We have to take some of it or word will get out, and men will swarm to this place in search of riches, especially dwarves. They're greedy for treasure more than any others," Layen said, filling his pockets with gold coins and small treasures.

Phin picked up a heavy bracelet and some silver trinkets. Balancing these he grabbed a handful more and a silver-bladed sword with a hilt too ornate for any real fighting. All he held in his hands was probably worth more than he was, he thought, as he touched the splendor and tried to identify it by touch alone. He couldn't, because he had never held such wealth.

They all filled their pockets and stared mournfully at the rest of the pile. Then Layen spotted the corner of a cloth sticking out between the pieces of gold and costly stores. He pulled it out and found yards of deep purple cloth, most likely from some murdered king.

"There's cloth in the pile, men!" he bellowed. "Dig! We can carry more treasure!"

The three dug frantically, throwing aside everything in their haste. Benji and Phin found more, and soon the four men were so possessed by greed they didn't notice when night came.

"I could buy a kingdom with this!" Benji said, holding the treasure he couldn't carry in his lap. They all were resting against the walls of the cave, comparing their wealth and riches.

"This is very good," Layen sighed. "All the hardship is worth this."

Phin sifted his fingers through his sack of treasure leisurely. His head suddenly snapped up, his ears straining again for the sound he heard. A sense of cold uneasiness settled over him like a shroud of dark, thick cloth.

"This may all be lovely," Phin said, getting to his feet and throwing his sack over his shoulder. "But we are still in a dragon's cave while the Princess of the Elves suffers in a cell somewhere."

Salgo and Layen sat bolt upright. "We have been fools, utter fools to neglect our duties," Layen said and started toward the entrance of the hole. Salgo and Benji followed firmly behind him.

The fall of Varisi the Great had shaken loose the rubble of the entrance again. Up the slope the four men trudged, holding their sacks of treasure, and then scampered over what dirt and rocks remained in the opening. Outside, the air had a bout of cold, while the sky above was dark and swirling with heavy clouds. The hill Varisi had lived in was on the very western edge of the Death Backs. In only a few steps the group reached the grassy plains again. Phin smelled the freshness of the open plains once more.

"There is almost no chance of us finding the horses again," Layen said. "And unless we do, we have to learn to eat grass or go back into the dragon's cave."

This idea was dismissed instantly.

"Either they – they being the horses – fled back toward where we started, ran and got lost in the Death Backs, or ran this way," Salgo said. "We haven't much chance."

Benji shook his head. "This gold doesn't do us much good if we just die with it."

Phin listened mournfully into the still night. He had thought he had heard the sound of a horse's hooves, but it may have been only his imagination. How he would have liked to climb onto Mage's back right now and just run! How long had they been with the dragon? One daylight? Two? A week? Because it wasn't winter he knew it couldn't have been a month, but who knew how long Varisi had slept?

"We need to think this through," Layen said sharply, dropping his sack to the ground. "We won't get far on foot and without food."

"That's already clear," Salgo said, rather irritably.

Layen continued speaking his thought process. "We could split up, one to this side of the eroded hills, one to the other, one into them . . ."

"Bad luck for the man forced to go through the Death Backs," Phin commented dryly.

"Or," Layen continued, "we could all go each way, but that would take up a fair amount of time and possibly starve us all to death."

"Oh yes, let's take that suggestion," Benji said bitterly, the happiness of being free and having the treasure wearing off with the thoughts of their predicament.

"We may as well call for the horses and hope they come," Salgo said, shrugging.

"And wake every foul beast in a surrounding mile with the racket?" Phin said. "Don't forget, we still have those bats most likely on our trail."

Layen rubbed his fingers along his stubbly chin thoughtfully. They had faced goblins, dragons, and two-headed snakes, but a simple thing like finding their horses was defeating them. There had to be a simple answer.

"All right. You all know your horses. What do you think they would do with what happened with the dragon?" he said. Just saying the word 'dragon' was strange and alien to his tongue.

"Mage would get spooked and run, of course, toward the safest area. When he'd calmed down he would just wander aimlessly, waiting for me to find him again," Phin said, adjusting the sack of treasure on his shoulder. "The khcalk would be with him."

"Storm runs for the safest area, a stretch of trees or a human village." Benji kicked at a clump of grass, fearing for the saddle sores on his horse when they found him again.

"North Wind would run like a blind, frightened deer until she couldn't even smell the danger," Salgo said. "She could be anywhere."

"And mine," Layen said last, "He'd do what Storm would."

"Sorry," Benji said, "but what does this have to do with anything?"

"It's drawing *me* to the conclusion that we should just go toward the forest. That way we at least have a chance of finding two of the horses and the khcalk, who has our things, and maybe the others on the way," Phin said diplomatically.

Layen pointed toward the Western Forest, a blur of shadow leagues from them. "Then that is what we will do. I'm feeling the same as Phin," he said, again shouldering his pack.

"Too bad we can't eat jewels," Benji said as he fell into step beside Phin. His older brother laughed, concealing his own hunger and unease.

21

A Helpful, Old Man

Phin rubbed one hand over his sightless eyes and tried to stifle a yawn. He had lost complete track of time during their stay with the dragon and the trek through the night. Dragging his legs over the grassy ground, the young man longed for their mission to be done, to be able to go back to his regular life.

He ran a hand through his filthy, dust and dirt-caked hair with disgust. Phin had never felt so dirty and scraggily before in his life. It had been a long time since he had washed himself or his travel-worn clothes.

There was suddenly a murmur on the wind. It whispered softly as it danced about the men, the breeze rustling their clothes and hair. Phin lifted his head, his finely tuned ears catching the voice, missing the words. The night fell still again.

Only Phin seemed to have heard it, though Salgo's eyes seemed a little more alight than before, and he was looking forward more often. Phin shook his head thinking he must have been hearing things from his drowsiness. The small group trekked on, shoulders bowed against the weight of their sacks of invaluable treasure. Phin used Benji's breathing as a guide to follow, though he would have preferred a simple staff. It seemed like the one hundredth time he had wished for one. He almost laughed at the irony.

The wind breathed again, whispering and murmuring words. Suddenly they became clear.

"Rest and safety lies only feet before you," the wind whispered.

Phin shifted his bag on his shoulder and strode forward again. He could rest soon. That was something worth keeping on for, because for some reason he believed the voice.

The four men dragged themselves up a slope in the plains, forcing their tired legs onward beneath the weight of their gold and gems. At the top of the hill, not far from the forest, was a stone-like cottage. The walls were made purely of large earthen-colored bricks, except for a door of smooth wood and one small square window. Dawn's light glanced off the glass pane as they drew close to the cottage.

"That's an odd sight," Layen said stiffly, stopping just short of the cottage. "Could be a goblin's home or the hideaway of some foul beast from the Westland."

Benji walked up to the door, staring intently at the top. "Would something like that have a winged horse carved into its door?" he asked skeptically, tracing with his finger the shape of a horse with out-furled wings that was cut intricately into the wood.

The door swung open suddenly, and a rather odd-looking man stepped out. He wore dark robes that contrasted with his white hair and short beard. His fair, wrinkled skin bore a cheery smile that twinkled in his beady eyes.

Benji was so startled that he almost fell over in his haste to step away from the door.

"Welcome, travelers," the old man said, all smiles and joy. "I see you have been through many trials." Before they could answer, he continued. "Hunger." He seemed to look at Phin's starved appearance, which was looking worse than usual. "Fire." He looked at Salgo's singed hair and Layen's burned boots. "Dirt." Each of their faces was smeared with it, and their bodies were coated with dust. "I am here to help those who need help," the man said and then laughed. "And you, my friends, are in great need."

He led them briskly into the cottage, which was much larger than it looked from the outside. The floor was hard-packed dirt and comfortable, with the new sunlight and a few burning candles lighting the first room. It was furnished with a table and two chairs, a cooking stove, and one very comfortable looking couch with soft cushions.

"In the next room," the old man instructed, "is a basin of water and a mirror. Behind a curtain in that same room is a small tub. Wash and come out clean."

"We are forever in your debt, sir," Layen said gratefully.

"But I must ask," Salgo said, "have you seen any horses? Three would be bridled and saddled, the other wild. If you could point us in the right direction?"

"Four horses are tethered behind my house. One black, one brown, one white, the last gray. By the packs and things they bare, I would say that they are yours. Oh yes, and along with them came a goblin's mount with quite a few packs on its back."

Salgo breathed out an audible sigh. Benji looked at him with a laugh concealed beneath his face. The elf would not have cared if he was filthy and starving as long as he had his horse.

"Now you go and wash!" the old man commanded. "You are dirtying up my clean room."

The four men went quickly to the chamber he had instructed and found the basin and the bath. Benji went straight to the tub behind the curtain while the others went to the mirror and basin. They each splashed their faces and shaved with the keen edge of a razor, staring up at their own reflections in the mirror.

Phin, though he couldn't see it, looked the worst for appearance. His usual thin body was to the skeletal point. Dirt and grime coated his skin and face, turning his skin a brick-like tan color and his hair a muddy, matted brown. There were a few small spots of blood on his clothes from the body of Varisi and some of his own from small cuts and scrapes. A bruise had bubbled up on his cheek from crashing into the hard wall. At least there was no longer short stubble along his chin and jaws.

Salgo cut the charred pieces of hair from his head, chopping his hair back to a shorter look. Each of them then followed his example and cut back their long, scraggily tangles.

Benji emerged from behind the curtain looking a different person. His skin was its natural color and his hair hung limp and clean on his forehead. The cloak he had worn for so long was now wrapped around his body like a towel so it covered his wet frame.

Phin went next, raking the grime from the roots of his hair and scrubbing it off his arms and legs, thinking the water would grow dirty, but somehow it remained clean. The scars across his lower chest and stomach stood out under his hands as he scoured himself with a hard bar of soap. Layers of grime fell away and he turned pink with the scrubbing.

Soon they were all clean and comfortable, cloaks draped around them, and walked into the back garden to retrieve fresh clothes. When they came back into the main room, washed and clothed again, the old man welcomed them gladly. They were so relieved to be fresh and clean that they couldn't worry about who the man might be. They felt that if worse came to worst, they could defend themselves now.

"That *is* better!" he said with a laugh. "You look more like men now, rather than creatures of the scrub; ah, elves as well I should say."

The four companions laughed, their temperaments having heightened with the feeling of cleanness and safety.

"Now, I'm afraid I haven't enough food or drink to last you through your journey, wherever that may lead," the elderly man said, a glimmer in his eye as if he really did know. "But there is good hunting in the forest near here and some apples and other such fruits. Of course an archer would be needed to take down any of the deer or wild boar that roams in the forest."

"I wouldn't dare hunt anything else in there," Benji said, startled. "I'm surprised there's *anything* that can be hunted and isn't tainted with evil."

The old man for the first time didn't look so merry. In contrast, he wore a frown and a stern look. "That's what you've been taught, isn't it?" he said. "All of you." It wasn't really a question, but his look was so sharp they had to answer.

They nodded uncertainly.

"Sit down," he commanded. The four travelers obeyed, Benji and Phin scrunching together on the couch while the elves took the two chairs.

"The Westland isn't fully foul or wholly evil," the man growled. "It is a place where creatures only there and in legend still dwell. Monsters and creatures as terrible as any in your most frightful nightmares –"

"See –" Benji began, but the man silenced him with a look.

"And on the opposite end of the pendulum, creatures more beautiful than anything in your wildest dreams. The forest teems with life . . . and magic. Magic is as real and as natural there as trees are in the East, or prairie grass is on the plains. True there is black, vile magic, but also there is white, good magic. In some places the black is stronger, and those places teem with monsters and darkness. In others white magic rules, and nothing could ever compare to the amazing sights you'll find in those places. I have seen it. The forest is not wholly evil, though magical creatures abound and travelers would most likely see more bad than good." The old man sighed. "Most bring it upon themselves; they come galloping in with war challenges, brandishing their swords and just asking to be eaten by a dragon." He gave a short laugh. "Or people come in and investigate business that was never theirs and they have no part in. They're asking for trouble, for there are many powerful forces in the Westland that don't like to be meddled with."

The men exchanged glances, but the old man pretended not to notice.

"I certainly hope if that is where you're going you won't put your noses in someone else's business. You won't see much good then, only bad. But know that the Westland isn't all evil."

The four men were amazed and bewildered. Somehow they knew that the place they headed was a place of black magic.

"So there are creatures like . . . like the winged horse on your door for instance?" Benji asked shakily.

The old man laughed again, looking again like the man they had first met. He nodded. "Many. Herds of them really. And unicorns as well, though they're shy and rare and stay away from people as much as they can." Benji looked both interested and surprised.

"But the dragon, Varisi, she was in the Death Backs," Phin said, "and she's a dragon. Shouldn't she have been in the West?"

The elderly man considered for a moment, stroking his short, white beard. "Yes, Varisi – I've heard the name. The natives spoke of her, said she was a very power-hungry dragon, always attacking her own kind to gain their land and treasure. She must have wanted to be the only powerful one in the area and get first rights to anyone passing through. Nasty temper and spirit, she had. How fares the brute?"

"Dead," Phin answered shortly, remembering the sound of her piercing death scream. It made him shiver.

The man grunted. "Serves the monster right. She was one of the worst of the lot, always wanting to steal the natives and treat them as her 'guests'," he said.

"'Of the lot?'" Benji asked.

"'Natives?'" Salgo asked at the same time.

The elderly man laughed, finding the double questions funny. The group was beginning to think he was very well informed, but a little on the peculiar side.

"Yes, lad, there are more dragons. Too many, and a load of different kinds. But they all love treasure, and hate their own kind unless forced to band together," he said. "Now to the other's question. Yes, there are natives. A small, shy race that lives in the forest and has broken off – or been forced away – from the other races. They understand the creatures and the magic. My bet is that they have some themselves, but I don't have a chance to talk to them much, and they seem to be the only people that can maneuver the forest. Strange they are, and distant. They stay holed up in their one city, afraid of any strangers.

"Now I'm sure you men would like a bit of rest before anything else," the elderly man said. "Second door. There are mats on the floor."

The four men gladly accepted, feeling the heaviness in their legs and eyelids again and forgetting their hunger.

When Phin awoke it was afternoon, and he felt again refreshed. He pulled himself off the mat on the floor, nearly tripping over their sacks of treasure, which had been brought in and set at the foot of their 'beds.' He could hear the sighs of his friends as they slept, sprawled across the floor like animals. The young man rubbed his legs to work out the stiffness, picked up the vine-bow where he had tossed it when he went to sleep, and pushed through the door. He wanted to visit his stallion.

"Out the front door and around the house," a voice said.

Phin stumbled over a chair.

"Oh, hello. How'd you know I wanted to see the horses?" he asked. "It is true, isn't it? You are a mage? Or a sorcerer even?"

The old man chuckled. "No." It sounded like a lie to Phin's ears. "Those are even rarer than they were in the old tales. I can just read facial emotions well."

The young man wasn't convinced. He righted the chair after groping around for a moment and sat down. "But I heard your voice on the breeze last night. I'm sure it was you," he said.

"It was. That calling is only a tool I got from the natives, an even more different race than the other ones that live even deeper in the Westland. Magic yes, but not my own. When I found the horses, I knew you men had to be out there somewhere," the old man answered.

"These natives – do they have a name?" the young man asked.

"They do. They are called 'Shifters,' though I don't know why. My opinion is that it has something to do with their magic. Either that they shift *themselves* or can shift *things*," the elderly man answered, shrugging. "And I haven't a clue about the ones that taught me how to call in the wind. I saw them only once."

Phin felt a strange tug on his heart at the word 'Shifter', as if it was the key to everything.

"Well, thank you . . . I'm afraid I missed your name," Phin said politely, rising from the chair and pushing it back into its place beneath the table, still holding the bow tightly.

"Because I haven't told it. My name is Morren," the old man answered candidly. His eyes fell on the bow in Phin's hand, and his brow furrowed. "May I see that?"

"What? This?" Phin held out the bow. "Sure." He passed it to the old man, who took it with reverent fingers. There was a moment of silence.

"What a beautiful piece of handiwork. It almost looks Shifter-made," Morren murmured. He handed it slowly back. "And you are?"

"My name is Phin," the young man said. "But now I think I shall visit my horse. I've been worried for him."

As the half-blood left, Morren rubbed thoughtfully at his beard. Something about the lad stumped him and confused him as well. He was familiar in some way, yet he didn't know how, and somehow the bow seemed to fit him.

Phin circled the cottage, one hand on the rock wall, until he heard the stamp of horses' hooves and their snorts and nickers of the familiar equines. The travelers' mounts grazed peacefully on the grass behind the house, ropes around their necks. Mage grazed a few feet from the others, a rope, chewed through, dangling from his neck, while the tiny khcalk grazed beside Storm. Phin called for Mage, and the stallion came willingly, his tail high. The young man threw his arms around his soft white neck, like a boy hugging a favorite dog. Mage smacked him hard with his nose in a way he seemed to think was affectionate, and Phin rubbed him in the middle of the forehead like he liked. The little khcalk brayed welcomingly.

When the other three men awoke, the smell of cooking meat and rich bread flooded the small cottage. They got up and went into the main room, the thought of food leading them.

Phin had just inspected the saddlebags of all the horses, finding that most of them were intact (only two were ripped or broken) when he too smelled the cooking dinner. He left Mage and the others, circled the house and went in through the front door. The half-blood was only a few paces in front of his friends.

"I thought you might like some food," Morren said, plunking down two plates of meat beside a jug of water. Beside it was a platter of bread and a bowl of apples. The small table groaned under the food.

The meal was wonderful. The four men ate until almost the bursting point, and the food never ran out. It seemed like the first meal they had had in a long time.

Salgo and Layen left after that, they being the only ones who would be any good at hunting, and started for the forest. Phin and Benji went back to the horses, enjoying their company.

"When do you think we'll be leaving again?" asked Benji, working off Storm's saddle and gently rubbing the small sores.

"I'm not sure," Phin answered, twining his fingers in the albino stallion's tangled mane. "Tomorrow?"

"Probably," his younger brother answered. "Layen and Salgo really feel this is their responsibility, and they don't want to make the princess wait any longer than she has to." He stopped to take a long breath before turning his dark eyes on Phin. "I wish we could stay here for weeks, but we really should do what we were sent to do. How are you with all this?" He produced a rag and began to rub it over Storm's back.

"If you mean with it being Yaja we have to rescue?" Phin answered. His now-seldom-seen half-smile flashed brightly in an almost teasing way. "I'm fine with it. We'll have to see if she'll even be willing to be rescued by someone so 'unworthy.'"

His head suddenly snapped up. They had fought almost six years ago, and he was still bitter. Just then he noticed how pointless it all seemed now. That fight had been about a stupid childhood infatuation too! Phin shook his head. He felt like a foolish, stubborn child, because after all that he'd been through – fighting monsters, escaping a goblin camp, killing a dragon – he was still feeling angry with Yaja. He wasn't even considering what she must be going through, trapped in a cruel cell by an evil man bent on world conquest. "If I ever see her again, I'm going to apologize for being such an idiot and holding a grudge for so long." Phin shook his head again, wondering how he could have been so self-centered. Yaja would probably welcome *anyone* who could set her free.

Benji raised an eyebrow. "You think too much," he said seriously, returning to working on his horse.

Phin laughed. "I'll agree with that. Maybe I should be more like you and not think at all."

A well-aimed rag, covered with dirt and matted horse hair, hit him in the face.

22

Into the Westland

"Leave your treasures here. There are creatures in the woods that would be after you in a moment, just for your gold. Besides, it is safe here, and it would only weigh the horses down," Morren said.

Saddlebags had been fixed and repacked, extra clothing mended or discarded – everything was prepared. The men agreed to the old man's suggestion and left their precious sacks of treasure at the foot of each mat, though they brought a pocket full of gold just incase the need should arise. They were rich men.

They had eaten another meal with the kindly man, Morren, and he had informed them about other important things in the Westland that he felt needed to be taken into account. Salgo and Layen had taken down a deer, treated it by a strange method Morren suggested so that it would stay good, and packed it away in their saddlebags.

"Be off!" the old man suddenly commanded sharply. "It will be a perfect day for riding, and you will make good time."

The companions all stepped into their saddles and started for the forest. Phin's body, so used to walking now, felt stiff and uncomfortable so suddenly thrown onto horseback again. Layen took to the front again, as if they had never stopped their journey. Ghost-foot was again tied to Mage's saddlebags.

The trees were all into their brightest stage of color. Burnt oranges, deep reds, and laughing yellows blended artistically above the riders in a thinning canopy as soon as they stepped into the shelter of the forest. Leaves covered the ground like a thick, crunching carpet, obscuring any trails or paths if there ever had been any.

"Morren said there was one main trail that was used long ago. He said it leads to anywhere of importance," Layen said professionally. "We should get on that."

"Do we even know where the princess is?" Phin asked suddenly.

"No," Salgo answered calmly, considering the odds that were against them. "Everything's a pure shot in the dark."

Phin then realized how much more difficult this was going to be. Anyway they took *was* 'a shot in the dark', especially if black magic was involved.

Benji looked thoughtfully at the area around them. "You know," he said, dismounting, "I think this *is* the road." Slowly he began scraping the leaves aside with his boot. Beneath the crisp twigs and leaves was bare ground, long since abandoned and ill taken care of, but usable. Small stubborn weeds poked through the packed earth. "So we just follow this," he said, smiling with a triumphant look that said purely, 'You thought I was stupid – just the *younger brother* in this little company.'

Layen shook his head as Benji remounted and then started forward again. The trail was only wide enough to go one at a time. Layen led, followed by Benji, then Phin. Salgo made his way back to work as rear guard. All that Morren had said made them only more wary than usual, for even if there *was* good, evil was sure to want to find them. The looming thoughts of the giant bats and two-headed snakes still wormed through their minds. For really, they *were* meddling in a business that wasn't really theirs.

The air was still. Not a leaf rustled; not a bird sang. There was no sound except the constant crackling and crunching of the brush beneath the horse's hooves. Phin fingered the vine-bow, enjoying the smooth sensation it gave him. Something was wrong with these trees, but he couldn't put his finger on why.

Then he smelled it. Something foul like mist that hangs over a poisoned swamp. It was faint, but pungent enough to be an annoyance. The young man breathed through his mouth.

"Do you smell that?" he asked to the back of Benji's dark head.

"Smell what?" the younger man answered, sniffing the air. "I don't smell anything." The foul smell was diminishing, floating away on the nonexistent breeze. Phin breathed again, scanning with his ears for any irregular sound. The forest came alive once more, a bird beginning to cheep in one of the trees ahead, while insects emitted their drowsy hum from the brush and weeds beside the path. Phin still felt uncomfortable. Mage's white ears twitched.

The group wound down the leaf-covered trail, checking every so often to make sure that they were still on it by rubbing aside the thick piles of debris to reveal ground below. Layen was still leading sternly, ever sure of himself and back in his role. Salgo stayed a few paces behind Phin's albino stallion, listening intently and looking over his shoulder.

Day progressed on, showing little to no change in the woods about them. A sense of security settled into them as the golden sun dropped through the thick trunks of the autumn trees. They began to believe what Morren had said about the Westland not being fully evil, for an everyday mourning dove began to coo at the top of a tall oak, just as it might have far away in the Northland.

The bat crawled along the ground, its claws scraping through the leaves a bit louder than it would normally have moved. But it was angry, and that caused it to be less cautious. That and that it was now back in its own territory and felt no fear of the Western forest.

Three times . . . three times . . . their prey had slipped through its claws, sliding away like sand in the wind. It growled. They had not succeeded in killing him in the human village. He had driven them away with weapons and fire in the forest to the East. Even the great two-headed snake had been killed by the prey and his other companions.

The bat snarled, the foul smell of its rage seeping through its skin. It tore into the bark of a tree with its hooked claws, using all four of its feet to climb up the steep wood. Crouching on one thick branch, the creature watched the road below. Signs of horse's feet plodding through the thick leaves stood out on the usually undisturbed piles.

The bat spread his leathery wings and swooped down, tasting the air. He could smell horses mingled with the smell of the prey. Instead of a snarl, it smiled, cold and murderous. The trail was hardly old. It would have the half-blood yet.

Tonight it and its fellows would attack, either destroying the prey, or dying in the effort.

“Don’t light a fire,” Layen commanded, “If Morren is right, then there are many foul things in these woods.”

“There’s no need anyway,” Benji said, throwing his cloak to the ground to serve as a blanket. “For now we have blankets and the air’s warm, and when we get home with parts of Varisi’s hoard, I’ll buy a kingdom in the South where it’s always warm, by a beach.” Phin chuckled.

“Have you ever even seen a beach?” he asked teasingly.

“No, but it doesn’t matter,” Benji said simply. “They have to be as good as people say they are.” Phin laughed again.

“Um . . . speaking of Varisi,” Layen said thoughtfully, “I’ve been meaning to ask, but what was Kern?”

Salgo nodded in agreement, though without much interest, as he leaned against the bark of a tree.

“All right. Kern was a human city: grand, spacious, advanced . . . They had the most beautiful libraries and gardens, the richest people, and the most royal treasures. I guess that’s why Varisi took it, for the riches. They were ill prepared, and all of them died or were scattered,” Benji said sadly. “They were one of the finest places in the North. The King’s City hardly compares, dirty and cramped like it is.”

“I see why you struck with such vengeance,” Layen said, nodding.

Salgo rested his head against the tree trunk, his blue eyes closing. “Wake me at the morrow,” he sighed. “If I don’t wake up, kick me.”

“We’ll hold you to that,” Phin teased, half smiling.

Salgo chuckled. “You do that . . .” then he drifted off to sleep, more comfortable under the shelter of trees again, even if they were foreign trees.

The younger man nodded his head toward Salgo, looking at Layen questioningly, or at least where he guessed Layen was by his voice.

"He likes forests more than the plains," Layen said, shrugging.

Slowly all of them began to drop off. Phin was the last to sleep. He lay awake for quite a while, listening to the night birds that sang both songs he knew and songs he didn't. The air of the forest was fresh and closed in the way he liked, and he breathed calmly, assuring himself he would be able to find and rescue Yaja, running all the dark scenarios over in his mind to prepare himself. He sighed softly, trying to relax. As strange as the place was, it seemed safe, almost homey. For a moment he thought he heard something. But he was too tired; it was probably just his imagination anyway. Phin rested his head against the ground and his arms, and slept.

CRACK!

Phin leapt off the ground, stumbling into Salgo who rested still against the tree. On reflex the elf reached for the knife at his belt, forgetting that it hadn't been there since Varisi had captured them and taken their weapons to add to her hoard.

"What is it?" he hissed, barely able to see the young man in the dark, even with his sharp eyes.

"Phin? Layen?" Benji's soft voice whispered. "Salgo?"

"Phin and I are over here," Salgo said.

They heard Benji crunch through the leaves, most likely crawling, and stop near them. "What's going on? Did you hear it too?" he asked, trying to make out anything in the dark. His eyes were taking a long time to adjust.

"If you mean that loud 'crack' – yes. But I haven't the slightest idea what it was," Phin answered, listening harshly to the blank silence.

"Look, it was probably just a bird, or a falling branch, or something," Salgo said, now able to discern Phin's face with its trademark unkempt hair. He also detected Benji's head and dark eyes.

There was a sudden swooping of large wings right above them. The three figures ducked, each set of eyes (with the exception of Phin's) shooting upward, but there was only darkness and the faint rustle of branches above.

"Grab a weapon, and somebody wake Layen!" Salgo commanded. "That man would sleep through a tornado."

"Mine's back near the horses, but I'll get Layen," Benji said, crawling back to his first place.

"Phin," Salgo now turned to him, "do you have flint stones?"

"They're with the ghost-foot!" Phin snarled, not in anger, but in exasperation. "And he's tied to Mage, and you know how Mage wanders."

Salgo cursed under his breath, reaching for his bow and quiver that he always kept beside him. The air seemed full of wings and creatures now. Slowly, the elf put one thin arrow to the string and drew it back. Aiming upward, he fired into the dark.

There was a screech and a yelp as something tumbled to the ground, landing with a crunch in the autumn leaves. It wriggled and shrieked, Salgo's arrow protruding grotesquely through its arm. The creature was a bat, coal black with flaming orange eyes.

Fire suddenly flared from the end of a stick Layen held. Dozens of bats began shrieking and flittering around, dodging the light and the branch Benji was swinging at them.

Suddenly three more appeared, only these were large as cats, with fangs that dripped with thick, white saliva. Their eyes gleamed in the torch's flickering light, their claws shining like new forged steel. Three mouths snarled, three noses quivered, and three minds were set upon this one goal: to destroy the prey that had so eluded capture.

The first monster leaped, spreading great leather wings. Without thinking, Salgo reached down and grabbed an arrow from the quiver and fired it before the bat had a chance to move out of its deadly path. The thin, elven arrow pierced through the creature's blackened, distorted heart. It fell to the ground silently, landing in a heap in the piles of foliage.

But by this time the other two large bats and all the smaller ones had begun to fight. It was a mad swirling of bats and the arms and weapons of the men trying to keep them away. The smaller bats were easily taken care of, for they were only the small breed that fed upon insects and could bite humans, but do no real harm. Their tiny fangs were merely like a pinprick, and as they flew, it was easy to throw them aside and continue.

The larger bats were far more of a problem. They swooped down upon the men, claws tearing, teeth bared. Benji drove them off with his straight branch, hitting them as hard as his sleep-filled arms could. Phin had grabbed a branch as well, as soon as he had heard the bats rush down. He was now whacking wildly toward the source of the flapping and cackling noises. Twice he had nearly hit Layen or Salgo and now the two elves were shouting at him in a wild line ofboth warnings and threats.

Most of the little bats by now had fallen, either hit so hard their frail bones were crushed, or slashed by the arrow Salgo was brandishing as a kind of long, sharp-ended knife. The two giant bats still raged forward, their claws having already lacerated the skin of their victims many times. But still the four men, slowly weakening, fought on.

One of the creatures leaped for Benji, and he only swung his branch barely in time. It connected with the creature's wing and gave a sickening 'snap'. The large bat floundered on one wing before falling, crippled, to the ground.

Some wild urge came over Benji, and he cast aside the branch, leaping instead upon the injured bat's thrashing form. There was a wild fight, claws slashing, wing flailing, as Benji fought to stay pinned over the creature, one hand holding down the bat's throat and trying to restrain the flailing legs.

"What are you doing?" Layen bellowed, aiming a blow with the torch at the other giant bat.

"Get . . . a . . . line of," Benji panted, sweat dripping down his face, ". . . rope." He pressed his weight into the arms and body of the creature he was pinning down, keeping its claws from his eyes and throat.

Phin jumped toward the horses, following orders and brushing small bats away from his face as they shrieked and tangled in his hair. The horses were pulling at their ropes, kicking and whinnying in fright as the black shapes darted about around their ears and wild, white-rimmed eyes. Whispering soothing words to the spooked equines, the young man dug through the nearest saddlebag, his fingers finally connecting with a line of rope.

"Benji!" he yelled and threw it to the young man who regrettably had to let up one of his arms.

The creature struggled, nearly freeing itself before a rope wound tightly around its neck. At that moment an arrow pierced the last large bat through the throat. As if some spell had been taken off, the remaining small bats scattered wildly, cackling and screeching, leather wings sweeping silently through the startled, silent forest. Just then did the four men realize how much noise the battle had been making.

Salgo tossed his bow (which he had been using rather as a staff) and the arrow he had been holding to the ground. Layen leaned against a tree heavily, still holding out his torch, which was now burning low and near his hand. Phin wiped the sweat off his forehead and ran his hands through his hair, which had become a nervous habit of his.

"I think," Salgo said, taking a heavy breath, "we've seen the last of those bat creatures. Except, of course, for the one Benji has decided to keep as a pet."

The young man scowled, looking down sharply at the broken creature on the end of his rope. It growled and lifted a claw to lash into his leg. Benji aimed a kick at the monster, and it scuttled aside, limping on its shattered front leg. The wing on that same leg bore a shiny, healed burn where no hair grew.

"It worked with Salgo, kidnapping someone on the inside. Why not to find where they have the princess?" he said, wiping aside blood that bubbled from a thin cut on his cheek.

"You can *not* be serious?" Salgo said, aghast.

"The monster probably can't even speak," Layen said mildly. "Just kill it Benji, and let's be off. It'll only slow us down, or betray us to something worse."

"No! I have a feeling it can, talk that is," Benji snarled. He looked again at the creature at his feet, cowering like a dog that had been beaten and was planning revenge. "Speak. If you can understand, speak, or I will kill you."

It snarled, staring up at him with cold, blazing eyes. "I do not . . . fear . . . death," it growled, the voice harsh and raspy. "Kill me . . . I challenge you . . . weak two-legged."

"If you do not fear death, then we will tie you to a tree with a tight knot and let you starve," Layen said. "Or you can lead us."

The monster spat, tearing into the ground and leaves with its claw.

"Choose," Benji commanded. The little compassion he possessed had been squashed by the recent battle.

The bat growled and hissed to itself in its own language before saying, "I will . . . lead you . . . but only . . . to the . . . cas-castle." A strange, bubbly growl welled up in the bat's throat.

Benji raised his eyebrows while wrinkling his nose. It was a look rather of disgust. "Then lead now," he commanded, slapping the rope lightly against the creature's back.

The men quickly untied the horses, leading them by their reins as the bat scuttled forward. Phin called for Mage, and the white stallion trotted forward obediently, leading Ghost-foot behind with irritation. The stallion didn't like being bound to the little, slow donkey. Phin grabbed Mage's mane and led him after his already-leaving companions.

The bat creature was hissing to itself, but knew it had to do what it had said. By the light of Layen's smoldering torch, the four wary men watched the beast's crumpled form lead them deeper into the woods, away from the main road. Sleep left their limbs as they traveled through the dense wood that was the Western forest in the weak hours of the morning, and nocturnal animals made noise behind the rustling of the trees.

Phin hurried forward until he was side by side with Benji, who only glanced at him once. The half-blood sighed, attracting the bat's attention. It turned its head just enough so it could see the skinny, young man – its illusive prey – with one yellow, hateful eye.

Phin spoke to it in a soft, insulted voice. "How many times do we have to kill you?" he asked the monster coldly.

It hissed. "You will . . . never . . . be rid . . . of . . . me," it growled. "Not . . . until . . . I . . . kill you."

Phin sighed again, feeling his fate was becoming less and less pleasant. "I thought as much."

23

The Dark Castle

The castle was dark and foreboding, spires looming like many sharp, chipped knives pointing toward the sky. It was black and stone, quiet like a grave, with only a faint sound of scratching and low growls and quiet screams. Dawn had dragged itself forward, but it was a smoky dawn upon a pale sky. The sun seemed to have lost all power here, and everything was dark and dusky, as if some shadow hung permanently over it. Over the castle soared a black creature with wings that cloaked parts of the dismal sky, weaving back and forth like a prison guard.

The bat had led them through the rest of the night, leading like a driver of slaves. The four men had not complained and now crouched behind the brush near the castle at the first fingers of morning, forgetting their hunger and the wounds they still bore.

"This is the place?" Benji asked quietly, staring with dark, anxious eyes at the monstrous towers. There could be no other.

The bat nodded, sniffing the dry ground.

"I will go alone," Phin said firmly, taking the vine-bow in hand and a quiver from Salgo, whose eyes were hollow. "Stay here. If I die and the princess is free, at least she can run to you three."

The young man stood up from his crouched position, hearing his heart beat like war drums against his ribs. This was it – his last chance to turn back and run, leaving the princess to her fate. And he couldn't. After all this time, he couldn't leave now that he was finally here, on the brink of the most insane thing he had ever done.

Benji stood up sharply too, dropping the rope that held the bat. Salgo was watching the beast closely. In an instant it had slipped into the trees again, the gleam of its eyes on Phin and Benji all the while. Soon it was nothing but a shadow with tiny points of light for eyes. Since it had left and done nothing, the elf decided to ignore its departure. "I'm coming too," Benji voiced.

"No," Phin said, shaking his head. "I have to do this alone. Stay where you're safe."

"Safe?" Benji challenged. "I've ridden cross country, been stalked by bats, fought giant snakes, been tortured by goblins, kidnapped by a dragon, and *now* you're worried about my safety? Phin, listen to yourself. Has *any* of this been safe?"

Silence followed Benji's speech, until slowly his brother nodded. "All right, Ben," he whispered, gripping his brother's shoulder. "You've made your point. Come on. I could use your eyes."

Benji smiled, knowing this was what he wanted, not sure if he could trust his will. "At least with me there you won't go blundering into walls and tripping over broken stone." Phin nodded soberly and didn't laugh. There was no smile on his narrow face, but he knew he couldn't stop Benji if his brother was determined. He grudgingly agreed that it would be helpful to have someone along so he wouldn't accidentally step on a sleeping monster's tail and get himself killed on his first steps into the evil place.

After one quick glance at the winged guard above, the two brothers proceeded out into the clearing, galloping quietly over the dewy grass toward the entrance to the evil palace. There seemed to be no guards besides the one on wings, and they hoped they were grubby enough with sweat, dirt, and forest debris that they would go unnoticed.

The door was of molding wood, scratched by claws like cats and hanging slightly open on rusted hinges. Benji pushed the door open only a fragment more. It admitted a screech that seemed to hang in the air. The two young men froze, waiting for some phantom or monster to leap out and slay them. Nothing came.

Benji slipped through the crack between the door and the frame, sucking in his breath, then pulled his brother behind him. They stood in the dark of the castle's first hall, both realizing that they still didn't know where Yaja was. The evil palace was huge.

The hall was wide and cracked, gray pillars holding up the ceiling throughout the room. A spacious staircase ran up to the next floor, some of the steps marked with scratch marks or dirty 'foot' prints. Behind the staircase were two long passages, both with many doors on either side. For some reason the smell of fish and raw meat hung heavily in the wide room, all the way up to the tall ceiling, so high it was cloaked in shadow.

"The hallways or the staircase?" Benji whispered, trying to hold his breath so the pungent fumes wouldn't get to his lungs. His quiet words seemed to reverberate through the emptiness.

The smell was nearly choking Phin, and he obviously couldn't see the staircase or the passages. But he did know he wanted to get away from the smell, whatever it was and wherever it was coming from. "Stairs," he hissed, holding a hand over his nose.

Benji grabbed hold of his brother's arm, and they jogged across the chamber, their steps muffled by the layer of grime and dust on the floor. It seemed too quiet – too still and peaceful. Shouldn't there be more monsters or guards? Shouldn't something be waiting specially for them, just to obliterate them from the face of the earth? Phin shook his head. The only thing that seemed to occupy his mind were thoughts of death.

Little did they know that the smell of fish and flesh came from a monster, a large creature, asleep, shrouded in gloom, on the far side of the hall. If they had taken the hallways they would have crashed flat into it. So far, their luck was holding, though that was a scant comfort.

The stairway to the next floor led them to more dark hallways and a spiral staircase.

"Check the left hallway," Phin commanded. "I'll check the right. Scream if something attacks you and you can't handle it."

"I've no need to be coaxed," Benji said and started down the hall, his hand wrapped around the hilt of his sword.

Phin's steps were shaky, his heart pounding fiercely in his chest. His left hand trailed close to Varisi's scale, which was still stuck into his belt. He touched the handle of the first door, feeling grime and dust of ages past, as if no one had used the room for a very long time. "The princess most likely wouldn't be there, would she?" he thought. Phin moved to the next one, and it too was covered in grime. The castle seemed empty, but why would the "Master" occupy an abandoned palace? Where were all the prisoners? He shuddered, clutching tightly to the vine-bow.

Suddenly, there was the sound of harsh voices, a shrill laugh, and footsteps. The air suddenly smelled of dirty hogs or a rain-soaked hound. Maybe there were guards after all.

Phin felt fear seize him; he pressed himself against the wall and froze. The voices drew closer. The smell of ale mingled into the other foul smells. The approaching guards laughed uproariously, most likely drunk. The young man still didn't calm down. Drunken guards were probably even more likely to kill a stray half-blood on a whim, especially if he was blind. Phin opened the closest door, fingers sliding on the smooth metal, and slipped himself inside just as the guards rounded the corner.

"– elf girl? Yeah I've seen 'er."

Phin pressed his ear to the spongy wood to hear more of the guard's conversation, his finger nails biting into the door.

"The lord is making us feed 'er some, says she 'as to last longer," said another guard. Each had the same thick accent. Phin barely breathed.

"Did 'e say why we're keeping 'er 'ere?" asked the first.

"Nah, doubt anyone knows," answered a third guard. He belched loudly. "Got to get back on duty. You checkin' on the elf?"

"Yeah, makin' sure she's comf'table," answered one. Was it the first? Phin couldn't tell them apart.

The guards laughed loudly and passed out of his hearing. Phin swore, cursing the foolish drunken guards for not saying where the princess was and would have hit his fist into the door had he not had the need to stay quiet. He turned the handle. It was stuck. The young man shook it, but it was futile. Phin forced his shoulder into it, but that did no good either. He was as trapped as the princess now.

That was when he noticed quiet breathing and the sound of strange, hard feet shifting right behind him, treading slightly on the bones of those who had occupied the cell before it.

Phin spun around, reaching for the knife that wasn't there and instead finding Varisi's spine. It flew out of his belt and into his hand as if it had a life of its own. He heard the strange feet take a step back. They sounded like a horse's, only heavier.

"What are you?" he strangled out, trying to look threatening, brandishing the spine.

"Peace, human. I am no enemy of yours," said a deep voice, rich like velvet.

"How do I know I can trust you?" he asked shakily.

"I believe I know where your princess is," the voice said calmly.

"How . . . what, do you really?" Phin gasped.

"Yes, if you can get us out," the voice said. There was a shifting of heavy feet, and Phin wasn't sure how to answer.

"Phin, Phin, you idiot," came Benji's voice. "Where are you?"

"Benji," Phin said, trying to speak loud enough that he'd be heard, but not loud enough to attract the guards. "I'm locked in here."

"Good job. Lock yourself in a deserted room," Benji hissed, pulling the door open with a creak.

"It isn't really . . . deserted," Phin said moving back into the passage, the heavy feet behind him. Benji gasped at the shape that emerged.

It was nearly as tall as the ceiling. A human head and torso connected to a sleek, white horse's body. The man was fair skinned, with hair that was pale yellow. His eyes glowed with a strange silver radiance, and his horse coat gleamed like moonlight. He flicked his tail, shifting his large hooves and picking the bits of bone from his feet.

"You – you aren't evil, are you?" Benji asked unsteadily, feeling very small and insignificant looking up at the noble horseman.

The centaur laughed, which sounded rather like a neigh, and shook his head. "I was a prisoner as your princess is," he said. "I will take you there. Time is precious."

He started down the hallway in large steps, followed by the two brothers.

"What, are you called?" Benji ventured.

The centaur turned his head, looking back with silver eyes at the young man. "Apollon," he said. "Now make haste."

Apollon went into a trot, his hooves clattering on the stone. The brothers winced, afraid of guards and monsters. He went into a jagged canter, forcing his followers to run to keep him in sight. The horseman turned around corners, jogged down abandoned hallways, and stopped in front of what looked like a solid wall. Raising up on his front legs, he kicked the wall with his powerful hind legs. There was a crack like something breaking, and a hidden door, made to look like the wall, crunched. The centaur reared up and kicked again, and the wall door fell in with a crash that must have awaken the entire castle.

"Go up those stairs; I do not do well on them. Rescue your princess and return. I will stand on guard," Apollon said, pointing toward the dark, rickety staircase behind the door.

"How did you know about this?" Benji asked, awestruck.

The centaur shrugged. "I have listened long to the wearisome talk of the guards. I ask only in return that you lead me out of the castle, for that I have not gathered from the trolls. Now go, or we will all be killed."

Phin and Benji nodded, taking their weapons in hand and not daring to ask any more questions. The noise of the breaking door was sure to draw attention to them, and they had no time to waste. Slowly they mounted the steps, feeling them sag beneath their weight. Benji's eyes had finally adjusted to the gloom, and he looked up at the coiling staircase above. He desperately hoped it wasn't a trap.

A horn rang through the castle, bounding through corridors, ducking in rooms, leaping off the banisters of stairs, and finally reaching the ears of the two young men. Its sound laughed at their attempt at saving the princess, all malice and mockery.

"Hurry!" Phin gasped. "Someone knows we're here!"

Phin leaped into the lead, galloping up the old steps, barely touching them with his light feet. Benji ran behind, feeling the rotting boards nearly breaking beneath his weight. His older brother continued urging him on, gasping for breath and holding the stitch in his side. They had hardly slept the last night, been in a fight, and been led without rest.

The heat of their exhaustion was catching up to them, but they forced themselves up the crooked, winding stairs.

A board snapped beneath Benji's foot. He fell through, the shards of wood cutting into his leg and twisting his ankle. Phin spun around and made a grab for his brother. The grab missed the young man's arms, but caught hold of his shoulder. Benji grabbed for his brother's wrist and was hauled from the broken step.

His leg and ankle were mangled, blood seeping from the cuts the wood had made. The foot was twisted strangely. Benji closed his eyes tightly and leaned stiffly against the wall.

"Stay here," Phin commanded. He tried to cheer him up. "With you here and Apollon guarding the door, the princess is as good as rescued."

Benji nodded, forcing a smile. "Go ahead. I'll protect you from here," he said, bravely clutching the hilt of his sword. "But when you come back, you had better be ready to support me back down."

"Of course."

Then there was another horn call – louder and more urgent.

"Go!" Benji incited, giving him a weak shove.

Phin let go hesitantly from his brother's shoulder and turned back up onto the stairs, feeling them creak beneath his feet. As he ran again he offered a silent petition to God to protect his brother from whatever was coming for them in this evil castle.

The stairs seemed to go on forever, always curling upward, and he felt it must lead to the top of one of the highest spires. His legs ached from climbing. Just as he was about to collapse from exhaustion, he reached a door. It was wood, not molding or dirty, but sleek and strong beneath his fingers. Phin yanked on the handle, but it was firmly locked. He pulled at it, turned it, pushed it, throwing his shoulder against the wood grain, but it was to no avail. This was starting to get annoying, all these locked doors.

Finally, he took one of the arrows from the quiver Salgo had given him, and jammed it into the keyhole. He turned this until he heard a snap, but it was only the arrow having its head broken off. He cursed the door and the lock and the whole blasted castle.

"There are rocks," said a girl's voice from behind the locked door. "If you're out there, there are rocks set up into the wall. Push three in a certain order, and the door will open. It's the only way."

So the princess was in there! Phin pressed his face toward the door. That wasn't the voice he remembered.

"Which three, princess?" he asked, settling his hands against the wood. There was a soft answer. "Sorry, I didn't catch that. What three?"

"I don't know!" wailed the voice. "Just go slowly."

He found the stones she was talking about by reaching out with his hands and gently, almost in a relaxed way, he began touching them one by one. First, second, third . . . nope. Third, fourth, fifth . . . not right either. This could – and would – take hours! Phin continued pressing the stones, still unsure about how many stones there really were. His legs were achy under him, and his pulse throbbed in his throat. The horn call still rang in his ears.

The sounds of battle hit him suddenly. Apollon's hooves smashed against the stone. Guards yelled and attacked. A blow, most likely of the centaur's hooves, shook the steps, which groaned like living things. There were yells and bellows. Sometimes sounds like neighs and screams and sometimes noises like human shouts escaped the centaur's human throat. They had been found.

Phin pressed stones faster, randomly hitting things beneath his now shaking hands, hoping . . . hoping . . .

There was a yell and a dull thud. Had Apollon fallen? If he had, Benji would have to fight with his broken leg. He didn't have enough time.

Footsteps pounded on the creaking stone steps. Armor rattled on the ascending guards' stout bodies. Weapons clinked against the stone walls in the attackers' haste. They were flooding up the stairs like a deathly river.

Phin wanted to scream. There wasn't enough time! There wasn't enough time! His mind swam and fogged with the tension. He couldn't take this! He punched his hand madly into the stones, making his knuckles smart. He felt a drip of blood as they cut on one of the rocks.

Click . . . whoosh . . . .
The door was open.

Benji swayed uncertainly. He had never broken a bone, not even sprained anything. But this time it felt like he had snapped his ankle, like the board he had cracked beneath him. The young man shook these thoughts from his head and held his sword at the ready, though his palm was sweaty. Be brave, he told himself.

The sounds of battle surged toward him: yells, crashes, and some wild bellows in Apollon's velvety voice. Benji wondered if the horseman could really hold off however many guards there were. The centaur, of course, amazed him. There was no doubt about it; he was certainly powerful, maybe even magical, but that strong? Benji shook his head again.

He thought vaguely of Salgo and Layen. They were probably crouched in some bushes outside with the horses, waiting apprehensively for their return. Salgo would be pacing, Layen silent. Then his mind landed on his life before this, and he almost laughed. If his departed mother could see him now!

But more than anything else, he worried about Phin. He knew it was stupid because on a million occasions his brother had proved that he was just fine without sight. But he still worried. He loved his brother, and though they fought and argued often, they had a bond even stronger than blood. Could Phin really save the princess without having eyes that saw?

Apollon bellowed, not a war bellow, but a bellow of pain. Benji cringed, tightening his grip on the sword hilt. There was a clatter of heavily booted feet on the steps. They were done for.

A guard, a scraggily, large-handed, short-legged troll, was coming for him, sword out. Benji heaved a blow at him with all the strength in his arm, cleaving in the armor along the guard's side. Trolls surged all around him as he tried to hold them off, giving wild swings of his sword as he balanced precariously on one leg. There was a sweep of dark cloak. He struck at it, his sword catching on the edge of the thick cloth. Then someone grabbed hold of his shoulder from behind. Thinking it might be Phin, the young man didn't strike.

But it wasn't Phin. A cloaked man grabbed him hard over the mouth and nose so he could scarcely breath, twisted the sword from his grasp, and put a knife to his throat. "We'll see if your *valiant* little friend values your life," the cruel voice sneered.

24

Transformation

"Yaj . . . Princess Yajandalay?" Phin asked cautiously, pressing the door open a fraction of an inch. "Is it you?"

"It is," said a meek female voice. "But who are you, hero?"

Had she called *him* – skinny, blind, 'unworthy' Phin – "hero." He smiled and for the first time truly wished to help her, which made him feel selfish and uncaring. He stepped carefully into the room.

"You know me, or you once did," he said mildly.

"I really am not in a state to guess," Yaja voiced wearily.

"I am blind, and have been as long as I can remember," Phin continued.

The princess's head snapped up. She studied the stranger outlined by the doorway again. "No. It could not . . ."

"I was there when you were on horseback through the forest," Phin said taking a few steps forward through the door. "A branch cut your face." He walked until he was right in front of her. "You had a scar." The young man ran his thumb across the bridge of her nose and onto her cheekbone, right along the scar, and then he gently traced the outline of her face. It was Yaja all right, older and dirtier, but it was her. He felt both worried and relieved.

Yaja choked back tears, letting her head fall again to rest on a large metal piece that held her neck back, bolted against the wall.

"No . . . Phin," she sobbed. "Why did you come? You hate me!"

"Not anymore," the young man said. "It was stupid of me. I shouldn't have held it for so long."

Yaja snarled, suddenly angry. "I still hold it. You vile excuse for a human being. Traitor to the elves. How *dare* you parade about gloating your freedom and thinking yourself worthy enough to come near me!"

Phin had a sudden urge to slap her and leave her there. Why was she so angry at *him*, so against him helping her? Had anyone *else* come to save her? He swallowed the feeling and only stepped back. Red anger still burned on his narrow cheeks. "If that's how you still feel, Princess," he said coldly, "then enjoy rotting here."

"Why didn't my father send a real man, an elf, or someone noble?" Yaja snarled with a vengeance that could only come from being bolted up in a dark room with only guards for company. "You can't do this. You just can't." Her voice took on a bitter, mocking tone. "I've certainly had plenty of time to think about it."

Phin was glad he couldn't see.

"You know what, Yaja?" he said. "Your father sent me – commanded me! I would never have come, risking *my* neck, being chased by bats and nearly starved, just for you. Believe me, girl, you aren't worth that."

Yaja looked away, stung.

"So you come here . . . to . . . to tantalize me with freedom and insult me to my face when I can't even fight back." Tears of pain and anger streamed down her face. "Just leave me alone, you cold-hearted jerk. I'd rather die here than watch you torture me with words. I thought you said you didn't hate me. Ha!"

Phin took a deep breath and let it out, along with his temper. It always had been a problem with him. "Yaja," he said in a calm, restrained voice. "I'm sorry. You're probably right about me. I'm *not* worthy of you, and I probably never was. Just . . . just, I'm sick of carrying this around. Please forgive me, and I'll forgive you in my turn. At least let it be a mutual 'friendship', nothing else, just so I can save you, leave this blackened place, and get whatever reward your father's willing to give me. Then you will be free of me for the rest of your life. You can go on with your life as Princess of the Elves, and I will continue my lowly life as a blind carpenter with plenty of money." He almost smiled.

There was a long, silent moment of indecision. The fluctuating emotions of the cell were wearing on the captive princess. It was all happening so fast. Months she'd been stuck in that room with scarcely the presence of another being, let alone an elf, and now a rescuer finally turns up, and it ends up being her long hated, ex-best friend. Yaja would have liked to lie down, eat a full meal, and talk to him about this later. But time was against them. There *was* no time.

Yaja sighed. "I don't know. Yes, I suppose. Let's talk in more detail about it when we *don't* fear for our lives." For the first time in years, Phin heard a shade of the old Yaja.

Horror suddenly dropped on her like a bucket of cold ice water. "No! No! This can't be possible. You can't rescue me!"

"Wha-" Phin started angrily.

"No, it isn't you, really. But you have to shoot the cuff around my neck, the metal part, with an arrow from some special bow! It's bonded by . . ." She hesitated. "Magic."

"But I could shoot you in the face! I mean, I can't see . . ."

"That's the problem!" Yaja yelled, knocking her head against the wall. "Come on, Phin, keep up!" They both almost laughed, but not really. Laughter was devoid in that place.

Phin didn't know what to do. He had to free the princess, but he didn't know how. He could kill her because of his blindness!

"Try, Phin," Yaja said, tears spilling over her cheekbones. "You'll have to try. Death like that would be better than staying here."

The young man grabbed onto the cuff around her neck and pulled, but it was firmly fastened. He tried rapping an arrow against it, but it did no good. A full minute he hesitated, afraid to do what he feared he might have to do. Slowly, he raised the vine-bow, taking an arrow from the quiver on his back. His hands shook. The sounds of battle still raged in his ears, though the stairs behind him had gone quiet. He swallowed, but what else could he do? There was no other way.

"Aim toward my voice, but a little lower," the princess said shakily. She shut her eyes, bracing herself for whatever was to come by pressing herself against the wall.

Phin swallowed again, pulling back the string of the vine-bow, praying more than he had ever prayed in his life. If he killed her . . . no, he told himself. He couldn't think about that. He stepped back to give himself room to fire, one finger brushing across the engravings in the smooth wood.

The young man tried to steady his hand. It was no use. He couldn't stop shaking. His heart pulsed in his ears, like a deep gong, tolling repeatedly . . . dong . . . dong . . . dong. The taut string quivered expectantly, the arrow pointed at the princess. He was going to kill her. It was going to be his fault that she died. The bow wavered and then held firm. He had to try, for his stepbrother, for Salgo and Layen, for the Elven King, for Yaja, and for his honor. He had been assigned to this task, he alone. What choice did he have? With all it had taken to get here, could he simply accept defeat? Never.

Phin took a deep breath and let the arrow go.

It struck the metal so near Yaja's neck that she screamed and tried to jump back, which was impossible in her tight bounds. A golden light suddenly swirled through the room, engulfing the two people. Phin felt the heat, like when he had stepped through the dragon's fire, hot wind billowing his hair and tugging at his travel-worn clothes. He was spinning, swirling, tumbling through warm, golden light that felt like cloud beneath him, like pollen on the wings of the breeze.

Then it stopped, and he was standing exactly where he had been, though slightly dizzy and lightheaded from the experience. The chains on Yaja's arms, legs, and neck snapped. She collapsed onto the stone floor, her legs too unused to movement that they wouldn't support her weight. Phin rushed forward, grabbing onto her to help her up, though his mind was still smeared with vertigo, and a simple thing like walking seemed suddenly difficult. The young woman was crying, clinging to him, and sobbing into his shoulder.

"Phin, I am so sorry. I've never hated you! I-I just wanted to stop liking you so much." She sobbed again. "So I replaced liking you with hating you, forcing you into anger, so you'd leave. But, Ph . . . Phin, I'm so sorry. I was so wrong. I just had so much pressure to be perfect and to get every *imperfect* thing out of my life. I kept hearing that a princess shouldn't-shouldn't be seen around a blind, useless boy. I guess . . . it caught up to me. I couldn't take it! I . . . I'm sorry I hurt you so much. Please, please forgive me, pl-please. I was so wrong to reject your friend-friendship just because of the image people wanted me to be. Can you ever, *ever* forgive me?"

"Yaja," Phin said sharply. "Take a breath! I forgive you, and I'm sorry too. I'm sorry I acted like a jerk, but please calm down. You're getting all panicky on me, and frankly, I'm panicky enough as it is."

Yaja looked up at his pale, blind eyes and smiled. "Thank you." She wiped the tears off her dirty face and hugged him. "Good old Phin, even after five years."

"Now," Phin said, helping her up gently. "We have to escape and get Benji."

"Benji?" Yaja asked.

Phin shook his head and said, "Later, I promise."

The two figures mounted the stairs and went hastily down, avoiding the step Benji had broken. Yaja kept a hand to the wall, still unstable on her long-unused legs.

"Where is he?" Phin said quietly to himself. "He couldn't have gone back down, could he?"

At the bottom of the stairs there was no Benji or Apollon. Phin was getting worried. Everything was quiet again, quiet and deserted like a grave. They started down the silent passage. Suddenly, someone yelled. The voice sounded like Benji, yelling his name.

"My brother!" Phin shouted, dragging Yaja behind him. She stumbled along but followed. Phin drew forth Varisi's scale, feeling the need to have some weapon in his hand.

Benji yelled again. It was wild and heart piercing, cutting into the stone walls like knives. Phin ran, forcing his exhausted legs to perform. Benji was in danger, probably dying! Someone had him at the point of yelling for help, or had forced him to, to get Phin to come. What if it was a trap? Phin found he didn't care.

They raced down the corridors, following the screams that continued coming toward them. Phin turned a corner sharply and burst into a room, stumbling over a bit of uneven floor. A strong man with a sharp face, cold eyes, and an expression of pure evil, smiled at the two of them as he held a knife at Benji's throat. The young man's eyes were wild, and he struggled like a caught bird. Yaja held Phin's arm and muttered under her breath what she saw for his benefit.

The man took the knife from Benji's throat, still holding the young man fast with his other, gnarled hand. He twirled the knife between his free fingers, a violent, insane look in his gray eyes. "So you got past my monsters only to have me still with the upper hand. I must say I'm surprised a skinny, blind bastard would get so far anyway. I applaud your inane efforts." He cackled, still twirling the knife so the torchlight in the dim room bounced off its shining blade. "But, I'm sorry to say, the princess will remain in my *gentle* care until the proper time of the public execution while you feed my minions. Pity there's so little of you. You'd hardly feed a troll. But no matter. Give me the girl now, *'hero,'* and I *might* kill your little friend here in a quick and *painless* manner, or I could simply toss him to the spell weaver, who likes to play with his prey," the man said, mocking him. A shiver ran down Phin's spine. Somewhere, ages ago, he had heard that same voice . . .

"Let him go!" Phin snarled, moving Yaja behind him. "You will never have the princess or my friend!"

The man laughed, a sound that made their skin crawl and an ache run into the marrow of his bones. It was full of evil and darkness . . . and magic.

"'Have him?' I believe I already have him, half-blood, or has your blindness limited you that far?" the man said and laughed again.

"Wait!" Phin said. "What would you trade instead?"

"The girl only," said the evil man. "She is the key to the Eastland, the exact piece that will destroy them. Her murder – public murder I might add – will drive the elves to such a rage, they will do something foolish. And my minions will rush in and utterly wipe them out." The man laughed insanely. He was a mad man, a psychotic magician who had gathered a hoard of evil, stupid followers.

"It started with stealing the Shifter Prince, seventeen years ago. The Shifters were so shaken that they would do nothing to resist us. Instead, they kept to their forest, building up the tangled wall of trees until no one could get in to find them. But they've always been weak, and they pinned all their hopes on the little *prophesied whelp,* which *I* stole out from under their beastly noses. That would teach the little creature-lovers some respect, I decided, so I left the little beast to die on the plains, alone and helpless." He laughed at his own evil, proud of his murder of the innocent child. "Rumors of an evil, magic race began appearing. I fueled those rumors, of course, driving back the Shifters until they weren't even considered a race any more! Then I got the leader of the centaurs, and they ran deeper into the Shifters' little hideaway as well, as skittish of evil as the bloody horses that are their better half!" The man laughed madly again. "The elves are the next key – the only other people who have any chance against me or the son I'm raising up in my footsteps. Men are easy to manipulate with gold and power, but the elves and Shifters – they were a threat. Shifters, weak as they are, are formidable in their other form, and those pointy-eared tree-huggers are hardy, stealthy, and will never give up to the *dark side*." His voice was mocking. "But they both had their weaknesses. One was a prince, long dead, and the other is the princess you're hiding behind you. But no longer," he said, singsong. Then he sobered. The knife pressed again into Benji's neck.

"Now you give me the girl," he commanded. "I have tired of this game, blind half-breed *child*. You have no right to stand any longer in my presence. Give up now, before more people get hurt." His smile was the most horrible thing Yaja had ever seen, and she cowered back.

Phin felt himself boil. For some reason this made him angrier than he had ever felt in his life. It was as if all the trials he had gone through, all the anger and frustration, all the torture, all the hardship, all those hours on horseback, feeling the sun bake the back of his neck, all the time he had spent risking his neck for some adventure he had been thrown into, had all burned into this one moment. Every act of betrayal, nonacceptance, harsh ridicule, snickers behind the hands of people who called him 'worthless', 'street dog', 'half-freak' and other names he had always endured. With all the trials he and his companions had been through to get here – monsters, hardship, long hours of travel – he would not stand here and be mocked! Not again! NEVER AGAIN! He was a human being, and they would banter no longer! Heat seemed to explode from his skin, and he bellowed. From far away, he heard a stallion scream.

It happened in an instant. One moment he was standing there boiling over. The next there was a great wolfish dog in his place. The beast's fur was the same color as the half-blood's hair, his mouth shaped into a toothy snarl. Sharply pointed ears pricked toward the man, the fur on the dog's neck and back standing up like spines. Great claws scraped the stone floor as he growled, snarling its hatred. Yaja jumped back in alarm.

But the strangest things that changed were his eyes. They turned deep, enchanting, and intense, like blue, sorcerer's fire. He blinked. Slowly, the world of darkness and shadow he had so long known shifted into colors and shapes and pictures. Gray floor, straight walls, dim light, a man in front of him, a young man in the evil Master's grasp. Phin didn't have time or thought to celebrate over this. He could only stare at the evil man's shocked, insane expression and watch him lower the knife. Every muscle in the hound's body was taut with rage.

"No," the man said. "No! I killed you!" He threw Benji aside. "I watched your huddled, blinded form as I rode away. We left you for dead! You were DEAD!"

But these were the last words he ever said. Phin, still in the great bear-like dog form, leaped at the man with powerful back legs. His broad, front paws striking the man's chest with the full weight of the blow, his needle-like teeth closed on the man's throat, and tore clean. Blood filled the dog's mouth as the body of the evil man fell to the floor under the beast's weight, gore spilling all over the cold stone. Phin rolled off, trying to stop himself with his clawed paws, but he hit the stone wall with force, causing his head to spin for a moment.

All the flaming anger simmered away, and Phin spat the blood out of his mouth, the taste revolting and somewhat victorious at the same time. His mind suddenly registered everything.

For one, he was a dog – a huge, scruffy-haired dog. Second: he could see! The world was clear; he was looking at it! Phin staggered up and looked around him, aware that his canine tongue was hanging out of his mouth. How could it feel both so odd and so natural to be in a form that wasn't his? He shook his head again, wondering if this was all some strange hallucination. But how could a blind man have such a clear and logical delusion?

Phin wanted suddenly to be a human. And he was, without a feeling or a twinkle of magic light. It was instant and effortless, as simple as breathing or thinking. He shook his head again and knuckled his eyes, just to be sure the sudden sight was for good. It didn't change once he opened his eyes again.

He stared at who must be Benji, trying to shake the scraggily hair from his eyes. The young man had hauled himself off the floor and was staring in disbelief at his brother. Phin saw his younger stepbrother for the first time in his life, the shell that held the voice and personality he knew so well. They couldn't take their eyes off each other, though Phin was feeling a little dizzy.

Benji hobbled forward, grabbing hold of Phin's shoulders with both hands. His dark eyes studied his brother's face.

"Phin?" he asked softly, waving a hand in front of his face. Phin blinked and flinched, pulling back. "It's true! You *can* see!"

Phin blinked again and couldn't speak. All he could do was stare into his best friend's face, memorizing each of the parts he had at some point felt beneath his skillful hands. This was the most amazing moment of his life, yet also the most mad and unbelievable.

"B-Benji?" he stuttered. He grabbed his brother's arm, almost in panic. The young man smiled and nodded, looking like he wanted to laugh and cry at the same time. Phin shook his head in wonderment.

"Hey, brother, is this how you thought I'd look?" Benji asked, smiling. His hair was rumpled and tangled, his face smudged with grime, but there was a gleam in his dark eyes that Phin would have recognized anywhere, even without having seen it before.

"I didn't know, but it fits," Phin said, and they embraced like long, unseen friends.

25

Mage's Valiancy

"Phin?" asked a meek, female voice. The young man turned, using his new eyes to take in every aspect of the room, ugly and dingy and gory as it was. Then they landed on Yaja.

Her hair was dirty and matted, the fine dress she had started with now shabby and ripped. She was thinner than usual and her skin was pale, with bags below her eyes from crying. But she was smiling, and her bright eyes shone as green as summer grass. Her stance somehow still retained its nobility.

"You must be the most beautiful thing I have ever seen," Phin said truthfully, because the little he'd seen was rather ugly in comparison. He walked to her and took her hands.

Yaja blushed and pushed a strand of grimy black hair behind her ear. "Don't tease," she said quietly.

He pulled her closer. "I'm not. Imagine being blind and then seeing something as pretty as you . . ."

"Stop, Phin," she said, smiling with embarrassment. Phin kissed her hands, dirty as they were, and smiled up at her through his wild array of hair.

"Sorry to break up this romantic moment for the two of you, but remember, we're still in an evil castle, even if the main man is dead," Benji looked with disgust at the bloody body. "Phin, did you really just turn into a hound-wolf . . . animal?"

Phin raised his eyebrows. "I guess I did," he said. Something was puzzling him about the 'Master's' last words. "I killed you. You were dead . . ."

"You don't think, *I'm* a Shifter?" Phin asked, surprised and confused and slightly afraid all at once. "*The* Shifter?"

Benji bit his lower lip. "It makes sense. 'Shifter' is someone who turns into an animal . . ."

"Right now it doesn't matter!" Yaja said sharply. "We need to get out. We can talk later." She pointed to Phin. "*You* promised."

Phin smiled at her. To think he had set her free. And he could see! And he could turn into a dog . . . maybe.

"Where's Apollon?" Benji asked apprehensively, looking around as they entered the passage. Phin stared around at it all like a half-wit.

"I am here," said a rich, velvety voice.

The three people turned. The centaur stared down at them with glowing, silver eyes. Phin tried to keep in his awe as Yaja gasped. Everything was so amazing!

"But how do we get out?" Benji asked.

"I planned for this during the months I spent here," Yaja said and shuttered. "If we go to the hidden door I can lead us out."

So they did. The odd group backtracked and followed Yaja's directions, the centaur keeping them at a hurried pace. The castle was sure to realize soon that the Master was dead.

Phin was surprised to find that it was difficult to do something as basic as walking because of this strange new ability to see. He kept finding himself walking into people as he hurried along or tripping over bits of floor that *weren't* uneven. Ironically, he found that he had to shut his eyes to get his bearings. When this happened, Benji would just smile at him, his eyes laughing in that mocking, patronizing way Phin had come to recognize by his sound rather than sight.

Still, Phin couldn't help looking around at everything. No one would ever understand how wonderful it was to suddenly see. No one possibly could.

Salgo paced from a tree to another, hands folded behind his back, which was his natural reaction to stress or uneasiness. Layen was still crouched in the brush, eyes pointed on the castle's door. Once in a while his eyes wavered toward the swooping guard or the sharp pinnacles. Then they would snap back to the door and linger there.

It had been very quiet since the two young men went in. Day had come fully, still pale and smoky, but full. Still no birds sang, and not an insect hummed. The world was utterly still, except for a possible cracking of leaves or a twig under Salgo's feet. Even the dark wings of the monster overhead were silent in their beating.

"There!" Layen suddenly snapped, pointing toward the door. Salgo jumped and lunged down into the brush beside him.

"Do you see them? Three figures, one tall and the others shorter, with dark hair. Look, the third one's a girl. They have the princess!" Layen said joyfully.

"The other creature, the hugely tall one, it looks like it's half-man, half-horse. I bet Benji's loving that," Salgo said. "Should we go out to them?"

"No. They're waiting by the door. Let them come to us."

Phin rubbed his shaggy forelock out of his new, seeing eyes, taking in the almost mind-blowing colors and shapes that unfurled around him like a glorious tapestry. Benji, who leaned against him for support, grinned at his wonderment.

Apollon eyed the sky warily, watching the black, winged creature circle and hover above. "Go, one at a time. The spell weaver will be less prone to notice," he said wisely.

"Spell weaver?" Benji started.

Apollon put up a hand for silence. Then he pointed at him. "You go first," commanded the centaur. "Do not run."

Benji nodded and tried to start forward. His wounded ankle buckled, and he winced from the flare of pain. Phin grabbed him and held him still, protectively.

"Get on my back," Apollon then said. He kneeled and Benji climbed on. The pain of his leg was soon forgotten for the awe of sitting upon the noble horseman's back.

It was tedious work as the centaur picked his way along, trying to look inconspicuous, trying not to make noise. Benji had enough sense not to look up at the spell weaver. He instead concentrated on the back of Apollon's sun-bleached blond hair. Suddenly, there was a scream that rang off the spires of the evil castle.

"The spell weaver! It's the spell weaver!" Yaja screamed, stopping up her ears and cringing. Phin looked up as the sickly black, slightly decayed-looking monster soared down at them. Yaja shrieked as another scream pierced their ears. Apollon leaped forward, Benji clinging around his human torso, and with monstrous strides, cleared the distance to the forest and leaped inside.

"Run!" Phin yelled, grabbing Yaja by the arm and hauling her to her feet. The spell weaver was not far above them, and it came at them with claws stretched like withered hands to snatch them up and stuff them into his wide maw to destroy them with one bite. Phin couldn't follow his own advice, so petrified he was by the monster's approaching form. It was the end.

Mage, still with the elves and now Benji and Apollon, bit easily through the rope that tied him to the tree with his fellows, kicked off his saddlebags and the khcalk's rope, and bounded out of the forest, chewed end dangling from his neck. Salgo yelled at him to get back, but the proud, white stallion didn't listen and instead charged bravely at his master and the Elven Princess. The horse gave a war scream at the giant monster that soared down on the pair, stretching his already long legs to their fullest. His mane lashed in the wind that his strides were creating, furling back like a pallid banner. He trumpeted again, raising his head to challenge the black monster.

Phin saw Mage and knew by his war scream that it was his valiant stallion coming to try and save them. But regular horses weren't that smart, or brave. Were they? Phin reached out his hands to the charging stallion even as the spell weaver came closer. His hand caught the rope still tied around the horse's neck as Mage slowed enough to let them on. Phin swung himself on, dragging Yaja on behind him with an arm made strong by carpentry and travel.

"Hold on," he commanded, and she gripped his waist tightly in fear. Phin shut his eyes to get his bearings and felt Mage leap forward again. His legs fit over the stallion's muscles and his hands wound into his mane. Slowly he opened his eyes again, enjoying the sensation of hurdling along on his familiar horse's back.

The spell weaver hit the ground with clawed feet and swung around with the speed and accuracy of a snake. Long tail whipped around, and holed wings flew open like flags in a gale. Its jaws parted again, ready to engulf the stallion and its two riders in the dark cavern of its mouth. But Mage kicked it in the face as he sprang into the forest, causing the monster to shriek in rage and pain.

"Away!" Phin shouted, hardly breathing because of Yaja's frightened grasp. The two elves grabbed their mounts with expert horsemanship, the equines already saddled, and tore off after the white stallion, Salgo holding Storm's reins while Layen had Phin's saddlebags and the khcalk. Apollon bore Benji as he ran with the rest of the company. The spell weaver, unable to follow in the dense trees, turned in hurt and anger back to the skies, giving one wrathful scream to vent its frustration at losing a supposedly easy kill.

26

A Continuation of the Journey

The group realized in only a few minutes that the monster wasn't following. Mage stopped first, panting and shaky in the legs. The rest of the company followed, dropping slowly from their horses.

"Phin," Yaja said, breathing hard, "I love your horse." The stallion's rider smiled, stroking his mount with pride.

"Well done, Phin and Benji!" Salgo said heartily, recovering first and clapping the younger of the two brothers on the shoulder as he slipped off the centaur's back. "That was some phenomenal running from your stallion, Phin."

"I have never seen any animal except a unicorn run so fearlessly against a spell weaver," Apollon said, looking meaningfully at Mage. The stallion nickered. "That is indeed an amazing," the centaur grunted, "horse."

"Phin, you look different," Layen said, helping the princess loosen her arms from Phin's abdomen and off Mage's back.

The young man studied the two elves, absorbing all their features. Salgo was tall, and long legged with shinning golden hair and twinkling blue eyes. Layen was more heavy set, more muscular, with dark hair and sterner eyes. Phin had the same revelation he had first had when he saw Benji. These were the men he had saved and been saved by.

"Your eyes are darker," Salgo said thoughtfully. "You can't see, can you?" He waved his hand in front of the young man's face just like Benji had.

"Why does everybody keep doing that?" asked Phin, brushing the hand away. "Yes, I am able to see. I can't believe you men aren't constantly in awe of the world around you!"

"It's different when you've always seen it," Layen said quietly.

"How did all this come about?" Salgo asked.

"First, we should get farther away from the keep. The Master may be dead, but his minions still live," Apollon said. The four men stared up into the horseman's silver eyes, struck by the power and nobility he carried.

They each took their horses and led them back into the depths of the woods. Phin looked at his stallion, smiling and stroking his soft neck as they walked. Each place his hand had touched when he was blind now came together, forming the stallion he now saw. Mage nosed him kindly, seeming to sense the change as easily as anyone else.

"I no longer think he's ugly," Yaja said into the young man's ear, laying her hand against the stallion's side.

"Of course he isn't ugly. He has always been beautiful," Phin said lovingly, rubbing the stallion in the middle of his forehead where he liked to be stroked.

Yaja snorted, the same noise she had made nine years ago.

They stopped safely away from the castle, and stories were related. Apollon bid them a fond farewell, saying he had to return to his herd and rule them again. The group was struck once more by his aristocracy, understanding now why the Master had kidnapped the centaur. The horseman then turned and trotted away, promising to never forget how they had saved him, and taking one last, curious look at Mage. Then he disappeared into the forest.

After the centaur had left, Benji and Phin spoke off and on, back and forth, about the goings on in the castle while their companions listened intently. But they were no storytellers and often had to backtrack to put in an important detail they had missed. Phin finally took over after they had covered Benji breaking the stair (here Salgo made a wise crack about the young man's weight and just ducked a blow) and told about recovering the princess. Yaja put in a few things, but both smoothed over the fact of Yaja's breakdown into tears and apologies.

But what both Layen and Salgo wanted to know the most about was how Phin had gotten his sight and how the brothers had killed the Master of the dark castle.

"You tell them," Benji said. "It happened to you."

"All right. Yaja and I had just come down the stairs and we heard Benji yelling," Phin began.

Benji nodded in affirmation, shuddering at the thought of how the Master had threatened to feed him to the trolls.

His older brother continued until he got to the moment when he had become the dog. He shook his head.

"You tell them, Benji. You saw it," he said. Truthfully he was tired of talking, tired of moving, and tired of thinking, utterly exhausted from the work and worry of going into the castle. He still felt a nagging uneasiness, but without realizing it, he began to doze off, leaning against a tree. The last thing he remembered was feeling the weight of the medallion below his shirt, resting its cool metal against his skin.

A brown stallion, a wildness in his dark eyes, arched his sleek neck down toward him. Phin stretched out one small hand and rubbed it along the horse's soft nose. Then he was tottering beside a round lake, a silver waterfall roaring down into it from mountains that surrounded the lush valley. The sky was the clearest shade of blue he had ever seen.

"Phin, wake up," said Layen's voice. The young man mumbled something, still deep in his dream.

"We've done it!" Salgo's voice was cheering. "Mind you, Phin and Benji did it. I should say, poor men. Begging your pardon, Princess Yajandalay."

"Peace, Salgo messenger," said Yaja, using her formal name for the elf. "But I understand how much work it took."

"I do feel for the two men," Layen said, leaving Phin to wake on his own. "This is the most they've ever gone through . . ."

Phin drifted back to sleep, returning to his dream. Now he stood before a giant castle and a man, eyes bright and glowing, rushed toward him. The man wore rich silks and a long purple cape that furled out behind him. His face was broken into the largest smile Phin could imagine, his look one of pure love.

"My son!" he beamed. "My son, you are alive. You have returned to us!"

The man's eyes were brimming with tears as he embraced a rather shaken Phin. He suddenly woke up, again having the happy revelation that he could see.

Benji was sprawled on the ground, his breath rising deeply in his chest and stomach. He was using leaves for a pillow and some of them quivered as he breathed. Phin pulled his body away from the tree he had fallen asleep against, arching his back, cat-like. It reminded him suddenly of waking up the morning he had received the Eleven King's letter, that day seeming like it had been a lifetime ago.

Sun glittered through the thinning autumn leaves. Cobalt sky churned above mixed with streams and swirls of white clouds, like a painter who had whirled the two colors white and blue. The air was warm and seemed to radiate from the flaming oranges and reds of the leaves. It was as if he had just awakened, not from sleep, but from a dark past life. He blinked a few times and smiled up at the bit of sky that grinned back down at him.

"We've won, Phin!" Salgo yelled suddenly. "Won, I tell you! We can go home!" He grabbed Phin's shoulders and shook him, as if to be sure he understood the importance of his statement.

Benji snapped awake and rolled over. "Can't you let a tired man sleep?" he asked, covering his face to keep the light out of his eyes. "A man who just helped to save the world? Or is that not grand enough for all of you?"

"Oh get up, you great slug," Salgo laughed. "We're going home!"

Benji sat up, rubbed leaves out of his hair and got to his feet. Sleep still clung to his eyes, but his face was bright.

"What are we waiting for? Let's be off!" he said, grabbing hold of Storm and throwing on the saddle Layen had removed the night before. "We've a long road a head of us."

Phin felt something tugging at him, and he lifted the necklace out of his shirt. He had never seen it before, only felt it, and now he studied the strange markings. In the center was the head of a dog with a sharp ear and a layer of scruffy fur around its neck. The carving was so good it almost looked real, as if the hound might start barking at any moment. Ringing the outside were letters in a strange language he couldn't understand, dots and dashes making up parts of the letters. He ran his finger over the engraved signs, wondering if it was a dog's head carved into it because he had become a dog. Phin sighed, wishing it would tell him what to do, like it had in the dragon's cave. But the pendant was silent, as a pendant ought to be.

Somehow it pulled at him, urging him that he couldn't just go home. The dreams and necklace somehow were intertwined together, but he wasn't sure how. He had to find out.

"Phin, come on!" Benji urged. "We accomplished it! We can all go home." He was grinning broadly at him, Storm already saddled and bridled.

They were all beaming at him expectantly, ready to be out of the forest and back to their normal lives, but somehow he knew he couldn't. This was still a mystery that had to be solved. The young man wanted to know why he could become a dog, had magically gained his sight, and why he still had the medallion. Some kind of past was behind him, and he couldn't just go back to his old life without knowing what it was.

"I'm sorry," he said, shaking his head. "My journey isn't done. I have to understand."

The others stared at him blankly, their faces falling.

"Actually," Phin said brightly, "all of you can go home. I'll catch up later."

"Never!" Benji snapped. "If you aren't done, than neither am I."

"You'll need a guide to get you home," Layen said wisely. "I will stay with you."

"Well, Salgo? You could go and take Yaja with you," Phin said, watching the elf's face.

The elven messenger smiled and shook his head. "You have always been odd, Phin. Ever since I first met you and we nearly killed each other with our tempers. I will not desert you after all this time," he said. "And I'm sorry to say," he turned to Yaja, "but you don't really have a choice."

Yaja smiled demurely, which Phin knew she wasn't. Her beauty again struck him. "I will willingly be dragged along," she laughed.

"Then it's agreed!" Salgo said. "The journey continues!"

"This is what you get when the blind see," Benji said, rolling his eyes in mock annoyance. "I might have known."

They were traveling again, but deeper into the thick forest instead of out of it. Sunlight fell to the trail before them between the pockets of leaves. Phin had a hard time not turning to stare at everything around him in pure wonderment because, though the sounds and smells were familiar, everything was so new. The whole earth seemed like a different place.

Mage shook his streaming mane and snorted. The albino's pink eyes peered ahead as he led the rest, paying attention to the road and the trees. He shook his mane again and whinnied, as if in a place he had known forever and was heading home. The gleaming stallion fell into a canter.

Yaja grabbed a harder hold on Phin's waist and leaned into his back. For some reason the young man before her was not trying to rein in his mount. Instead he let him run and ducked beneath branches that came his way.

"Slow your horse!" Layen commanded. "He'll throw you into a tree!"

"Does he even know where he's going?" Salgo asked the back of Layen's head.

"I doubt it," the elder elf said.

"Mage seems to," Benji's voice said up toward them.

The white stallion's nostrils flared, and he continued his steady pace, hooves echoing on the packed earth and crackling over the leafy debris on the ground. His mane and tail flew, and Phin shut his eyes, remembering how to hold on, and kept his seat. Though it was difficult to ride Mage and see at the same time, he still found that his legs fit comfortably into the stallion's back. Suddenly, the horse lunged off the trail, slowing his pace only barely as he dodged the trees and bushes in his path.

Phin clung to the mane and the horse's neck. Yaja wrapped her arms around the young man and tried to stop concentrating on how dislodged she felt when the stallion swerved and jumped over fallen logs and low creaks. Only Mage seemed to have any idea where he was going, and he found no difficulty in maneuvering the forest, rugged, wild and overgrown as it was.

Salgo and his sure-footed mare were the first to follow after the running stallion. He leaned low on North Wind's neck and spurred her on. His legs gripped the horse's sides as she leaped along, her light frame ducking between trees with agility. Both their pairs of eyes were concentrating on the fleeing, white blur darting through the trees before them.

Benji turned his burly black gelding sharply also, and they ran, only a foot behind North Wind's pounding steps. Storm snorted and leaped forward, his neck extended as if he would catch North Wind's tail in his teeth. The brush clattered under the abuse of the horses' hooves. Layen was the last to follow. He hated running through thick forests because the prospect of having his horse cripple itself by tripping over branches or brush was not a prospect he liked. Still, he knew he had to follow and turned his horse off the trail, muttering gruffly under his breath.

Phin nearly lay on Mage's back as he stormed along, thundering over the hard ground and dense brush and bracken in their path. Suddenly, the stallion veered left, broke into the open, and stopped so sharply that Phin and Yaja nearly flew over his head. Phin grappled at the horse's neck as Yaja nearly strangled him with fear of falling off, her arms tight around his skinny waist. North Wind screamed out of the woods and was turned by her rider until she slowed, sweat frothing from her sides and neck. Storm made a crashing uproar just behind her as he broke out, his head pulled back by his rider so sharply that the bit jarred his teeth. He grunted in annoyance, chomping at the steel. Layen emerged a moment later.

Phin slipped from Mage's back and stared up at the valley they stood in, leaving Yaja sitting on the horse's back. His breath caught in his throat at the majesty of the place around him. Mountains, deep purple and regal, ringed three of its sides. The grass was glossy greenish blue, billowing like the waves of an ocean. Hills rose in sweeping humps scattered around the beautiful valley. There were scattered patches of forest and dancing fields. But the two things that stood out the most were the city at the foot of the tallest hill and the huge round lake that took up a good area of the valley. The water was silver and was provided from a cascading, sparkling waterfall.

Phin looked in wonder at all this, knowing this was the land of his dreams – the place of his destiny. But his eyes were finally drawn to the castle at the top of the tallest hill, one with windows that would look down upon the entire valley. It looked to be made of glittering glass or shining crystals, but was most likely polished stone. It could not have been more different than the evil keep they had rescued the princess from.

"Is this the place?" Benji asked, staring around at the sweeping hills and valleys. The horses began to graze on the sweet, blue-green grass.

"Yes."

"How are you sure?" Salgo asked. "I mean, what if you became a hound once, just because you were mad? Maybe it was just that one time?"

"He has a point, Phin," Yaja said gently.

Phin knew he wasn't wrong, but he didn't have proof. It seemed foolish to tell them about the dreams or how the necklace seemed to 'speak' to him. Maybe that had been just that once too. Maybe he *was* just imagining things and hoping for something greater than he was. It did seem strange that this place should be here at all if he had just thought it all up.

"There isn't anything wrong with trying again," Layen pointed out kindly. It seemed out of character for him to believe Phin more than the others. "Try, Phin; try to become the dog again."

Phin sighed and shut his eyes. The group gasped. Slowly he opened his eyes and realized that he was looking up at all of them, which happened with very few people. He stared down and saw paws, stared back and saw light brown fluffy fur running along what must have been his back. He couldn't believe what he was seeing. He was a *dog*! And it was as easy to see and move this way as it was when he was in a human form.

He took a hesitated step, fearing these alien legs would decide to dissolve beneath him just when he needed them. They held, as regular and sturdy as human legs. He turned in a circle, feeling as childish as a toddler who had just learned to walk, but it was amazing. Impossible. Magic. His tail wagged slightly, which was odd.

"It's true," said Layen softly. "He must be . . . what did Morren call them? Shifters. That's it. If he can do it at will . . ."

"Where should we go? Salgo asked. He reached down and patted Phin's head. "He certainly feels and looks like a hound. But we can't just dump him in the city."

"The insane man who wanted to take over the Eastland, said he kidnapped the Prince of the Shifters. You don't think . . ." Yaja said trailing off meaningfully. She stared down at Phin.

"He does have that magic necklace," Benji said, rubbing the back of his neck. "But what if they want him to stay here? I don't want to lose him just because he has some kind of power."

Phin cleared his throat, now back in human form, and said, "I may look like a dog, but I can still understand you." He hadn't liked the way they had talked about him, acting like he *was* some dog that couldn't make a decision for itself.

"Sorry," the others said in unison, their voices distant, for their thoughts were elsewhere.

"I'm going to go to the castle. I ask none of you to go with me. In my dreams –" Phin said.

"You've *dreamed* about this place?" Benji asked, surprised.

Phin swore at himself internally. "I've dreamed about it for a while, yes," he answered. "And now I'm going to find out about all this."

He took hold of Mage's mane and led him forward, forgetting Yaja was still on. She did not protest. Benji turned Storm and followed as loyally as a puppy follows its master. Salgo and Layen's eyes connected, and both understood that they would go too. The group started across the sloping prairies and mounted the hill toward the gleaming castle, twinkling against the cobalt sky.

27

A Lost Prince Found

"What do you mean, you can't let them in?" Phin asked, looking back at his companions.

The door guard, a burly man who shifted into a leopard, stared at him harshly with flaming gold eyes. Why was it anyone above Phin's standard acted like he was a meddlesome child? Phin, if he hadn't been intimidated, would have wanted to ask the Shifter all the questions he had about the race. But as it was, he held his tongue.

"Just as I said, boy. I won't let any of the other races into the king's castle. You may enter, Shifter – though few Shifters leave the Kingdom of Casan and wander around – but these others would never be allowed inside," the leopard man said sternly. He wore no armor and bore no weapon except a knife. The thought that he could instantly become a giant cat kept Phin subdued, the gold eyes constantly reminding him of that. Dogs didn't fight full-sized wild cats.

A lean, swaybacked, grizzled wolf trotted out of the woods at the base of the hill and walked up, circling the castle. When it laid eyes on the party of elves and men it snarled and galloped forward, prepared to attack without a thought. The Shifters had been driven away by these races! How dare they come here!

It knotted up its legs and prepared to lunge at them, light amber eyes blazing. Phin saw it and shifted, leaping toward the gray wolf, teeth bared, ready to defend his friends without a thought about how easy it was to shift now and that he had never seen a wolf before. His bulk hit the lean hunting animal and both fell. Phin rolled and got up again, as if he had moved and lived as a dog forever. The light brown dog was a few inches taller than the wolf and more bulky but not as long. Both canines circled each other, watching for the other to leap first. Phin felt the muscles in his back legs tighten, flicked his fanned tail, and jumped at the wolf. His teeth caught the beast's shoulder and held tightly, enough to be in charge. They rolled, clawing and biting, barking and snarling, growling and yelping, sound roaring from the tangled heap.

The group could only stand aghast. Suddenly, understanding dawned on the door guard's face. He too shifted and leapt into the scuffle. With great leopard paws, he cuffed both canines back and stood between them, needle sharp teeth prepared to bite either of the two if they dared to attack each other again. The party of elves and the one man all stood staring, not sure what to do now.

Then the door guard changed back.

"Howtan!" he barked at the wolf. "Do you not know who this is?"

The wolf turned into a rather crooked, sharp-featured man with dark gray hair. His light amber eyes stared hate-filled, first at Phin – still in the form of the great dog – then at the leopard man. Blood dripped from his torn shoulder and a few other scattered scratches.

"Who *is* he? A dirty traitor, friend of the enemy," the wolf man growled.

The leopard man looked over at the large, brown, bear-like dog. For a moment he studied Phin, who was still growling, and then turned back to Howtan. "No, Howtan, he is the one the prophecy spoke of. He is the king's son," the door guard said.

The fight fizzled out of Phin, and he shifted back to human form, too shocked to think of anything else. He looked over at his friends, who were watching the guard in disbelief, and then looked back at the two Shifters. The thought that he might be the prince had crossed his mind when Benji had mentioned it, but he had never *really* taken it seriously. He couldn't be. Could he?

Howtan looked, startled, at the door guard and then at Phin. His eyes narrowed. "How are you so sure" he asked, "that that brown whelp is the prophesied prince? You've held onto legend too long, door guard. The prince is dead."

"Every Shifter alive knows the prophecy: that the great brown dog with flaming blue eyes would be the one to bring the Shifters back up to their right place as one of the races. You remember how we began to fade, how people began to think that the Shifters were evil and the Westland cursed and vile, how we were chased out of our place as one of the races. More people got the endless shift, and our numbers lessened even more. Then the prince was born, just as we were beginning to accept our fate. The prince had the flame blue eyes the prophecy spoke of. His hair was the color of the promised hound's fur. Then he was swept away in the dead of night, and the Shifters were finally defeated and completely stunned –" the door guard related.

"Enough, Bastion! We all know our own sad history, but it brings no proof that this-this 'cur' is the prince," Howtan growled. Phin bristled, snarling. "He's got pointed ears, for the love of God!"

"Elves sometimes rub off on other races, putting a little of their own characteristics into people around them. He did grow up elven," Layen said. Phin and the two other Shifters had nearly forgotten the rest of the group was there.

"All right, all right!" Bastion said putting up his hands, drowning out Howtan's insults toward the elves. The door guard suddenly snapped toward Phin. "Show us your pendant, boy!"

"How-how did you know I . . ."

"Then he does wear the pendant!" Bastion said triumphantly. "Show it to us."

Phin drew it out slowly, protectively. The door guard came nearer and looked at it. He let out a soft gasp that drew Howtan over as well. They studied the markings and the shape in the center, the guard even touching the engravings.

"It is the prince's seal," the door guard breathed.

"Are . . . you saying . . . Phin is a prince?" Yaja asked softly.

Howtan looked at her coldly and wouldn't answer. "He could have stolen it," he said to Bastion.

"A magic necklace that can't be felt half the time?" Phin challenged.

Howtan and the supposed half-blood made eye connection and snarled darkly.

"Enough!" the door guard yelled, pushing the two men away from each other with one large hand to each. "The king will know. All of you . . . other races, come inside. Tie your horses to the rings on the wall."

The rest of the company followed orders as the door guard took hold of Phin's shoulder and steered him inside, followed closely by the sharp-faced man, Howtan. Phin felt like he was a prisoner again, this time utterly alone. If the king said Phin wasn't his son, would he just let Howtan kill him? Or would they fight until one of them died? Phin shuddered at the thought. But if the king said he was his son, did he want that? That would mean his mother wasn't his mother, he wasn't a half-blood, and he wasn't even Benji's stepbrother. That would also make him a prince and mean he couldn't leave. Somehow fighting Howtan sounded easier than excepting that.

Everything was marble and polished, gleaming pale gray and nearly white in some places. Hanging from the ceiling were seven tapestries. Each had markings like those that circled the perimeter of his pendant, and in the center was the shape of a creature's head or its full body. The last one matched Phin's necklace completely except that it was shrouded with a thin black cloth.

Bastion noticed his gaze. "The ten generations that have lived in this castle. The prince's is the tenth," he said.

Phin looked at him. "I thought the Shifters were pushed back into the Westland."

"Not physically, no. We have always lived in this valley and the forest around, but now our numbers are so small we fill only one city. The forest has grown thick and full of dark things, and no trails even lead outside. We have cut ourselves off and been cut off."

"What is the 'endless shift'?" Phin asked, surprising himself. "You spoke of it earlier."

"A person shifts and for some reason can never get back. Slowly their minds lose humanity, and they become witless animals," the door guard said. He sighed. "It happened to the queen. She was such a wonderful woman, full of kindness and joy."

"Soon he'll know every secret of the Shifters, and he'll go back to his pointy-eared companions and tell them everything, and they'll come and wipe out the last of us!" Howtan sneered. The three elves glowered at him for the insult, and the door guard silenced him with a sharp look.

"And you'll find claws in your back if you don't stop talking now," Bastion growled.

"Or an arrow," Salgo muttered, stroking his bow.

A servant walked up to them suddenly, breaking up what might have been another confrontation. "Very sorry to keep you waiting, good men," she said, smiling in a friendly manner. "What can I do for you?"

"Bring the king, quickly. We may have found his son," Bastion said, clapping Phin sharply on the shoulder.

The servant's eyes widened and stared wildly at Phin, as if he was something that had popped out of the ground unexpectedly. Her very expression seemed to show that she remembered everything about the prophecy that the prince would bring the Shifters back to their rightful place in the races. She mouthed things unintelligibly for a moment.

"Yes, of course," she finally got out, and she turned and trotted away.

"Hurry!" Howtan snapped at her back. The servant went up a large flight of stairs at a jog, her skirt flying behind her as she lengthened her stride to a run.

Phin continued looking around the rich room. There were stone benches near the door, but no one felt much like sitting. The young man was twisted into three emotions: fear, excitement, and pure bewilderment, the third being the strongest. What would happen if he was the prince all the Shifter's wanted?

Only forty-eight hours ago he had been a blind half-elf, going into a haunted castle with his brother. Now he could see, could change into a dog, and was possibly a prince. It was mind-boggling, not to mention frightening. If he was a prince, would he be expected to live in the castle and stay in the Westland? What would Benji do without him? What would he do without Benji? He swallowed nervously, looking up to the top of the stairs.

They stood silently for a few moments more, no one daring to speak. Suddenly a man dressed exactly like the man in Phin's dreams came rushing down the stairway. He had dark hair flecked with gray, a fairly large nose, and eyes that were bright, rich gray. A circlet of gold and silver twisted together rested comfortably on his head.

"Where is he? Where is my son?" the man yelled as he reached the landing.

Bastion took a step aside. Everyone followed his example, except Phin who was left alone to face the king. Howtan sneered at him. Yaja and Benji smiled worriedly. His legs seemed to have turned to water, and utterly alone, he could only watch as the king came nearer. The king stopped in front of him, a few inches shorter than the young man before him. He raised one hand, the fingers covered with rings, and placed it against the young man's cheek. He studied him like he might a horse he was considering buying, and Phin wouldn't have been surprised if he had started walking around him, taking in all his traits. The young man stood still, as stiff as a board with nervousness, and studied the man's face for familiarity. Could he be his father? Phin couldn't even guess.

"You look so much like your mother," he said quietly. "We always knew you would. The ears are a surprise, but you look just like her . . ."

The king slowly traced the chain down to the pendant that hung against Phin's shirt. It seemed to glow through the ragged, thin cloth. He lifted it and looked at it for a moment, the gold medallion gleaming radiantly, the carvings looking alive. His eyes lifted, surprised and happy almost to the point of crying. "My son, my dear Karaden Par. I have mourned long for you . . ." said the king. He raised his voice. "Let it be known – Prince Karaden Par has returned!" Then he embraced his newfound son. Startled, Phin couldn't hug him back (the king's arms pinned his own firmly to his sides), but he knew his life from now on would never be the same. He wasn't sure if he liked that. He gave a wry smile. At least Howtan wouldn't kill him.

28

A Sad Parting and a New Beginning

Mage seemed delighted to be led into a corral, his saddlebags taken off, and Phin was completely surprised. The stallion really seemed to feel at home, and Phin thought that might be a good sign, though his throat felt closed up from nerves and strain. He was amazed at the change in Mage since the beginning of their travels, but he was also happy the stallion still kept the same stability of character that he had always had, a trait Phin thought must be true in all horses. He tossed Mage's saddlebags across his shoulder, undid his pack from the khcalk's back, and stared at the other horses and their riders, who busied themselves with the equines. There was a bit of stiffness in the way they worked that made the young man realize how uncomfortable they felt in the presence of this strange castle in this strange land. Phin chewed on his lower lip. Would he ever see them again?

Benji, seeing that Phin was becoming more ill at ease by the second, left Storm in Salgo's good care and walked with Phin up to the castle. They entered inside, and a servant led them through the labyrinthine hall of the castle to what would now be Phin's room. The young man had never seen a building so large, or one it would be so easy to get lost in. He thanked the servant tightly as they went inside. The room was far too spacious for Phin to live in, or so he felt. His mind was still in turmoil as he and Benji brought up his things to the large room that was now his and dropped them on the lavish feather bed. Benji was looking around the room with a combination of awe and envy.

"Well, Prince Phin, I mean, *Karaden Par*, this should be wonderful for you," Benji teased. He kicked at one of the rugs on the stone floor.

"You aren't helping, Benji," Phin said tossing down the saddlebags with something like distaste. "It might be good to get away from you." But he didn't mean it. As he studied the tapestries on the walls and the empty chests on the floor with fresh eyes, he noticed how very empty the place felt. It was a wide and vacant room.

Benji rolled his eyes, watching Phin toss the rest of his things to the floor. "Like you won't miss us and be crying your eyes out when we leave!"

"So will you, Benji, so will you," Phin said, lightly punching his best friend's shoulder. It seemed strange that he had seen him for the first time not long ago.

They both stood for a moment in silence, surveying the room. The lavish trappings stared back at them.

"Maybe all the rich food will fatten you up," Benji commented dryly.

"Or make me sick," Phin answered. "It seems lonely, doesn't' it?"

Benji nodded. "I really will miss you."

Phin nodded as well. "I'll miss you, too."

True, no one was crying in the end, but it was a painful departure. The four friends didn't in any way want to leave each other, the two "brothers" least of all. They embraced and smiled toughly while the two valiant elves wished Phin the best of luck.

"That room will seem quite large without you," Benji said. "Your mother is going to faint when I tell her that you're actually a prince of a forgotten race!"

"Maybe she'll just hit you with something," Phin said. "Wish I could be there to see it."

He laughed and cuffed his brother teasingly on the arm. Salgo and Layen promised to visit as often as they could, Salgo joking about how he might have to detour to the Westland when he was delivering messages. Though it was nice to hear, Phin still felt sad. He would be alone in this strange, new place after all. Yaja walked up to him lastly, almost shyly.

"Well, Yaja, you were wrong all those years ago," Phin said firmly.

"How so?" she answered cautiously.

"I *was* worthy. I'm a prince, and I was your 'rescuer'," he said, half teasingly, half seriously. He smiled his trademark half-smile.

"Yes, and you still are, hero," she said and kissed him gently on the lips, having to rise up on her toes to reach his face.

Phin grinned broadly, reddening only slightly.

"We still haven't had that talk you promised, when you'd explain everything to me," Yaja reminded him. "But I forgive you."

"Letters," Phin said. "You have your own personal messenger after all." He glanced at Salgo and saw him wink.

"I just stopped hating you, and now we'll be separated again," the princess said, sighing overdramatically.

"But we don't hate each other," Phin acknowledged and hugged her boldly. After a moment they separated, and she stepped away. "Goodbye, Princess."

Now he stood at the doorway to watch them go. Mage and Ghost-foot were taken care of, the other horses had been packed and prepared to leave, all good-byes said, and all mysteries solved, except how Phin was going to survive in this strange, new life.

Phin looked out at the area around: the mountains, the forests, and the rolling, blue-green hills. Most of all he watched the three horses start down the hill, their tails flipping in the breeze in rhythm with the waving grass. He wanted to be down there with them, but knew it wasn't possible. He had found his destiny, strange as it was, and there was no turning back now.

A breath of autumn wind rustled the hanging seeds on an ash tree right near him, and some of the seeds scattered, spiraling to the earth. Phin watched them for a moment before turning back to the horses and their riders. Benji turned and waved, smiling. Phin waved back, knowing they would always be bound by spirit, even if they weren't by blood or family.

Because when the blind see, when it's possible for men to become dogs and back again, and when a half-blood can find that he is really a lost Shifter prince, interesting things can and will happen. And Phin, as he turned back to the castle to begin an entirely new chapter of his life, was looking forward to their coming.

The son of the Master held his father's limp form in his arms as he knelt on the cold, blood-stained floor. His eyes were wet, the sleeves of his shirt stained from picking up his father's corpse. The young man rocked himself back and forth, clinging to the body as if it were his last lifeline, as he sobbed uncontrollably. How could this have happened? He cried all the more because all that his father had patiently, lovingly trained him in would be for naught.

"I will avenge you, father," the young man breathed into his father's corpse, tears rolling like raindrops down his pale cheeks. "I will kill those who killed you, and then I will finish what you began. I must. I will. The world will still be ours."

He bowed his head a moment more in mourning, eyes closed with internal pain, a need and longing and hunger for revenge. It burned in him like the embers of a forgotten fire. "We *will* control the world," the son said softly, the new Master, heir to all his father had had, "though now it is my turn."

THE END

BVG